WITHOUT WARNING

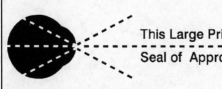

This Large Print Book carries the
Seal of Approval of N.A.V.H.

WITHOUT WARNING

LYNETTE EASON

THORNDIKE PRESS

A part of Gale, Cengage Learning

GALE
CENGAGE Learning·

Farmington Hills, Mich • San Francisco • New York • Waterville, Maine
Meriden, Conn • Mason, Ohio • Chicago

GALE
CENGAGE Learning®

LIBRARY OF CONGRESS CATALOGING-IN-PUBLICATION DATA

Names: Eason, Lynette, author.
Title: Without warning / by Lynette Eason.
Description: Large print edition. | Waterville, Maine : Thorndike Press, 2016. | Series: Elite guardians ; #2 | Series: Thorndike Press large print Christian mystery
Identifiers: LCCN 2016028838| ISBN 9781410493163 (hardcover) | ISBN 1410493164 (hardcover)
Subjects: LCSH: Bodyguards—Fiction. | Restaurateurs—Fiction. | Large type books. | GSAFD: Christian fiction. | Mystery fiction. | Suspense fiction.
Classification: LCC PS3605.A79 W58 2016b | DDC 813/.6—dc23
LC record available at https://lccn.loc.gov/2016028838

Published in 2016 by arrangement with Revell Books, a division of Baker Publishing Group

Printed in Mexico
1 2 3 4 5 6 7 20 19 18 17 16

Dedicated to my family. I love you all!

Many thanks to those on my wonderful Facebook page who gave their input on the name of Daniel's restaurant. Here were the top ten:

Rewind — Valia Jade Warren
A Taste in Time — Pam Wright Burke
Bygone Bites — Sarah Thomas
Moments in Thyme — Tana Porter
Generations — Tana Porter
Yesterday Café — Jenice Pearson
Time Warp — Cassie Chidester
Vintage — Candy Arrington
Candle Light Café — Lynn McJunkin
A Taste of Yesterday — Rachelle Gwinn
   THE WINNER

The name was chosen by the Revell staff and other voters on Facebook.

Thank you so much to all of my Facebook

buddies who gave their input. You all did a fabulous job and I appreciate it very much!

[1]

A TASTE OF YESTERDAY RESTAURANT
EARLY SATURDAY MORNING
12:26 AM
Chink, chink, chink.

Seated at the desk and studying the frustrating spreadsheet, Daniel Matthews had ignored the sound for the past five minutes. Until he realized it wasn't supposed to be there. It came from somewhere below him, a barely there noise, but one that annoyed him — and had him curious. He looked up from the computer. Everyone else had gone home for the night, leaving him alone in the building. Hadn't they?

Of course he was alone. He'd escorted his last-to-leave interim chef, Marie Stewart, out the door and to her car. When she'd driven away, he'd returned to the restaurant and locked himself inside. He tapped his pen against the paper on the desk and thought. Okay, so if he was the sole oc-

9

cupant, what was making the noise? Something with the water heater again?

Chink, chink, chink.

Didn't sound like a water heater noise, but what did he know? He rose from the desk and walked to the open office door. Just beyond the threshold, the steps to the basement and wine cellar were to his left. The door stood open because he'd promised his closing staff he'd take care of locking up. Before he left, he planned to check the wine inventory — he just hadn't gotten to it yet because the numbers on the spreadsheet had captured his attention.

He was working late, having come down to the restaurant after putting in a full day in his fifth-floor office at the headquarters building in downtown Columbia, South Carolina. He might be the CEO of A Taste of Yesterday, Inc., but he still liked to keep his hand on the day-to-day operations of all six of his restaurants. This one in particular, since it was his newest establishment — and losing money. Thanks to a business trip cancellation, he had a chunk of time he could devote to finding the problem and coming up with a solution. Was the loss strictly due to the theft he'd discovered by his former chef? Or something more complex?

The *chink, chink, chink* sounded again. He frowned and flipped the light on in the stairwell, revealing brick walls that were original to the old 1860s building. One of the few structures in Columbia that had survived Sherman's 1865 march when he and his troops had nearly burned the city to the ground.

Daniel started down. His hand slid along the rail and he tried to listen over the echo of his shoes on the matching brick steps. At the bottom, he paused, the chill of the basement penetrating the wool sweater he had on over a long-sleeved T-shirt. At the bottom, he stopped. Listened for the sound.

Heard . . . a footstep? "Hey! Is someone down here?"

He walked past the wine cellar. Just beyond that, rows of storage shelves greeted him on either side of the brick path that ran between them. He continued toward the back of the basement, his heart picking up speed, his blood humming a little faster through his veins. As he got closer to the back, the temperature dropped. A lot. Why was it so cold in here? A shuffle of a footstep up ahead made him pause. "Hello? Who's there?"

No answer. But he knew someone was there.

Uneasiness crept through him and he wondered at the wisdom of continuing on in his search for the source of the noise.

Chink, chink, chink.

What *was* that? The noise was louder now, so it was definitely coming from down here. More footsteps. But faint, like they were moving away. Daniel slipped back to the wine cellar and grabbed a bottle of wine from the nearest rack. Not much of a weapon but better than nothing. He patted his back pocket. He'd left his phone upstairs. He grimaced. Of course. And the Beretta M9 he'd removed from his shoulder holster and placed into the now-locked top drawer of his desk wouldn't do him any good either. He rarely went anywhere without the gun on him but had gotten too comfortable in his office. Too complacent in a life without danger around every corner. If he went to retrieve the weapon, whoever was down here would get away. If he confronted the person, it could be a deadly mistake. Then again, it was highly unlikely the person up ahead would know Daniel had once been a Marine. And Daniel planned to use that to his advantage.

He gave a low grunt. So be it. Hand-to-hand combat it would be. No one was going to break into his restaurant and not

12

expect to face consequences.

With his adrenaline surging, he made his way back toward the sound. The recently replaced exposed pipes above his head rumbled. He'd never noticed that before. True, he'd had everything checked out before he'd bought the place, but since it had been renovated and opened to the public, he'd spent little time in the basement.

He finally came to the end of the row of shelves. The room opened up and light from the parking lot filtered through the open basement door. He heard the roar of an engine and a chill that had nothing to do with the physical temperature swept over him. He raced to the door in time to see taillights fade into the distance. Someone had been in the basement. But why? Who?

A gust of wind caught him full in the face and he flinched. Goose bumps pebbled his skin.

Chink, chink, chink.

Daniel spun toward the sound. His eyes landed on a body hanging from the ceiling pipe, held there with a chain wrapped around his neck. Daniel inhaled sharply and backpedaled as he recognized the grotesquely distorted features on the body that gently swayed back and forth. The dead eyes

13

stared at him, as though accusing Daniel of letting him die.

Another heavy burst of wind came through the open door behind him and the extra length of the chain knocked against the exposed pipe.

Chink, chink, chink.

Katie Singleton fought a yawn as she crossed the Broad River on 76 and headed home. To her left, and up ahead off Elmwood Avenue, the road that ran parallel to 76, blue and red flashing lights caught her attention. Briefly she wondered what was going on but was too tired to think any more about it. At least it was a good tired.

She'd just come off a job that had ended well. It had been a fun concert with a well-behaved, well-mannered celebrity who appreciated — and listened to — her security team. A dream assignment. As far as she was concerned, it was the perfect way to start her week of vacation. Well, week of renovation. Which was vacation to her. She'd just purchased the home she'd grown up in as a child. A 1920s Charleston-style home on Gadsden Street that was "livable" but still needed a lot of work. Next on the agenda was her kitchen. The cabinets had been ordered and were due to arrive on

Tuesday.

She glanced in her rearview mirror, the law enforcement lights catching her attention once again as she passed them. She gave a slight start. Was that Daniel Matthews's restaurant? A Taste of Yesterday?

Riley Matthews, Daniel's niece, was one of Katie's students in the self-defense class she taught twice a week at the local gym. Katie pulled off the highway at the next exit, then drove to Elmwood to head back toward the lights. She passed Elmwood Cemetery on her right and slowed. The cemetery sloped downward. At the bottom of the hill, a brick retaining wall separated the burial grounds and the back of the restaurant. She could see the action focused on that part of the building.

She pulled into the parking lot and stopped when a uniformed officer lifted his hand and frowned at her. Behind him she recognized Detective Quinn Holcombe, a man she worked with in a professional capacity on a regular basis. She rolled to a stop on the outside of the yellow tape and caught Quinn's eye. He raised a brow and jogged over. The officer who'd waved nodded at Quinn and stepped back when he saw that Quinn knew her.

15

She lowered her window. "What's going on?"

"Katie." He placed a hand on the top of the car and leaned toward her. "What are you doing here?"

"I was on the way home from the concert across the river and saw all the lights. It looked like it was coming from here. I know Riley Matthews, Daniel Matthews's niece."

The light went on for him. "I see." He glanced back at the building. "Apparently someone broke into the basement of the restaurant and hung himself."

"Apparently?" Katie blinked. "*Hung* himself?"

"Well, that's what it looks like, hence the word 'apparently.' I'm not saying that's what happened."

"Murder?"

He hesitated and she knew it wasn't because he was afraid he was talking out of turn. Thanks to the mayor and her work with the Elite Guardians Agency, Katie had special credentials that allowed her to be "read in" on cases, even contracted as a professional in certain circumstances. She knew Quinn was just pausing, trying to figure it out in his own head. "Maybe," he finally said. "I think so, but that's just speculation. We'll have to wait for the ME's report, of course, but —" he shrugged — "Matthews said he heard footsteps and made it to the door just in time to see a car drive away. Like I said, we'll see." He nodded to the cameras mounted on the side of the building. "I'll be real interested to see what those show."

"Do you know who the victim is?"

"The chef Matthews fired week before last." He consulted his notebook. "Maurice Armstrong. It seems they had words after Matthews caught him stealing from him and confronted him. Armstrong denied it, but Matthews had it on video. He told him if he ever set foot on one of his properties again, he'd turn him in and have him arrested."

"Ooh, that doesn't sound good." She frowned. "Why *didn't* he call the police and have him arrested?"

"Armstrong has a fifteen-year-old daughter he's got sole custody of. There aren't any other relatives that will take her — at least none that are in good health. I think there's a grandmother, but she's pretty sick, from what I understand. If Armstrong was to go to jail, she goes into the system."

"So what happens now that Armstrong's dead?"

"No idea. Either the sick grandmother or foster care."

"That stinks."

"Don't I know it."

He did. Better than most. "Sounds like Matthews isn't such a bad guy." Which was the impression she'd already gotten from what Riley said about him.

"First impressions indicate he's one of the good ones," Quinn reluctantly admitted.

Katie lifted a brow. Quinn didn't say many positive things about anyone. "He made an impression on you."

Quinn shrugged. "He's a former Marine who served two tours in Afghanistan and one in Iraq. I'm former military. I want to believe he's on the up-and-up. I think he's tough and can have an attitude, but the jury's still out on whether or not he's a cold-blooded killer."

But he *was* a man who could take care of himself. And while his actions sounded honorable — even compassionate — were they? Or had he not reported the theft for ulterior motives? From what little she'd picked up from Riley, the girl adored her uncle. But she might be wearing rose-tinted glasses. "Matthews — Daniel — was here alone? And he found the body?"

Quinn pursed his lips and nodded. "Yeah."

"You think he killed him and staged it to look like a suicide?" She didn't want to

18

believe it for Riley's sake, but she lived in the real world and knew Quinn had to consider the possibility even while his gut was telling him something different.

"I think someone did. But like I said, I don't have the feeling it's Matthews." He scowled. "I've been wrong before, so I'm not ruling him out, of course. We'll know more as time passes."

"If it's truly a suicide, I can see the guy hanging himself in the restaurant as being some sort of freaky revenge for Daniel firing him. But other than that, why would anyone kill him, then decide to string up his body in the basement of the restaurant where he was fired from?" she murmured.

"Good questions. The only answers I can come up with for now would be to make Matthews look bad. Guilty."

"Frame him?"

"Or paint him as responsible for the man's despair. I don't know, but we'll figure it out."

"No doubt. Did Armstrong leave a note?"

"Haven't come across one yet."

"Any more security cameras on the other side of the building?"

"Two. I'm hoping they picked up something. If not, we're not going to have much to go on other than what the crime scene unit finds."

She glanced past him. "Where's Bree?"

Brianne Standish, Quinn's partner, was usually on scene with him, but Katie hadn't spotted her.

"Her sister had a DUI, she's dealing with her — and her mother."

Katie winced. "Ouch."

"Tell me about it."

Bree had some family issues that were making her crazy, but she was coping as best she could — and she had a partner who understood and had her back. She'd be all right. "Okay, I'll get out of here. I just wanted to . . ." What? She shrugged. "I don't know what I wanted. Guess to make sure Riley wasn't somehow involved and that she didn't need anything. And see if I could help in any way."

Another officer rushed from the building. "Quinn!"

Quinn straightened and turned. "Yeah?"

"We've got another development."

"What's that?"

"One of Matthews's other restaurants is burning over on North Lake Road."

"You've got to be kidding me."

"Nope. Fire trucks are already on the scene."

Quinn tapped the hood of Katie's car.

"You want to join the fun?"

Katie's first reaction was a resounding no. Before the word left her lips, she considered it. Did she *want* to? Yes. *Could* she do it? As a former agent with Alcohol, Tobacco & Firearms and a trained arson investigator, the thought of the fire intrigued her, fascinated her. However, flashes from the past during her stint with the explosives squad made her hesitate. "Um . . . no. I don't think so."

Quinn studied her for a moment. "That's not the answer I'm looking for. You know you want to."

Yes. Yes she did. "It's not a matter of want to, you know that."

"Come on, Katie, you can do this."

"Quinn . . ." She sighed.

"Just come. Stand there and watch the fire. Give me feedback on it. You don't have to do anything else."

His furrowed brow and intense stare didn't faze her. Her internal struggle did. Very few people knew the reason she was no longer with ATF. Quinn was one of those people. "Fine. I'll ride over. I know where the place is." She pursed her lips, wanting to recall the words. But she didn't.

She caught the brief flash of surprise in

his eyes before he nodded. "Good. See you there."

"Where's Daniel?"

"Still answering questions. He's pretty shaken up."

"Are you going to arrest him?" she asked.

He blew out a puff of air. "No. Like I said, I don't think he did it. But even if I did think him guilty, I've got no evidence to support an arrest tonight."

She hesitated. "Why don't I give him a ride? I can come back here on my way home and drop him off to get his car."

"I'll tell him."

So much for her renovation vacation.

[2]

Daniel sat in the passenger seat of Katie's Jeep. He inhaled the scent of new leather. She had good taste. He blinked. Was he really noticing her car when a man had been hung in A Taste of Yesterday's basement and one of his other restaurants was now burning?

It must be some kind of coping mechanism. His brain couldn't handle reality right now. Kind of like when he'd been on active duty in the Middle East. He drew in a deep breath and forced the images he'd seen there from his head. He closed his eyes and pictured Riley's sweet face, her smile, thought about her robust laugh that had been all too infrequent since her parents' deaths. Katie's face slid over Riley's and he jerked. Blinked. Then glanced at her.

She was of a mixed heritage, with her dark

23

hair and eyes and light brown skin. A combination of genes that made up a physically gorgeous woman. She wore her long wavy hair up in a tight ponytail that pulled just enough to enhance her high cheekbones. From what Riley had to say, her heart was just as beautiful. The fact that she'd been concerned enough to stop when she saw the flashing lights at his restaurant spoke clearly to that.

Katie drove in silence, her features tense. He appreciated that she didn't spout platitudes or even try to offer comfort. He'd met her only a few times when he'd gone to watch Riley at the self-defense demonstrations her classes had done. He remembered being impressed by Katie's students — and her. Detective Holcombe hadn't explained anything to him when he'd told him to ride with her, just that she was going to the scene at the detective's request. "What made you stop? The lights? The fact that you know Riley?"

She glanced at him, then back to the road. "I recognized the restaurant as being yours," she said. "So, all of the above."

"I appreciate that." He paused. "Riley really looks up to you." Small talk? But what else was he supposed to do? Bang on the dashboard and demand an explanation from a God he wasn't on speaking terms with?

"She's a great girl who's got her head on straight, her priorities lined up well," Katie said.

The blaze just ahead caught his attention and all thoughts of conversation fled. Law enforcement and emergency vehicles swarmed the area. Katie flashed some kind of badge and an officer waved her through. The strobe-type lights blinded him, bringing on an instant headache. Daniel opened his door and stepped out. Cold air blasted him, even through the heat and smoke from the burning building. He processed the sight, his heart thudding a heavy beat in his chest. A sick feeling swept over him and he drew in a deep breath. Then coughed on the smoke that filtered into his lungs.

"Unbelievable. Please tell me no one was in there," he whispered.

She flicked a glance at him. "I don't know. We'll find out soon enough."

How she'd heard him over the roar of the fire and the organized chaos he didn't know. Firefighters were already on the scene and working to get the blaze under control. Two ambulances stood ready. His mind flipped through the names of the employees who worked at this location, but he had no idea who would have closed the store. The

25

manager took care of the schedule.

Daniel stared, struggling to process the devastation in addition to the murder. What had happened to his world?

"Hope they can keep it contained," Katie said. "It's getting pretty close to the building to the left."

"At least there's no one in the lot to the right." The area was in the process of being cleared and a large backhoe sat waiting for someone to fire it up to finish the job.

Katie stared at the fire and shook her head. "This can't be a coincidence." She pulled a phone from her back pocket and punched in a number. "Hey, Olivia, sorry to call so late, but I need a favor."

Daniel didn't know who the person on the other end of the line was, but he listened as he tried to think. He heard her explain the situation.

"Yeah, I know. I think someone needs to go by his house and keep an eye on it. As well as the other restaurant downtown."

Daniel finally processed what she was saying. He faced her. "Wait a minute. What? Go by my house?"

She met his gaze. "Okay, thanks. I'll let you know when he heads that way." She hung up.

His eyes narrowed. "You think Riley's in

danger?"

"I don't know, but if I were you, I'd consider it a slight possibility. And even a *slight* one is a possibility to pay attention to. It's no accident someone hung a body in your basement." She nodded to the fire. "I'm willing to bet that's not an accident either."

He looked her straight in the eye. "So who did you send to my house?"

"A friend and partner. Her name is Olivia Edwards. She'll show Riley her identification, but Riley's met her a couple of times when Olivia's taught the self-defense class, so she'll know her." She looked back at the fire. "If I were you, I'd want someone there with her, because this definitely concerns me."

"So you're saying what I'm thinking."

"If you're thinking that it's entirely possible you've become a target, then yes. And until it's proven otherwise, I'm saying I think you should be smart. Nobody does stuff like this without a motive. Until we learn what that is, you need to take some serious precautions."

Her words hit him hard. He wanted to protest but had no rebuttal that sounded logical. He couldn't deny what had happened tonight — was happening in front of

27

his eyes at that very moment. "Okay, I can't talk about this now. If there's even a hint of a possibility that Riley's in danger, I've got to get home. Can you take me? If not, I can call a cab." He looked back at the burning building, sadness and loss threatening to overwhelm him.

"Even if you left right now, Olivia will still beat you there. But it would be a good idea to let Riley know she's coming."

He pulled his phone out of the clip and sent the short text. He'd let Olivia go into more detail when she got there. He waited for Riley's response, which came lightning fast.

Olivia Edwards? What? Seriously? She's a BODYGUARD. WHY DO I NEED A BODYGUARD??? Where are you? WHAT IS GOING ON????

He winced. She was still up, probably waiting on him to get home. Sometimes she acted more like his mother than his niece.

I'll explain as soon as I get there, I promise, just ask for identification when the woman gets there.

I know Olivia, I don't need to see her ID.

Daniel Matthews, you're scaring me. Call me.

Detective Holcombe approached, his tight lips and narrowed eyes not boding well for whatever he had to say. Daniel tensed as though getting ready to ward off a blow. He shot Riley a quick reply.

> Have to go. Talk to you soon. Text me when Olivia gets there.

As soon as he hit send, his phone rang. He glanced at the screen. "It's Riley. I need to answer." He paused. "But I want to hear whatever it is you've got to say." He stepped away from Katie and Detective Holcombe and pressed the phone to his ear. "Hey."

"Uncle Daniel, are you all right? First I get your crazy text, then Beth texted and said one of the restaurants is on fire!"

Beth Sawyer, Riley's best friend. And perpetual night owl and news junkie. He glanced at the news vans already on the scene. He was surprised they hadn't been clamoring to get to him. Beth had either seen something on television or — more likely — a breaking news banner that had come across her iPhone. "I'm fine," he said. He kept his voice low and reassuring. "And yes, it's been quite a night. I'll tell you more

29

about it when I get home."

"When will that be?"

"I'm not sure. Just go to sleep. I'll be there when everything calms down."

"Go to sleep? Really? I'll come to the restaurant. You need someone there with you."

"No," he barked. Silence. He drew in a breath. "Sorry, didn't mean to snap. Katie Singleton is here."

"My self-defense instructor?"

"Yes."

"Oh. But how —"

"It's a long story, I'll give you all the details when I get home. There's nothing you can do right now. Just stay home, okay?"

"Fine, but I'm going to keep my phone nearby. Call me if you need to."

Again he wondered who took care of whom. "I will, Princess, I promise." The detective and Katie glanced at him. "Now I've got to go."

"Fine. Bye. And don't call me Princess. I love you."

"Love you too, Princess."

He hung up on her groan and turned to find Katie and Detective Holcombe in deep conversation. He moved closer to hear. It was his restaurant, he figured he needed to be in on the details. He started to listen, but his phone buzzed again.

Riley
GET MOM'S BOX.

Then a second text on the next line.

PLEASE. If you can.

I'll do my best.

Her mother's marble box. The one he'd kept at the restaurant. The box was a lovely antique marble keepsake that Riley had spent hours playing with as a child. When he'd started opening his restaurants, he placed one item that had belonged to his brother and sister-in-law in each store. It had been like having a piece of them with him in every location. He glanced at the destruction that had once been a thriving business and sighed. Would the box survive? He hoped so. For Riley's sake. But he'd have to worry about that later.

Katie and Holcombe stopped talking at his approach. "So what now?" he asked.

"Once they get the fire out, there'll be an investigation," the detective said.

"Of course." Daniel nodded, his eyes sliding back to the fire. "No one was in there, right?"

31

"Not that we can tell. It looks like the fire started in the kitchen. When the firefighters got here, there was an explosion. When they tried to get in the back, there was something barricading the door. By the time they made a way in through the wall, the flames were hot and high, but they think the explosion came from the gas stove. Right now, they've got the blaze under control."

Daniel thought his blood pressure might just cause him to stroke out. He swiped his forehead with the back of his hand. Thirty degrees and he was sweating. "So there's no doubt this is deliberate."

Katie pressed a Kleenex into his hand and then slipped the packet back into her jacket pocket. He pressed the tissue against his upper lip and forehead, then crumpled it into a ball, his fist tight.

"I'm not an arson investigator, but it looks pretty suspicious to me. We'll have to wait for the official report before making that call." Holcombe cleared his throat. "So we talked to a couple of your employees."

"You woke them up?"

"Yeah. We have to do that sometimes. Like when we're trying to solve a murder."

Daniel met the man's gaze. "Why the sarcasm?" he asked.

"I don't like it when people don't tell me

everything."

"Such as?"

"Such as I'm still thinking about the argument you had with the dead man."

"Okay, what about it?"

"So you fired him."

"I did," Daniel growled. "You already know that. And you know why. I caught him stealing from me."

"But you didn't call the cops."

"Again, you know that I didn't."

"Because his daughter would go into the system if you did."

Impatience threatened. "Yes. Partly."

"What's the other part?"

"I believe people deserve a second chance."

"Is that why you went to his house a few days ago?"

Daniel drew in a breath. "Well, if you've talked to his daughter or his mother, you know why I went to his house."

"Actually Mrs. Armstrong said you and her son talked privately, and after several minutes he yelled and ordered you out of the house. She said he never told her what you two argued about, but she overheard you tell him you hoped he didn't wake up one day with nothing but regrets."

"Yes. That's true."

"So what did you argue about?"

Daniel massaged his temples. "I offered to set up a college fund for his daughter if he'd go to counseling."

"And that made him mad."

"Yep." Daniel's temper had been ignited and he was struggling not to punch the guy. He saw where this was going. But he'd left his hotheaded reactions in his youthful past. He would control himself. With effort, but he would.

Detective Holcombe tilted his head and narrowed his eyes. "Why?"

"He said it wasn't any of my business and told me to stay out of his life."

"I see."

"I don't think you do, but you're going to believe what you want anyway, aren't you?"

Holcombe ignored the dig. "Did Armstrong come back tonight to confront you?" He glanced down at Daniel's rock-hard fists. "Maybe you lost your temper and took things a little too far? Or he reached for a weapon —"

"And so I killed him and hung him in the basement to make it look like a suicide?" Daniel gritted the words through his teeth. The detective lifted a brow. Daniel snorted. "That's the dumbest thing I've ever heard. Why would I kill someone and hang them in my own restaurant when I own a gun and could've shot him miles away from here and not be under suspicion?" Daniel stepped forward, locked his eyes on the detective, and made sure he had his full attention. "Look, Detective, my brother and sister-in-law were killed by a drunk driver. A drunk driver who suffered a slight concussion and walked away to drink again — and will probably kill someone else when he gets out of prison next year. If I was going to kill someone, Armstrong wouldn't have been my first choice."

The detective stilled but kept a steady gaze on Daniel.

Daniel let out a sigh, shook his head, and uncurled his fists. "Yeah. I have a temper." He took a deep breath. "But it's one I've learned to control."

"Really?"

"Really."

"How do you figure?"

Daniel placed his hands on his hips. "You're still standing, aren't you?"

Katie, who'd been silent and watchful during the entire exchange, let out a low sound, either a snort or a chuckle, Daniel couldn't tell which. Quinn lifted a brow and Katie cleared her throat. "Quinn, this isn't getting us anywhere. Chill." She looked at Daniel.

"You too."

Holcombe rubbed his bloodshot eyes and nodded. "Right. So you had an argument with the guy because he was stealing from you."

"Yes," Daniel said, the word short and clipped.

"Your employee also said you threatened him."

That stilled Daniel. "What? Threatened him how?"

"Said you threatened that if he didn't straighten up and fly right, you'd make sure he lost everything he had."

Daniel blinked, his brain churning. "I never said that."

"What did you say?"

"I told him if he didn't straighten up and fly right, he *would* lose everything he had. Quite a bit of a difference in meaning." His frown deepened. "Who's the employee anyway?"

"She didn't want her name revealed to you."

Daniel stared, then shook his head. "Unbelievable," he muttered. He ran through the list of employees in his head but couldn't pick out a specific one who might have a grudge against him. He'd be sure to find that out as soon as possible.

The detective wrote something else down and looked back up. "You own a gun?"

"Yes."

"Where is it?"

"Locked in my desk drawer at the other restaurant."

"I'll want to see it."

"Then we'll need to get back over there."

"We'll do that as soon as I can leave here," Holcombe said.

He felt Katie's gaze on him and looked at her.

"You've become a target," she said. "Why?"

"That's the million-dollar question for the night, isn't it? What do you think?"

"I think you might be the only one who can answer that. You have any enemies?"

He flinched before he could stop it. Then sighed and ran a hand through his already seriously mussed hair. "Probably a few."

"Shocking," Holcombe muttered.

"Shut up, Quinn," Katie murmured.

Holcombe's complete about-face, going from believing him not guilty to thinking he had something to do with Armstrong's death and the fire, had Daniel's blood boiling. He turned his back on the detective. "Most of them are overseas, though. Then

37

again, they consider all Americans the enemy."

Katie blinked. "All right." She pulled a small notepad from her back pocket and handed it to him along with a pen. "Make a list."

"Now?"

"While you're thinking about it. Start with Armstrong's family."

His jaw tightened and he consciously relaxed the muscles. "Yeah. Maybe." He looked at the blank page, then back at his ruined building. Shaking his head, he wrote *Armstrong family.* Then paused and sighed. He scribbled through the name and handed her the notebook. "Look, I have people I've clashed with. Business issues, things that didn't go well or as hoped, people I've fired, of course, but —" he shook his head and she repocketed the items — "no one who would do this. I just don't have any names right this minute. Not even the Armstrongs. Maurice's daughter came to me and thanked me for not sending her dad to jail. Her grandmother, who has terminal cancer, came with her the day after I fired him. They both were grateful I'd let him off. It's not them."

"What about a male relative?" she asked. "Someone Armstrong was close to who

38

might want to strike back at you for firing him?"

"I just don't know." He glanced back at the burning store. "But, I'll admit, I just don't see how this could be a coincidence. Someone kills Armstrong and hangs him in my basement while one of his family members wants revenge so he burns *this* restaurant down? That's not even plausible."

"No, it's not, although stranger things have happened. But someone's angry and I have a strong feeling once all the evidence is in, we're going to see these two events are related somehow."

"I have no doubt you're right." So obviously he'd made someone angry enough to lash out in a major way.

But who?

[3]

Nolan Swift, another detective Katie had worked with on occasion, motioned Quinn over. Quinn held up his index finger, indicating he'd be there in a moment. "One more question," he said to Daniel.

"What's that?"

Katie could see the tension in Daniel's stance. He'd had just about enough of Quinn's questions.

"If you didn't have anything to do with Armstrong and had no ill will against him, do you know anyone who does?"

Daniel shook his head. His sandy blond hair was cropped close in a military style and his green eyes were narrow. "No. Other than the bit I've shared with you, I don't know much of anything else about him. If you want to know any more personal stuff, that would be a question for the employees he worked with."

Quinn nodded and snapped his little notebook shut. "I'm sure I'll have more questions before we're done."

"I'm sure I will too," Daniel muttered.

"Give me a little bit longer, then we'll head over to the other store and you can show me the gun." Quinn left them and Katie turned to Daniel.

"So," she said, "let's talk about why you didn't call the cops on Armstrong."

"It doesn't matter." He shot a malevolent glare at Quinn's back. "What's his problem? At first, he was pretty decent. Then he did an about-face and became the clichéd surly cop. Why?" He shook his head.

She sighed. "It's the way he is. He has a lot of respect for those who serve in the military. You were in the Marines. You were even with the Criminal Investigation Division as an agent for a while. You know as well as I do the reasons for his turnaround. Finding out about your clash with Armstrong doesn't help."

"Not to mention the faulty report from one of my employees casting aspersions on my character, making Holcombe think I was lying by omission." He drew in a deep breath. "Yeah, I get it." His eyes narrowed. "You've done your homework on me."

41

"No, not in the sense that I went snooping."

The light went on. "Riley's been talking about me."

"Yes. I don't ask a lot of questions, though. Some of the information has just come out in our chats."

He tilted his head. "I don't have a lot of secrets. Ask all the questions you want."

"But you'll only answer the ones *you* want."

He didn't bother to answer, just lifted one corner of his mouth and stared at her.

She paused. "Why aren't you working as a detective now that you're out of the Marines? According to Riley, you have an exemplary military record, closed most of the cases you were handed in a timely manner. Any police department would be eager to hire you."

"Yes, that's true." There was no pride in the statement, just a fact. "I have my reasons."

"Riley?"

"She's one of them."

Okay, for a guy who didn't have a lot of secrets, he sure was giving her short answers. She could respect that. She had no real business or reason to dig into his past other than to satisfy her own curiosity —

and figure out if he was a killer. But that was Quinn's job, not hers. "Regardless of Quinn's suspicions," she said, "I believe what you said."

He quirked a brow at her. "Why? Because you like my niece?"

"Nope, she has nothing to do with it — well, maybe a little." She shoved her hands into the pockets of her khakis and looked him in the eye. "But I believe you because it's not logical that you would catch the man stealing from you, not call the police about it, but threaten to make sure he lost everything. You had proof of his guilt, right?"

"Yes. Still do."

"So if you wanted him to lose everything, you would have just turned him in to the cops as the first step in the process, right?"

He blinked. "Oh. Well. When you put it that way."

"Unless, of course, the more you thought about it, the angrier you got and finally decided to take matters into your own hands and get revenge on him for betraying your trust." His nostrils flared and she held up a hand. "But I don't believe you did." She gave him a small smile. "Riley's the best character witness you could have. She adores you."

His expression softened. "The feeling's

mutual."

Not that Riley's adoration meant the man was innocent, but she had a pretty good gut instinct about people, and her instinct wasn't coming up with any red flags. In her eyes, he was innocent until the evidence proved otherwise. She drew in a deep breath. "Come on, I'll take you back to the restaurant to pick up your car."

He turned back to the still-burning building. "Is Olivia with Riley yet?"

She checked her phone. "Yes, she's been there for a few minutes."

"Then I'll stay here a little longer." He fixed his gaze on the flames. "I really need to know there wasn't anyone in there. And I need to look for something Riley wants me to bring home to her."

"You'll have to wait on that last one. Everything needs to cool off first. Then the fire investigator will come out. Then you can look for personal items."

"I know the routine." He glanced at her. "Are you still planning to take a look like your detective friend asked?"

She stared at the now smoking building. Felt the tremor deep in her belly, the fear threaten to choke her at the thought of donning her gear and heading in. She shook her head. "Not for hours if I do. And only after the investigator has done his job. After that . . ." She shrugged. "We'll see." It looked like they had the fire under control at this point, but she wasn't going any closer. "I'm sure when Quinn asked me to come along, he didn't picture the enormity of the fire or how long it would take to put it out." She didn't know what Quinn was thinking when he'd asked her to come along. Or maybe she did. She pulled in a deep breath. "If he wants me to come back, I will." Another maybe.

"How much longer do you think he's going to be? Once I know everyone's okay, I'm ready to get this night over with. Watching years of work go up in smoke isn't doing much for my attitude." He grimaced. "Not to mention that hundred-year-old building and all of the precious antiques that were in there." He shook his head. "Breaks my heart."

"Let's hope that's all that gets broken," Katie murmured.

He shot her a black look and turned his back on the depressing scene.

"Hey, Matthews!"

Daniel turned to find the detective coming toward them. "Yeah?"

"Just thought you'd like to know that all

employees are accounted for."

Relief swept him. He nodded. "Thanks."

"We can leave now. I'll meet you back where all of this started — or you can ride with me."

"No thanks. Katie can take me." He looked at her and she nodded. They headed for her vehicle, Daniel's heart heavy, his mind trying to process everything.

Once back at the site of the murder, Daniel led them to his office while his nerves twitched. He had visions of the gun being missing. Of him opening the drawer and staring into the empty spot. The way his night was going, it wouldn't even surprise him at this point.

Katie and Holcombe stepped into the office after him. He pulled his keys from his pocket and opened the desk drawer. And there was his gun. His freshly cleaned weapon he hadn't fired since his last visit to the range.

The detective leaned in. Held out a hand. "You mind?"

"Help yourself."

Holcombe did. He emptied the weapon, checked it, then snapped pictures of it.

"Maurice wasn't shot," Daniel said.

"I know." Holcombe handed the weapon back to him. "And this hasn't been fired lately. It's clean as a whistle."

"I clean it often."

"Like tonight?"

Daniel bit his tongue, chose his words, and held onto his temper. "No. Like last night." He pulled on his shoulder holster and slid the weapon into it. He then snagged his wallet from his back pocket, pulled out his concealed weapons permit, and handed it to Holcombe.

The detective looked it over and gave it back to him. "Don't leave town."

"Ugh, Quinn, really?" Katie said.

The detective let his hard gaze swing between him and Katie. "Really."

Daniel swung his SUV into his driveway and pressed the button for the hangar door. It slid open and he rolled into his spot — right next to his Cirrus SR22. The hangar served as storage for his vehicles and his plane. Seeing the small plane parked in its spot in the hangar never failed to give him a thrill. But tonight, he couldn't take any pleasure in it. He felt . . . flat. Numb to the events. He'd felt that way before and knew it would pass. It was just how he dealt with severe emotional hits. Watching years of hard work go up in smoke was a tough one. When Katie had insisted on sweeping his

SUV for explosives, his anger had nearly gotten the better of him. Not at her — at the events of the entire night.

He climbed from the vehicle and saw Katie stop at the edge of his drive. The wind blasted him as he exited the garage, and he shivered, pulling the edges of his coat tighter against his throat. He walked toward Katie and she rolled down her window.

"You didn't have to follow me," he said.

"I know." She held up her phone. "But as soon as Riley learned I was with you, she texted me and asked me to make sure you got home safely."

He shook his head. "That girl."

She frowned. "Be careful. Watch your back. Something's not right about tonight in more ways than one."

"Yeah. I know."

"My opinion is that someone's started playing a pretty twisted game, and until you figure out if it's the restaurants he's targeting or you personally, you need to be on constant guard." Her eyes dropped to where he would wear a shoulder holster should he have it on. "Carry your weapon."

"Twenty-four seven." He took in her concern, the way she tilted her head, the dark hair pulled back into that severe ponytail. And felt his attraction meter kick in. Strange he hadn't ever noticed her before. He shook his head, pushed the feeling away, and chalked it up to the craziness of the night.

"You have it?"

He blinked. Have it? Oh right, his gun. He patted the shoulder holster. "Yes, I've got it. I kept it after Holcombe looked at it."

She nodded. "Good." She gave a low laugh and shook her head.

"What?" he asked.

"Me. Telling you what you need to do. Sorry, it's a job hazard."

He smiled and glanced around. "It's okay. I don't mind."

And surprisingly enough, he found the fact that she wanted to look out for him . . . interesting. He'd never experienced that before. He had a feeling Katie wasn't like most of the women he'd been around. A few he'd worked with in the Marines were tough enough, but there was just something about Katie . . .

A noise at his front door distracted him and he turned to look. A woman stepped onto the front porch. Riley tried to slip around her, but the woman shifted her body to block Riley's, then whispered something in her ear. Riley hesitated, stuck her head around the woman's frame, and shot him a glance.

"I'm fine, hon," Daniel called. "Go back inside. We'll talk in a few minutes."

Riley lifted her chin, then let her gaze bounce between the three adults. She narrowed her eyes and shot him a look that Daniel knew meant she wouldn't be put off for long. Riley flounced back into the house and the woman stayed on the porch, pulling the door closed.

Daniel assumed this was the Olivia that Katie had told him about. Her straight blonde hair blew around her face. She stood tall, around five feet nine inches, and wore loose-fitting jeans, a black turtleneck, and a man's gray sweater. Strong and slender, she glanced to her left, then the right. She loped down the steps and crossed the lawn to join them. "Everything's been quiet here."

"Thanks for coming over. I'm Daniel." He held out a hand and she shook it.

"Olivia. Happy to do it." She looked at Katie. "Anything else you need?"

"No, I think we're good."

"Then I'm headed home." She patted Daniel on the shoulder. "I'm sorry about all the trouble tonight. If you need anything, you know where to find us, right?"

"Of course. Thank you." He knew it had

been a stressful night, but he had to admit it touched him that these two ladies who didn't know him had gone out of their way to help him and Riley tonight.

Olivia climbed into her SUV that she'd parked across the street from his house. "I told Riley to rearm the alarm when she went back in. Be sure to turn it off."

"I will. Thanks."

Olivia climbed in her car and drove away. Daniel turned to Katie. "I owe you."

"I didn't do anything."

"Yeah. You did. Thanks."

She frowned a little, then smiled. "Sure." She nodded to the plane, visible in the open door. "Nice."

"Yeah, it is."

"I noticed the runway in your backyard — and the yards of a lot of people in this neighborhood that connect to the main one. Do you fly a lot?"

"Every chance I get. Wanna take a ride in her one day?"

Her eyes sparked. "Don't offer unless you're serious. I love to fly."

"I'm serious. Maybe I'll let Riley pilot us."

"She has her license?"

"Yep. She got it the day she turned seventeen." He shook his head. "She's a natural pilot."

"Wow, I'm impressed. She's never said a word." Another smile lifted her lips. "And I'd love to go up with you and Riley one day. But for now, I'll say good night. I'll see you later, Daniel."

"Good night."

She waited, and he knew she wouldn't pull away until he was safely inside. He jogged up the steps and into the house. He shut the door behind him and looked out the window.

She caught him watching and pulled away with a wave. He watched her taillights disappear around the corner after a brief pause at the stop sign. She'd circle the neighborhood before heading for the exit. He didn't know why he knew that, but just knew she would. Probably because it's exactly what he would have done in her place.

He waited for her to roll past his home one more time, then he opened the door and stepped outside. Standing on the porch, he probed the area. Everything looked exactly as it should. His eyes scanned the neighboring properties. The houses were close enough to know who lived nearby, but not so close one felt claustrophobic. Strategically placed trees denoted the property lines and well-manicured lawns sprawled along the street. It was an aviation community where pilots and their families could live and fly on a daily basis if they chose to do so. It was a good place to live. A safe place. He hoped.

He breathed in and smelled the crisp air. It smelled like a snow that wouldn't happen this early in the year — and something else. Something he couldn't put his finger on but reminded him of the day he'd been riding in a Humvee in Iraq and decided to take a different route. He'd radioed to the vehicle behind him, but they hadn't wanted to deviate from their course. Less than thirty seconds after Daniel had turned onto a side road, the explosion shattered the air. The Humvee behind him had gone straight instead of following Daniel and they'd all died. Gut instinct. Divine intervention. He'd learned not to ignore it. And now the training he'd never put behind him kicked in. He released the strap on his shoulder holster and pulled the weapon from its home. With light steps and ears tuned to the night sounds, he moved to the garage, punched in the code, and listened to the door come down. Also from the outside, he armed the hangar, then he slipped around the corner of the house and into the shadows, avoiding triggering the motion lights.

He stayed still, listening. He heard nothing — and didn't really expect to, but the incidents of the night had made him a little paranoid. Understandably perhaps, but he didn't like the feeling and definitely wouldn't ignore it. He continued to scour the area, double checking, knowing he'd rest better if he was thorough in his assessment. Leaves rustled behind him and he tensed. Turned. Held his weapon out and ready. He moved toward the bushes, not really expecting anything or anyone to be there, but wouldn't be surprised if there was.

But nothing. He relaxed slightly. Just the wind.

And yet . . .

He continued to clear the area around the house, and when he made it back to his front porch, his nerves were tight. But at least no one lurked in the shadows. For now.

He unlocked the door and stepped into his home, shut the door behind him, and punched in the code for his alarm to deactivate it. He rearmed it, then shrugged out of his heavy coat and gave it a toss over the back of the nearest dining room chair.

"Uncle Daniel? Can we talk now?"

He turned to find Riley coming from the hallway. He blinked. As always he was struck by her physical beauty. Her dark hair and blue eyes were a wicked combination, and

54

he was surprised he wasn't finding guys parked on his front porch. What really hit home was how remarkable the resemblance was to her mother. He nearly gasped aloud at the sharp stab of pain the memories evoked. "Hey, Princess." She grimaced at the nickname and he winced at his forgetfulness. "Sorry. It's a hard habit to break. I've been calling you that since you were born."

"Just don't do it in public." She shot him a ferocious frown. "Are you all right?"

"Yeah. You?"

"I am now that I know you are." She crossed the kitchen, slipped her arms around his waist, and laid her head against his chest. "You scared me," she whispered. "What if I'd lost you too?"

He held her tight, her fears valid. He could have been hurt had the intruder had something else on his mind. Checking out the yard might not have been the best decision. He really had to get used to thinking about the fact that another person was depending on him. After eighteen months one would think he'd have gotten the hang of that. "You're not going to lose me."

She pulled away. "Don't make promises you can't keep. You and I both know life is fleeting and can be snatched away in the blink of an eye."

His heart squeezed. She shouldn't have to worry about that kind of stuff, but then again, maybe it was good she was so aware. "Yes, that's true. Let me put it to you this way. I'm going to do everything I can to make sure nothing happens to me, all right?" Or at least he would from now on.

"Fair enough. Olivia didn't say much, just that it looked like the fire was on purpose. So who's the jerk that burned down the restaurant? Did you find Mom's box?"

"To the first question: I have no idea. The police are looking into it. As to finding the box, no."

Her shoulders slumped.

"Hey, I just have to wait for everything to cool off, then I can go back and find it."

"It's probably gone."

He chucked her chin. "It's not gone 'til it's gone. It's marble so it might be all right. Maybe singed and sooty, but all right. Stay positive."

She looked away. "I put her Bible in there," she whispered.

Daniel stilled. "Why?"

Her shoulder lifted slightly, then dropped. "I don't know. I guess I was hoping it would . . . make a difference somehow. I don't know." She tucked her chin. "Stupid, I guess."

"Definitely not stupid. I promise I'll go back and look for it as soon as I can get access, okay?"

She sniffed and nodded. "So what now?" She pulled his jacket from the chair and walked behind him to the hall closet, opened the door, took out a hanger, and hung up the jacket. When she turned around, her slight frame shook. She was fighting tears.

"Aw, Riley, I'm sorry, hon. Come here, let's go into the den and have a seat."

She sniffed and shook her head. "No, you have an interview in the morning, remember? For the new cook you need?" She looked at the kitchen clock. "Or rather, in about four hours."

He kissed her forehead. Right. His secretary, Bridgett Holmes, had scheduled the interview after his trip to Charleston was canceled. Riley had instant access to his calendar so she knew where he was at all times. And sometimes she saved his hide by reminding him of appointments. "All right then. If you're sure."

"I'm sure." Her eyes widened. "Oh, I almost forgot. This guy named Tim Shepherd called. He said it was urgent that you call him back."

Daniel stiffened. Tim Shepherd, a real estate developer who wanted Daniel to sell his prime piece of land that now held a burned-down shell of a restaurant. "What time did he call?"

"Around eight o'clock."

"Okay, thanks." He pulled out his phone.

"You're not going to call him now, are you?" Riley exclaimed.

He paused. "Why the outrage?"

"The time, Uncle Daniel. Remember what time it is?"

Daniel blinked. "Oh right."

She shook her head, took his phone from his hand, and powered it down. "You can call him tomorrow. Today." She frowned. "In a few hours. Go to bed. You need your beauty rest."

He snorted, secretly glad she'd lightened the moment. "You go to bed too, kid. I'll see you in the morning."

"No you won't. I'm sleeping in."

"Playing hooky?"

"It's the weekend. Today is Saturday."

"Oh. Right. The weekend." Her exasperation amused him. He hoped he hid it well.

She shook her head. "You really need to work on the whole concept of time and days and stuff."

He sighed. "Hey, I'm getting better, aren't I?"

"Maybe a little." She gave a small laugh.

"But not much?"

"No, not much."

He paused. "Did Grandma call or text or anything? Does she know about this mess?"

"No, I haven't heard from her. She's probably asleep."

"But she watches the news every morning." He sighed. "I'll call her first thing in the morning."

"That would probably be wise."

He tweaked a stray lock of her hair. "Night, Princess. Love you."

She rolled her eyes. "Night, Danny boy. Love you too."

"Later, gator."

She glanced back over her shoulder. "Not saying it."

"After 'while, crocodile," he finished.

"Ugh." She disappeared down the hall to her room and the smile slipped from his lips. He turned his phone back on. Riley meant well, but he couldn't take a chance on missing any calls from anyone who might have news about the events of the night. He rubbed his eyes and walked from the kitchen into the living area to drop into his favorite recliner. Instead of picking up the remote and turning on the television, he stared at the blank screen while his brain finally processed the events. He had no idea how long he sat there, unable to relax. But he kept waiting for the phone to ring. Or for a knock on the door. Or for the security alarm to sound.

Something. Anything.

When no one called to give him a report on the conclusion of the fire, he unclipped his phone and dialed Detective Holcombe's number. Then hung up. The detective would call him if he had something to say. Daniel set the phone on the end table next to his grandmother's Bible. A Bible he hadn't opened in eighteen months but couldn't bring himself to put completely out of sight. He was sure a psychiatrist would have a field day with that one.

He turned his gaze from it.

Someone had set fire to his restaurant. That same someone — most likely, though not yet proven — had killed a man and hung him in the basement of one of his other restaurants.

Daniel was no stranger to death. He'd seen plenty of it during his three tours in the Middle East. He'd even been a target before, simply because of his country of birth. But this was different. This was personal. And the sinking feeling in his gut said it had only just begun.

■ ■ ■ ■

As he let himself inside his house, he breathed his first real breath since meeting Maurice Armstrong at the restaurant. The man had agreed to meet him after hours. When darkness would cover the fact that Armstrong was once again on Daniel's restaurant property. Money was a very good motivator.

He fancied himself pretty smart. Brilliant even. Usually he was a planner and always level-headed. He never acted upon impulse. At least not anymore. The fact that he'd done so tonight, had reverted to old habits, had knocked him off his game. Meeting Armstrong had been an impulse, a decision that had to be made without careful fore-thought or planning. Going to Daniel's house had been spur of the moment as well. He shouldn't have gone, but he almost couldn't help himself. He had to know, had to watch. It unnerved him that Daniel had sensed his presence and come looking for him. He'd managed to slip away, of course, but now it was time to regroup.

He headed for the fireplace and stripped himself of each garment and threw them into the cavernous hole. He used a small bit of lighter fluid and set the clothes on fire. He'd dispose of the ashes in the morning. He went into the master bath and bathed, scrubbing every square inch of skin. If they came to his house, they'd find no evidence on him. He meticulously cleaned his nails and hands — even though he'd worn gloves. Then washed his hair three times before deeming himself free of evidence. Once out of the shower, he dressed, then grabbed the bleach from beneath his sink. He poured the remaining amount of liquid into the shower, then scrubbed it as well as he had his body.

He replaced the bottle of bleach back under the sink, grabbed the damp towel, and returned to his living area. He tossed the towel into the fireplace with the clothes and watched the lot burn. He enjoyed the warmth from the flames as he thought.

He hadn't planned the events that had unfolded. Not all of them anyway. He certainly hadn't planned on having to kill. But once he'd seen what Armstrong had to show him, he'd had no choice. The plan had jumped into his mind as though it had been waiting for him to embrace it. And that was when he'd known that Armstrong had to die. No, *that* part of the night hadn't been planned.

But now that it was done, he wondered at his lack of emotion. Shouldn't he feel bad that he'd taken a man's life? Probably. But the fact that there had been no other choice soothed any remorse that might be trying to rear its head. And truly, Armstrong had brought on his own death, insisting Daniel needed to know things that just weren't his business. There was no way he could allow that. So really, Armstrong had committed suicide, it just hadn't been by his own hand. He smiled. It was like suicide by cop. He'd been perfectly justified in killing Armstrong, so there was no need for regrets.

He walked into the kitchen and poured himself a glass of ice water. He chugged it and refilled it, then walked back into the den. He relived the moment he'd felt Armstrong's life seep away. Carrying him into the basement might have been stupid, but he'd thought the man wouldn't be discovered until much later. How was he to know Daniel would be there and would almost come upon him? He wanted to smack himself. He should have checked the front parking lot. He would have seen Daniel's SUV. But he hadn't even gone that way. He'd parked in the cemetery and had walked over to the back area. Maurice had done the same. He sure hadn't wanted his car on Daniel's property.

Ah well, at least he'd thought to avoid the security cameras. And at least he'd had a hoodie on to pull up over his head. A hoodie that had now been reduced to ashes, along with the rest of the clothes that might carry any evidence of his nocturnal activities.

He had to be more careful from now on. He had to plan, to calculate the risks involved in what he wanted to accomplish and be ready to act if he found unexpected obstacles in his path. And he expected he would. He rose from his sofa and walked to his desk. He set his glass on the coaster and pulled his pen from the holder. With his left hand, he opened the middle drawer and pulled out a brand-new yellow legal pad. He placed the pad exactly in the middle of the desk and stared at it while he thought.

Yes, it had all worked out for the best, but there could be no more unplanned scenarios. He tapped his lip with his forefinger and ran through all the different ways he could use everything to his advantage. The niggling at the back of his mind that he'd had when he'd set fire to Matthews's restaurant now blossomed into a full-blown plan.

He clicked the tip of the pen and began to write.

[4]

Katie looked up from the novel she was reading, yawned, and chugged another swig of her black coffee. She had the day off and intended to spend it doing nothing more strenuous than curling up on the lounger in her newly finished sunporch. She had been trying to find the time to read this novel for a month now. She popped another peanut M&M and glanced at the clock.

Well, the rest of the day anyway. She'd slept through the first half of it. She'd received a text from Olivia stating that all was quiet and peaceful at the Matthews household and Katie was instructed to enjoy her time off.

So, she focused back on the book and ignored the call of the rest of her unfinished house. Truthfully, she'd be working, but she couldn't do anything in the kitchen until the cabinets arrived. Until then, she was content to wait and be lazy with a good book. And wait for Quinn to call and let her know how the investigation was going.

Unfortunately, the words on the page ran together and her brain refused to process them. She reread the last paragraph, and when she found herself reading it yet again, she finally slammed the book shut and looked at her watch. Was Quinn going to call or not?

"Not that he's under any obligation to call," she muttered. Backdraft, her orange tabby with reddish coloring, leaped onto her lap and settled against her stomach. She scratched the cat's ears and thought about the events of the early morning.

She wasn't officially assigned to anything dealing with the case, but she couldn't get the burning building out of her mind, or the fact that Daniel *could* have killed Armstrong and hung him. Or wrapped the chain around his neck and held him there until he died. Or whatever . . . She really wanted to hear the official cause of death.

Regardless, no one in his right mind would do that and not expect to be a suspect. *Or* was it just a clever way to throw suspicion off himself hoping that the police would wave their hands and say no one was that stupid?

Unfortunately, the police knew people *were* that stupid, so if that had been Daniel's plan, it would eventually backfire and he'd be arrested. But . . . she really didn't believe he'd had anything to do with any of it. She sighed. Time would tell. The first thing Quinn would check would be Daniel's financial status. Those records would show if he needed the insurance money from the fire.

Her phone buzzed and she looked at the screen. Her stomach dropped and she grimaced. But she couldn't ignore the caller. "Hi, Daphne."

"So you *are* still alive."

"I am. And how are you?"

Her sister's sigh filtered clearly through the line. "I'm fine, Katie. It's the middle of October."

"Yes, I'm aware of that."

"So . . . are you coming home for Thanksgiving next month?"

Katie closed her eyes. Was she? She pictured the event. Her family seated at the table with five places for her, her sister, her mother and father. And one distinctly missing person. The tension would crackle, the atmosphere would be subdued. And she would feel the blame emanating from her parents. She drew in a deep breath. "No. No, I'm not."

As soon as she said the words, a deep satisfaction filled her. This was the moment she'd been dreading and now she felt almost . . . free.

Silence greeted her words. She could feel Daphne's shock reaching across the airwaves. Katie held her tongue and refused to give in to the desire to cave and do what her sister wanted.

"I . . . see." Daphne cleared her throat. "I . . . well. Um . . . are you sure?"

"Daphne, what will it accomplish if I'm there?"

"Well, I . . . don't . . . I mean . . ." Another sigh. "Mom's not going to take this lightly."

"I didn't make the decision lightly." She glanced at the clock hanging over the television. "I need to go." But she didn't. Not really. But phone calls to her family always stressed her out and she didn't want to be stressed today.

"You always need to go," her sister said.

The sadness in her voice struck Katie and she swallowed against the sudden lump in her throat. She was only a two-hour drive from her family and she never saw them. And while she had her reasons, she knew Daphne missed her. "What are you doing this weekend?" Katie blurted.

"What do you mean?"

"I mean, are you busy? What are your plans? Are you on the schedule?" Daphne was an ER nurse at the Grand Strand Medical Center in Myrtle Beach.

"Nothing terribly exciting. I'm off Friday, probably will see a movie with some friends Friday night, work on Saturday, and Sunday dinner with Mom and Dad."

"You want to come visit?"

More silence. "You've never asked me that before."

Katie blinked. "I haven't?"

"No. Every time we talk, you're always busy with some job. So I don't ask you to come home and I don't ask to come visit. And . . . neither do you. Until today."

"Oh." She stood and walked over to the window to stare into her backyard and the wooded area beyond it. "I'm sorry." Had she truly not? She closed her eyes. "I didn't know I needed to. I suppose I just assumed you would know you had an open invitation."

Daphne's small laugh reached her. "No, I wasn't sure." The hesitancy in her sister's voice nearly killed her. "I mean, aren't you working?"

"Yes, I'm working a case, but that doesn't

mean I don't want to see you."

"Then I'd love to come see you this weekend. I want to hear more about your job."

"Oh. Right. Well, it's, um . . . pretty boring. At least most of the time."

"All right, then we'll talk about Thanksgiving."

Katie closed her eyes and gave a silent groan. "Okay. Text me when you're on the way."

"I can come Friday morning. We could have most of the day Friday, but I would have to leave first thing Saturday morning. I have to work that afternoon."

"That's fine. I'll take what I can get." Katie paused. "It's been too long. I'm looking forward to seeing you, Daph."

"Same here. Bye."

"Bye." Katie pressed the button to end the call. She dropped the phone into her lap. She knew why she hadn't extended an invitation before now. She'd been sure Daphne would say no. But she hadn't. Wonder of wonders, she hadn't.

Her phone vibrated. Riley. "Hello?"

"Hi, Katie, I hope you don't mind me bothering you."

"Of course not. You're never a bother. What's up?"

"I saw you sitting outside my house last night and wanted to say thanks for keeping an eye out for us. It made me feel better knowing you were there."

Katie stilled. "Wait, what? What are you talking about?"

"Uncle Daniel told me to go to bed, but I couldn't sleep, so I came down to the kitchen to get some water. When I looked out the window, I saw your car on the street."

What? "Riley, I don't mean to scare you, but that wasn't me."

Silence. Then, "Oh."

"What else did you notice about the vehicle?"

"Nothing really. I just thought it looked like yours and I didn't think any more about it." She paused. "It could have just been the neighbor's. I think they have one like it, but . . ." She laughed. A jerky, self-conscious sound only a teenage girl can make. "Never mind, I guess I was just seeing things. Maybe things I wanted to see."

"Or maybe not, Riley. Don't discount it. Did you see someone in the driver's seat?"

"Just a shadow. Like a silhouette."

"But there was definitely someone there," Katie said.

Riley didn't answer right away and Katie

71

could almost see her blue eyes narrowing in thought. "Yes," she finally said. "Because I thought it was you."

"So it was a woman?"

Riley hesitated. "Um. Maybe. I don't know. I mean, I just glanced out the window and saw a vehicle that I thought was yours and someone in the driver's seat, so . . ."

She just assumed. Katie drew in a deep breath. "All right then. I wouldn't worry too much about it."

"You wouldn't? Come on, Katie. After all that happened last night — this morning — you can't be serious."

She wasn't going to be able to blow it off. Not with Riley. "Well, I was hoping I could ease your mind, then go about investigating it a little."

"I thought that might be what you were doing."

The girl was sharp. Too sharp sometimes. "It's not going to work, huh?"

"Nope."

"Want me to come over and ask a few questions of your neighbors? See if anyone else saw anything?"

"Do you mind?"

"Of course not." Katie picked up the bowl that had held her M&Ms and found it empty. "I need to make a chocolate run.

Can I bring you something?"

"Of course. I never turn down chocolate."

Katie smiled even though Riley couldn't see it. "I'll be sure to come by sometime today." She glanced at the clock. It was already a little after twelve. She could be there in a couple of hours.

"Thanks, Katie, I appreciate it." The girl's voice had thickened with emotion.

"Is there something else going on?" Katie asked.

"Um . . ."

"Tell me, hon, what is it?"

"I'm just scared I'm going to lose him too," she whispered.

Katie knew the story of her parents being killed by a drunk driver. She remembered the grief flashing in Daniel's eyes when he'd confronted Quinn while his building burned behind him. "Don't go there, Riley. It doesn't help anything. Stay positive and focused on the things you can change."

"Like what?"

"Like if someone is after your uncle, he needs to take precautions, be careful, stay alert. You can remind him of that. And when you're with him, you can be watchful and alert as well. Actually do that even if you're not with him. But you get the idea. That's being proactive. He's got skills too, Riley.

Good skills. He's a fighter, he's smart, and he can take care of himself. Remember that, because worrying about what might happen won't help the situation and can distract you from what you need to do. Does that make sense?"

"Yes." This time she sounded thoughtful. "Yes, that makes a lot of sense."

"Where's your uncle this morning?"

"At A Taste of Yesterday, the downtown restaurant. He, uh, told me about that man that was killed and hung there. He figured I should hear it from him instead of seeing it on the news." The girl sounded distanced from the fact, like she'd already thought about it, processed it, and was thinking about something else.

"What are you thinking, sweetie?"

"A lot of things. We've talked a lot. Had some good conversations on just about every topic there is, and I know you believe in God."

The statement caught her off guard. "Yes, I do."

"I know. And you know I do too. Remember I told you that my parents were missionaries?"

"I remember."

"Well, they taught me that God puts people in our lives for a reason. I really believe that."

The seventeen-year-old's insight brought a lump to Katie's throat. She cleared it. "I agree."

"Which is why I want to hire you to be my uncle's bodyguard."

5

1:00 PM

Daniel set his drink on the white tablecloth that covered an 1860s antique Chippendale dining room table. The table had belonged to his brother and sister-in-law. Now he considered putting it in storage until the fire at his North Lake Drive restaurant was solved. The last thing he wanted was to lose another piece of the people he missed so much. And he didn't think Riley could take another hit. He still hadn't been able to go out to the site to look for the box. But he would.

He studied the name and number Riley had given to him last night. Tim Shepherd with Shepherd Real Estate Developers. The man had called him at home, he must be getting desperate. Unfortunately, he'd just have to stay that way. Daniel wasn't selling. He picked up his phone to call the man when the device vibrated. His mother's picture flashed on the screen. "Hi, Mom."

"Daniel. You want to explain?"

"Hi, Mom, good to hear from you."

"Cute. Now explain."

"Nothing much to explain. If you saw the news, you know as much as I do."

"Is Riley all right?"

"Did you get her text?"

"Yes, but anyone can send a text."

"It was really her."

His mother snorted. "I know it was. I've already talked to her."

Then why ask if she was all right? "Gotcha."

"Daniel." Her voice softened. "Are *you* all right?"

"I'm fine, Mom, I promise. I'm not sure what's going on or why this is happening, but the police are working on it." He wondered if he should be worried about her as well. He frowned. Then sighed. "Mom, will you watch your back?"

"What do you mean?"

"I mean, I don't know who's behind the incidents or why. I don't know if I'm the only target or if he's going to start targeting the people I love. I just . . . I'm worried enough to mention it."

Silence greeted him. "I'll watch my back." He heard the seriousness in her voice and was glad she didn't just blow off his concerns. "Will you keep me updated?" she asked.

"Of course." Her heavy sigh came through the line. "I will, I promise."

"Does Riley need to come stay with me for a while? I can get someone else to go out on the next assignment." His mother was a paid companion who traveled with those who didn't have anyone else to travel with. The largest percentage of her clientele were women who'd lost their husbands. He smiled when he thought of how far she'd come since being a single mother who worked three jobs to make ends meet.

"No, Mom. Not right now. In fact, going on this assignment may be the best thing you can do right now. Get away. Be safe. If something changes, I'll let you know."

"And Riley's safe?"

"Yes." He felt like she was. Right now.

"All right then. If you're sure."

"I am. And I promise to let you know if there's any new developments that you need to know about."

"That sounds good."

He rubbed a hand across the back of his neck. "How long are you in town for?"

"Just today and tomorrow."

"Where's your next assignment?"

"Brazil."

"What's her name?" He always ran back-ground checks on the people she traveled with. He might not be in law enforcement anymore, but he still had friends in high places.

"Eliza Green. She's seventy-eight years old and this is a bucket list trip for her. She's terribly sad her husband passed away last year and was unable to go with her, but before he died, he made her promise to take the trip for him. She's honoring that request but doesn't want to go alone. I've already met her and she seems wonderful. A real firecracker too. I think we'll get along just fine."

"I hope you have a great time."

"I've never been to Brazil, I hear it's lovely. They speak Portuguese, so I've been brushing up." He heard her nails clicking on her keyboard. "Riley said she has to decide on her internship soon."

"Yes. If she works with Martin, she starts Tuesday, I think."

"So weird she didn't jump at going to Co-zumel, but to each her own, I suppose."

"I suppose."

"Take care of my granddaughter."

"You know it."

"Love you."

"Love you too." He hung up and pulled up Tim Shepherd's number again. The front door of the restaurant chimed.

Daniel looked up as his buddy Martin Sheehan, full-time archaeologist and part-time university professor, bounded over and slipped into the chair next to him. "Hey."

"Hey. You get bored playing in your sandbox?" Daniel asked him. He set his phone aside. Shepherd could wait.

"Cute. And never. Boredom isn't a word I'm familiar with." Martin waved a waitress over.

Sarah Durham, the pretty brunette and single mother of two young children, was one of Daniel's best waitresses. She wore an 1860s-style costume complete with hoop under the skirt. She had on one of the more fashionable items of history, with the skirt raised above the ground and cords tied around her waist. Daniel had wondered if the clothing would interfere with her movements and ability to serve effectively, but so far, she'd done a fabulous job. And some customers mentioned they came just to see what Sarah would be wearing that day. Finishing off her attire was a small hat with the popular ribbon streamers. Sarah had insisted she liked dressing in costume and had even made a few of her own.

If she stuck around, he planned to make her manager one day. Soon. She walked over and pulled her pad and pen out of her apron pocket. "What can I get for you, Mr. Sheehan? Same as usual?"

"Absolutely. Burger all the way, cheese fries, and a double chocolate shake. Oh, and let's go crazy. Add a large side of onion rings to it this time."

"You got it."

"Fabulous dress, Sarah. Did you make that one?"

Sarah flushed and gave them a slight curtsy. "Thank you ever so much, Mr. Sheehan," she drawled in her soft southern belle voice. "And yes, I made this one," she said in her normal alto. "So kind of you to notice."

"If it's history, he notices it," Daniel said with a smile.

"Be right back, gentlemen." She walked away, her hoopskirt swaying gently, the hint of citrus following in her wake.

Daniel shook his head as Martin took a long swig of his water. "Will you ever change your eating habits?" The man ate like a trash can and never did gain an ounce. Lean and muscled, with blue eyes and reddish blond hair, his rugged good looks turned female heads wherever he went. A fact he acknowledged but didn't seem to care much about anymore.

"Not likely."

Daniel chuckled. After his third divorce, Martin had declared he'd finally gotten his priorities in order. He was now hyper-focused on his work as an archaeologist and professor at the local university. "What brings you in?" Daniel asked. "Besides the free food and my charming company, of course."

"Came to see if you were wallowing in self-pity."

"No time for that." Daniel gestured to his open laptop and cell phone. "Crunching numbers, going back and forth with the insurance company, and scheduling the reconstruction of the restaurant."

"So you're going to rebuild."

It wasn't a question. Martin knew him well enough. "Of course."

Martin looked around. "It's good to see that the incidents from last night don't seem to be hurting business."

"No. Thank goodness."

"How was the interview? You find this place a new cook?"

"You talked to Riley this morning."

"How do you think I knew where to find you and that you had an interview?"

"Of course. The interview went well for a last-minute thing. I texted the guy yesterday morning when I found out my trip was going to be canceled and he arranged his schedule to meet me. Not only was that impressive, he really knows his stuff. He's a senior at USC getting his Culinary Arts degree. I hired him on the spot and he agreed to start Monday."

"Good for you." He took a sip of his water. "He wasn't turned off by the events of last night?"

"I made sure he knew what happened, and while he expressed regret for the loss of life, it didn't scare him off the job."

"Excellent." Martin rubbed his fuzzy chin and Daniel thought he saw a puff of dust erupt. He simply dipped his napkin in his water and handed it to his friend. Martin gave a sheepish grin and ran the napkin over his scruffy facial hair. When finished, he crumpled the napkin into a ball. "I have to say, I'm surprised you opened."

Daniel rubbed a hand down his cheek. "I thought about staying closed today, but what's the point? The crime scene was cleared about an hour before we were scheduled to open and I have workers who need to work. They have families to feed and bills to pay. Closing would have done more harm than good."

Martin nodded. "This whole business is a tough break. I'm sorry about Armstrong. Can't believe he was that depressed. And to hang himself in your basement . . ." He clucked his tongue. "Was it some twisted way to get back at you because you fired him?"

"I'm not so sure it was a suicide."

Martin lifted a brow. "No? That's what the media is reporting."

Daniel shook his head. "The cops are investigating. That's all I know right now."

"And someone burned down the North Lake location. What's up with that? That's crazy."

Daniel grunted. "Yeah. Crazy's a pretty good word." An accurate one that had been used way too much in the last twelve hours.

"How bad is the damage?"

"I'm not sure yet. I rode by this morning and several firefighters were still out there."

"Making sure the blaze is out for good."

"Yes. I know the arson investigator is supposed to get over there sometime today. Once he files his report, I'll hear from the cops. But I have a feeling the damage is extensive and I'm going to have to build it back from the ground up."

"Well, I guess we know where your focus

is going to be over the coming months."

Daniel grunted. "Yeah. No kidding."

Martin leaned back and crossed his arms. "So are the incidents related?"

"I don't know. Like I said, they're working on figuring it all out."

"Let me know if you need anything."

The compassion on his friend's face helped ease the sting of the past day. "Thanks." At least Martin didn't think Daniel had anything to do with the whole mess.

"Moving on to less-depressing topics. Has Riley made up her mind on which internship she wants to do? I'm all ready for her to come play in the sandbox." Martin smirked.

Daniel sighed. The private school Riley attended had a special month during the school year that they dedicated to internships. Students received hands-on training in their field of interest and it counted toward their high school units. "Riley is a very smart girl with a variety of interests. She's narrowed the field to marine biology and archaeology. The fact that she knows and likes you is weighing in your favor. The fact that they're offering marine biology in Cozumel is tilting the scales."

"Cozumel." He sighed. "I know which one I'd choose, but I still hope she picks me. I have tons I could teach her." Sarah approached and Martin's eyes gleamed with anticipation when she set the food in front of him. "That looks amazing. Thanks."

"Of course."

"You got your license yet?"

Sarah grinned. "Just have to take the test, thanks to Riley and Daniel here. Who would have thought little ole me would learn how to fly a plane?"

"You're a great pilot, Sarah," Daniel said. And she was.

Martin's gaze lifted to meet Daniel's. "What did you have? That grilled chicken salad that wouldn't fill up a gnat?"

"Yes." Daniel laughed and winked at Sarah. "It was good and it filled me up. And in ten years when your cholesterol is sky high, I'll be the one laughing."

Martin snorted. "I doubt it. What do you think, Sarah?"

"I think I'll stay out of it." She smiled. "Tell Riley I'd love to go up a couple more times before I take the test. Even though she's not a certified instructor, she really knows how to instruct."

Daniel nodded. "I'm sure she'd enjoy doing that with you. She said you were the best student she's ever had."

Sarah grinned. "I'm the only student she's

ever had."

"As soon as she turns eighteen, she can be certified, so it's great practice for her too." He slapped Martin on his shoulder. "Riley keeps trying to get this guy in the sky, but he won't budge."

Martin nearly choked on his mouthful of burger. He shook his head. "Not me. No way, no how. I'm a landlubber. No flying for me." He swallowed and wiped his mouth.

She shot a smirk at Martin. "On second thought, since I was asked, I'll go ahead and voice my opinion on your eating habits. I agree with Daniel." She laughed at Martin's look of dismay. "You know he's right."

Martin shook his head as though he felt sorry for the two of them. "I work it all off playing in my sandbox." Sarah made her way over to another customer and Martin stuck a straw in his shake. "But the food and the exceptional company aren't the only reasons I decided to drop in."

"No kidding."

"Nope."

"What other reasons could you possibly have?"

Martin took a huge bite of the burger and chewed. Slowly.

Daniel scowled. "You do that on purpose."

His friend swallowed and grinned. "Yep." Then took a large swig of his shake.

"Seriously, dude?" Daniel rolled his eyes.

Martin laughed. "Okay, okay." He leaned closer. "I found something."

"You dig in the dirt, you're always finding something. What's so special about this time?"

Martin glanced around the nearly full restaurant, then reached into his pocket to extract a clear plastic baggie. A small coin rested in the bottom right corner.

"Cool." He tried to pull the bag in for a closer look, but Martin snatched it back, hovering over it as though it would disappear if he let it get too far from his person.

Once again, Martin's eyes darted from patron to patron, table to table before coming back to rest on Daniel. "It's a coin. A rare coin. If I'm right, there were only fifteen ever minted." He slowly slid it toward Daniel, who stared at the coin.

"1804? Wow, that's old."

"Yes, but they weren't actually struck in 1804, they were all minted in the 1830s or later. If I'm right and it's not a counterfeit — which I'm 99 percent sure it isn't — do you know how much it's worth?" he hissed.

"No, but I'm guessing you do?"

"The Bust Dollar, Class I — last sold at

an auction for 4.14 million."

Daniel nearly choked. "What?" He straightened and let out a low whistle. "No kidding."

"No kidding. Edmund Roberts distributed the coins in 1834 and 1835. They were created to be special proof coin sets and were supposed to be diplomatic gifts during his trips to Siam and Muscat."

"How did they get all the way over here in North America?"

"I have no idea. I'm guessing that one of the Civil War soldiers had it with him. Maybe passed to him from a father who traveled widely. It wasn't just poor kids from the wrong side of the street that fought in that war. There were some rich kids too. Frankly, I don't care. I just know it's going to make me famous," he whispered.

Daniel thought the man might cry, he was so excited. "That's some serious stuff. What are you going to do with it?"

"Like I said, I'm going to let it make me famous, my friend." He let out a laugh and Daniel smiled. Martin finally seemed to be happy, to be in his element. "But," Martin said, "I'm going to keep it a little secret for now. I want to see what else is down there before I bring in the media."

"Good for you, Martin. That's incredible."

The man's eyes gleamed with the same glee as when Sarah had placed his food in front of him. "Indeed." He turned his attention back to the plate in front of him. Within minutes, he'd cleaned it off and downed his shake. "I gotta go. I'm spending the night at the dig."

"Are you crazy? It's freezing out there."

"I've got a space heater or two. I'll be fine." He rubbed a hand down his unshaven face. "Might need to stop by my house and reacquaint myself with a razor, though. Can't stand it when the stubble gets dirt in it. Itches like crazy."

"Good idea." He glanced around, mimicking Martin's subtle glances from earlier, then nodded toward his friend's pocket. "Do you have someplace safe for that?"

"Safe-deposit box, but can't get there until Monday."

"Well, don't flash it to anyone else. People have killed for less."

Martin paled. "I know. I know."

"You want me to put it in my safe at home until Monday?"

"No way. I'm not letting this baby out of my sight."

"Does anyone else know about it?"

"No. I probably shouldn't have shown it to you, but you're my best friend. I trust you and I had to tell someone. I just can't get over it. I found it, man, I found it." His hands actually started to shake. "Do you know what this means? This is my big break and it's all I can do to contain myself." He sucked in a deep breath and closed his eyes. "Okay, I'm out of here." And then he was gone like mist on the wind.

"Daniel?"

He yanked his eyes from the door and turned to find Katie standing next to his chair. "Hey there." He stood. "How are you?"

"I'm doing well, thanks. How are you?"

"Recovering." He waved a hand to the chair Martin had just vacated. He pushed aside the dirty dishes and they both sat. "Can I get you something to eat?" he asked. "It's on me."

"I'm not hungry, but I'd love a glass of strawberry tea."

"You got it." He waved Sarah over and she took the order. "How did you know I'd be here?"

"Riley told me."

"You talked to Riley?"

"A little bit ago. She's worried about you." Sarah returned with the tea and Katie took a grateful sip. "Thanks. That's wonderful."

He nodded. "Glad you like it." He sighed.

"Look, I'll admit, things were intense last night. Crazy. Unbelievable even. But —" he shook his head — "I don't think Riley needs to worry. I'll talk with her again when I get home."

She leaned forward, her dark eyes capturing his. "I don't think you understand just how afraid she is of losing you."

Daniel stilled. "Why do you say that?"

"She called me and wants to hire me to be your bodyguard."

That sentence packed a hard punch. "Oh man."

"Yeah." She hesitated.

He frowned. "What else aren't you telling me?"

She tapped her lip, then linked her fingers together and rested her hands on the table. "Riley said there was a car sitting outside your house last night. She thought it was me and didn't think anything else about it. She went to bed and asked me about it when we talked earlier."

His frown deepened. "But it wasn't you."

"No. And the police officer Quinn had posted to drive by your house on a regular basis last night remembers the vehicle but said he never saw anyone inside."

He stood. "So Riley could be in danger. I've got to go."

"No, she's fine. Olivia's with her. I asked her to stay with her while I tracked you down. And another officer is also driving by frequently."

He slowly took his seat again. "Okay. Thanks." He took a swig of water. "So. The officer who drove by my house last night . . . You talked to him?"

She nodded. "I called him a little while ago. Riley asked me to look into it."

He rubbed a hand down his cheek and studied her. "Seems like Riley's asking an awful lot of you."

"Not at all. She's a friend and I've grown to care about her over the last year she's been in my class."

"Riley's mentioned the time you've spent with her, drinking coffee and talking. I appreciate that. She really admires you."

The sudden pink in her cheeks endeared her to him. Sarah refilled Katie's empty glass, and Katie thanked the woman. "I think it's important to mentor young girls, to share the wisdom the years have imparted." She gave a self-conscious chuckle. "Such that it is. But Riley's a great girl with a good head on her shoulders."

"Thanks, I think so too." He cleared his throat. "The officer didn't happen to write down the plate number, did he?"

93

"Yes, actually, he did. He took note of all the vehicles on the street and ran checks on them. Nothing came back as a red flag, but I'm interested in tracking down the vehicle that caught Riley's attention."

Daniel looked away from her, his gaze on the now-black computer screen. "I don't understand this."

"What?"

"Any of it. Who would do this or why. And I don't like it when I don't understand something."

"I can understand that."

He gave her a small smile.

She grimaced. "Okay, that was bad, sorry. It was worth a try." She sobered. "Look, the investigation is going to take some time. I know that you're experienced in taking care of yourself and don't need me, but sometimes it doesn't hurt to have someone watching your back."

He tilted his head. "I'd agree with most of that."

She lifted a brow. "Most of it?"

"You're right. I can take care of myself, but that doesn't mean I don't recognize my limitations. I'm not invincible."

"So, do you mind if I just kind of hang around and keep an eye on your back — and Riley's?"

He studied her for a moment. "You want me to agree for Riley's sake, don't you?"

She gave a slight shrug. "It couldn't hurt."

"And it would offer her some reassurance," he said with a sigh.

"Yes."

He pursed his lips and gave a slow nod. "You can hang around . . ."

"But . . ."

"But if this guy comes near Riley with the intention of hurting her, he's a dead man."

6

Katie nodded. "I can live with that." She stood. "Do you mind if I take a look at the basement?"

"Why?"

"I just want to take a look. When you and Quinn are talking about the area, I come up with nothing to visualize. It'll help to have a picture in my mind of the place you or Quinn refer to. Have you been back down there since everything happened?"

"Yes. This morning."

Of course he would have. He'd have checked every nook and cranny after the detectives and CSU left and the scene was released. "Did you find anything?"

"No. Just cleaned up all the residue left by law enforcement and swept out some dirt that had been tracked in." He gestured toward the back of the restaurant. "But I'm more than happy to take you down."

"Thanks."

She followed him through the restaurant, then down the stairs, taking note of the fine décor detail. The brick steps, the wooden banister, the old pictures on the stairwell wall. "You like history."

"Love it. It fascinates me for some reason. I like to think that if I know the mistakes made by others before me, I'll be smart enough to learn from them."

"Hmm. I know what you mean."

At the bottom of the steps, she stopped and looked around. Full wine racks, storage shelves, and containers. "You're very organized."

He laughed. "You can thank my manager for that. She's amazing."

"You've got some good people working for you."

His eyes clouded. "And maybe some not so good."

"The woman who misrepresented you to Quinn?"

"Yes. I wonder if that was deliberate or if she just really misunderstood what I said to Maurice."

"I'd like to know that too. Can you think of who it might be?"

"No. Unfortunately. As far as I'm concerned, I have a good working relationship with all of my employees. I have about a hundred people working for me — just with this restaurant alone. Another hundred at the restaurant that burned. A mixture of full and part time. I don't know them all on a personal level, of course, but I *have* met each one at some point over the course of the time they've worked for me. I checked the records of those who were working that day. This is a large restaurant. We stay busy. Sometimes I have fifty people on duty. That day there were forty-three workers."

"Wow. It would take a while to question them all."

"Yes. Even going over the list, no name jumped out at me."

"It might not be important. If Quinn thinks it is, he'll work on it."

"Like a dog with a bone."

She laughed. "Exactly." Katie ran a hand down the interior wall. "What was this place before it was a restaurant?"

"An old inn. The second floor above the restaurant used to be living quarters. I plan to restore them with profits from the restaurant and then rent them out."

She nodded to the floor. "Looks like you didn't get all the dirt."

"What?" He walked closer, looked where she pointed, and placed his hands on his hips. "Huh." He went to a small closet on the other side of the room and came back with a broom. She opened the basement door and he swept the dirt out. "That's weird. Maybe one of the staff came down here after I did and had dirt on his shoes or something."

A thud at the back made him look up. "What was that?"

Katie shook her head. "I don't know. I think it came from back here." She looked around. "Or upstairs." She walked toward where she thought she'd heard the noise and placed her hand on the wall. "What's back there?"

"Nothing. Just storage. The access door is around here." He led her to the other side of the U-shaped section. He twisted the knob. "Locked." He knocked on the door. "Hey, is anyone in there?"

No answer.

"You have the keys?"

"Of course." He pulled a set of keys from his pocket. He started to open the door when a loud crash shook the floor just above them. "What in the —" He raced to the steps and Katie followed behind him at a fast clip. At the top, just inside the restaurant, he rushed over to the small crowd gathered around their waitress. Sarah, he'd called her. Katie watched him wade through and take Sarah's hand. "What happened?"

"I'm sorry, Daniel," Sarah said.

A pitcher lay shattered on the floor, with pieces of glass swimming in the tea. "It's fine," he told her. "Really. Don't worry about the pitcher. Are you all right?"

"Yes, I'm fine, just stupid. One of the customers grabbed my rear as I walked past, and even through all the layers of this silly dress, it startled me so bad I dropped the pitcher."

Daniel's eyes narrowed. "Where is he?"

Sarah waved a hand. "He left." She indicated his overturned chair.

Daniel righted it and slid it under the table. "Is he a regular?"

"No, I've never seen him before." Two other waitresses appeared with towels and a broom and began to clean up the mess. Sarah smiled at them. "Thanks, ladies."

Daniel walked to the door and looked out. Stiffened. "What was he wearing?"

"A flannel shirt and I think he pulled on a brown coat. But —"

Daniel strode out and Katie hurried to follow him. "Daniel?"

He kept going until he came face-to-face with a man who was wearing the clothing Sarah had described and getting ready to get into his white Buick. "You just assaulted one of my waitresses."

The tall man turned. Katie stood back, ready to jump in and help if Daniel needed backup. Bare hands against a gun or a knife sometimes ended badly for the unarmed person. Then again, Daniel had his gun on him but she was fairly certain he wouldn't pull it unless his life was in danger.

"I didn't assault anyone," the man sputtered. "What are you talking about?"

"Are you denying you placed your hand on one of my waitresses? That you grabbed her?"

The man bristled. "I didn't touch anyone, and if she says I did, she's a liar."

"What about the video footage I'm getting ready to pull up from my security camera? Is that going to lie too?" Daniel's soft voice belied the deadly intent displayed by his body language.

The man slammed his car door and swore. He faced Daniel, fists clenched at his sides. Katie shifted into a better position to watch his hands.

"What's your name?" Daniel asked.

"John Doe." The man sneered. "And I didn't grab anyone. You look at your video and see I'm telling the truth."

"If she said you did, you did. She's playing the part of a southern belle in an historical restaurant. And if you're a gentleman, you keep your hands to yourself. You're not welcome here again. I'll be getting your face from the video footage and making sure my staff knows it. You show up here again and you'll be charged with assault." He paused. "If she doesn't decide to press charges today."

"She's crazy! She brushed up against me, I didn't grab her!"

"Then why are you running?"

"Because my marriage is already on the rocks, and if this gets back to my wife, I'm done, you understand? I can't let that happen. And you sure don't have to worry about me coming back. I'm getting out of here before this day gets any worse." The man let out another string of choice words, opened his car door, and climbed inside. Within seconds, he was squealing from the parking lot.

"You get his plate?" Katie asked.

"Yep."

"Me too."

When he turned, a slow anger burned in his eyes. He looked past Katie. She turned to see Sarah standing in the doorway looking regal and southern — and a bit teary-eyed. "Thank you, Daniel. No one's ever done anything like that for me before."

He scowled. "Guys like that are creeps. Are you going to press charges?"

She flinched. "No. I just want to forget it happened."

"You could teach him a lesson."

Sarah shook her head and backed up. "No, I think you might have been the better teacher in this instance."

"Still think you should press charges."

She hesitated, then shook her head. "No."

"Fine. But next time, bash the pitcher over his head."

Sarah gave a short bark of laughter. "Good idea. Hopefully there won't be a next time."

Katie bit her lip, her admiration for the man growing the more she got to know him. Sarah disappeared back into the restaurant. The curious rubberneckers dispersed. Some back into the restaurant and some to their vehicles.

They walked back into the restaurant and took their seats once more while he closed his laptop. He looked at Katie. "I think I'm done here. Now what?"

"While Quinn's checking on Tim Shepherd, we can be proactive."

"What do you have in mind?"

"One, why don't we do a little digging into Maurice Armstrong?"

"And two?"

"I promised Riley I'd talk to your neighbors and see if anyone saw anything last night."

He shoved his laptop into his black bag. "I'm going to leave too. I'd feel better working from home and being close to Riley after hearing there was some unknown person outside my house last night."

"Of course."

He led the way, then held the door for her.

She lifted a brow. "Thanks." She stepped outside and pulled her coat tighter around her.

Daniel shut the door behind him.

A crack sounded and something slammed him to the sidewalk.

7

"Shooter! Run!" Katie screamed to those on the sidewalk, frozen and staring. Others had already taken off before she had a chance to call out the warning. "Daniel!" Her heart slammed into her throat. Was he alive?

She grabbed for him, but he was rolling to his feet with a grunt. He snagged her arm and pulled her behind the nearest parked vehicle. Another shot shattered the car window and Katie ducked. Screams echoed around her. When she looked back up, Daniel had his weapon out, already scanning the area.

"You're okay?" she gasped.

"Yeah. The bullet got my computer bag." He grunted. "And probably my computer, but I'm alive so I'm okay with that."

Katie made a mental note of the layout and where the bullets could be coming from. The front of the restaurant faced the frontage road with the interstate just beyond. Elmwood cemetery snugged up to the parking lot in the back. To her right was a large tree-lined field and another road past it.

"Where's he shooting from?" she asked as she grabbed her phone and dialed 911.

The operator answered before the first ring cut off. "911, what's your emergency?"

"There's a shooter targeting A Taste of Yesterday restaurant on Elmwood. I can't spot where he's shooting from, though." She scanned the area again, desperate to pinpoint the shooter.

"There." Daniel bumped her arm. "Behind the rail."

She followed his pointing finger and spotted the crouched figure. "He's on the guardrail on I-76. He's got a high-powered rifle —" Three more shots had her scrunching down into a tight ball. The bullets hit the building behind her. "— and we need officers here fast!"

Keyboard clicks came through the line. "We've got officers en route. ETA is ninety seconds."

"Make it sixty." She hung up as two more quick shots brought more screams. Sirens sounded, but Katie could tell they were still a good distance away. She kept her eyes on the shooter and gave a brief thought to going after him. Her mind calculated the distance, the lack of coverage, and her chances of reaching him without getting shot. They weren't good.

"Don't do it," Daniel muttered. A fine sheen of sweat covered his forehead and upper lip.

She met his gaze. He'd thought about it too, but the wide-open expanse between them and the vehicle they hid behind would make it a suicide mission. They were all effectively pinned down for the moment. The shooter had chosen well.

More bullets chinked the asphalt. Two slammed into the car they used for protection. She ducked again and looked at the others crouched behind vehicles. A man held his infant against his chest, head ducked against his small body. She wouldn't have thought it possible, but her adrenaline kicked it up a notch. Two teens huddled together behind the wheel of a truck. Anger flowed hot and swift. Putting innocents in danger was just wrong. Her eyes swept the area once again. On the heels of the anger came gratitude. So far she didn't see any wounded, so she prayed everyone had made it to a safe hiding place, out of sight — and range — of the shooter. Yes, definitely something to be grateful for.

The sirens screamed louder. Katie edged around the front of the vehicle to take another look in the direction of the shooter. He was gone. Blue lights flashed from the location she'd reported him. She pulled back and looked at Daniel. "He's gone."

Daniel scowled. "Yeah, but where?"

"I don't know. Don't give up your hiding place yet. Maybe a traffic cam got him on video or at least his license plate."

"I'm not holding my breath," he muttered.

She understood what he meant. After another long pause, when no more bullets came their way, he stood, cautious and watching.

Katie punched in a text to Olivia to let her know what was going on. "Do you want Riley to know about this?"

He looked skyward. She followed his gaze with her own. Already a news helicopter hovered above. It never did take them long. "Yes," he said.

Katie finished the text and told Olivia to stay close to Riley and assure the girl her uncle was — once again — unharmed.

By the time she hit send, officers had descended and the chaos bumped up to the next level. Law enforcement in SWAT gear held their weapons ready as they started clearing the bystanders from the area. Katie flashed her badge. The badge that afforded her law enforcement privileges when she needed them, thanks to the mayor.

"He's with me." She gave the officer a brief rundown of the situation and earlier incidents. "We're going inside the restaurant."

The officer nodded. "Go. I'm right behind you. I need to get everyone's information and a statement." He waved over three other officers and asked for their help in expediting the process.

Daniel marched into the restaurant. Katie followed.

"Everybody listen up," Daniel said. The patrons cowering under booths and tables slowly started to emerge. "A Taste of Yesterday is closed until further notice. If you have a business card, leave it on the bar. If you want to write down your name and email address, that's fine. Once the trouble is past and I reopen, you're all invited back for a free meal. I apologize for the scare. Don't leave yet, though, until we receive the all clear from the police. I know they want to talk to you."

The police got busy. Conversation buzzed as the diners placed their information in the designated area. But no one ventured out the door. Less than a minute later, an officer stepped inside, weapon drawn.

"It's all clear in here," Katie said. She flashed her badge again.

The officer holstered his weapon. "Anyone hurt in here?"

"No," Katie said.

He nodded. "The shooter is no longer in the area, as far as we can tell. As soon as the officers are finished in here, everyone is safe to leave."

The officers were professional and quick. One by one the customers filed out the door, and soon everyone was gone, leaving her and Daniel and his workers alone in the restaurant. Some gravitated toward him. He motioned them all to join him in the large dining area and they filed in.

"Daniel?"

He turned and Katie saw the young waitress named Sarah approach him. "Yeah?"

"Are you really going to shut down?"

His jaw tightened. "I have to. Someone's targeted me and those around me. I can't take a chance on someone getting between him and me." He looked around, his eyes connecting with each person. "You're welcome to find another job, of course, but I hope you'll give the police a few days to catch the person responsible. I'll continue

110

to pay you for now. If this drags out, we'll talk about what to do at that time."

"You're going to pay us not to work?" One of the cooks behind the counter scratched his head. "That doesn't seem right."

"Shut up, man." Another co-worker nudged him. "If he wants to pay us to chill, I'm good with that."

Daniel smirked, but his eyes remained hard and cold. "Yes, I'm going to pay you not to work until you hear from me. Your paychecks will be mailed to your home addresses."

One by one, his employees left, each one stopping to either shake his hand or offer a hug. The police officer spoke with someone over his radio. Once the last person was out the door, he turned to Daniel. "Detective Holcombe is here to talk to you."

"Of course he is." Daniel sighed and rubbed his eyes. "Fine."

Katie took note of the new lines on his face since last night.

Quinn stepped inside the restaurant and the officer left. "You again, huh?"

"Yeah. Lucky me."

Quinn looked around. "Someone said you shut the restaurant down."

"I did."

"I think that was probably a smart move."

"I didn't do it for you."

"I know." Quinn's tone was easy, concilia-
tory even, but Daniel didn't give an inch.
She watched him. Given his law enforcement background, he knew being investigated was part of the process. She also knew
he didn't have to like it. Or the detective
doing the investigating. Although, Daniel
had to realize this latest incident worked in
his favor. He would now be seen as a victim,
not a suspect.

Quinn pulled his notebook from his
pocket. "Are you all okay? I don't see any
blood."

"Fortunately, I think my laptop was the
only casualty." Daniel handed it to Quinn,
who studied the bullet hole. "The bullet's
still in there for ballistics."

Quinn motioned for a crime scene tech.
The young woman hurried over. "Bag this.
It's evidence."

"Right away."

She took it and left. Quinn scratched his
nose, then pointed behind him. "There
aren't any cameras along the interstate that
caught the shooter himself." He turned
back. "The ones that caught his vehicle and
license plate aren't any help because he had
it caked with mud. He also parked his car
in such a way that it blocked his actions

from oncoming motorists. Anyone who passed him probably thought he was just waiting on help and couldn't see the rifle."

"Great."

"Yeah. He picked a good spot."

"In other words, he had this planned," Katie said. "He was waiting, watching for Daniel to come out of the restaurant."

"Which means he knew I'd be here today," Daniel said.

"Are you often here around this time on Saturday?"

Daniel shook his head. "No, not usually. I don't have a set schedule. Sometimes I come in, sometimes I don't. I have good managers and they keep me updated, so I have the weekends off most of the time."

Quinn frowned. "All right. Then maybe he followed you when you left your house earlier or picked up your tail along the way?"

"I doubt it. I was watching."

"And you're trained to spot a tail."

Daniel met Quinn's eyes. "Yes."

"Right. The Marines."

"And CID," Katie murmured.

Quinn's eyes widened a fraction.

Daniel crossed his arms. "You haven't gotten the DD-214?" His military record that would have his history on it.

"It's been requested." He studied Daniel

for a bit longer, then gave a short nod. "I knew you were military, but . . . all right then. You didn't have a tail when you got to the restaurant. But our shooter knew you were here."

"What if it was the guy you confronted?" Katie asked Daniel. "Would he have had time to muddy his car, pick his spot, and take shots at you?"

"And he just happened to have a rifle with him?"

"Maybe he's a hunter."

"What guy?" Quinn asked.

"A customer," Katie said. "He was a little free with his hands with one of Daniel's waitstaff, and Daniel let him know that if he came back, he'd be arrested for assault."

Quinn lifted a brow. "Really?"

"Yes."

"Does the waitress want to press charges?"

Daniel shook his head. "I don't think so."

Quinn frowned. "She should."

"I agree."

"So what's this guy's name?" Quinn asked.

"John Doe."

Quinn rolled his eyes.

"He didn't give it. Paid in cash. But Katie and I both got his plate number." Daniel gave it to Quinn along with the vehicle description. "If the vehicles are different, he's definitely worth checking out. He might have more than one vehicle."

Quinn nodded. "Hold on and let me request that information." He sent a text and looked back up. "All right. I should have that in a few."

"What if the shooter didn't know Daniel would be here?" Katie asked. "What if he didn't care? What if it was just a co-incidence?"

Quinn lifted a brow. "What do you mean?"

"What if the shooter was going to shoot at the restaurant anyway and Daniel just hap-pened to be here this morning?"

"Just like it was a coincidence I was at the restaurant last night when someone hung a body in my basement?" Daniel said.

"I'm not saying it as fact, I'm just stating it as a possibility."

Quinn shook his head. "No, he could have shot at anyone out there. He chose to wait for you."

"Yeah. I guess so." Daniel pinched the bridge of his nose. "You know what? The thing is, I wasn't even supposed to be there last night or this morning. Not just at the restaurant, but I wasn't even supposed to be in town."

"Where were you supposed to be?" Katie said.

"On a business trip that got canceled at the last minute Friday morning. I was scheduled to meet with a man who was interested in opening another restaurant in downtown Charleston. But his eighteen-year-old son was in a car wreck that landed him in ICU. We postponed indefinitely."

"So it's someone who knew you were supposed to be out of town but knew you didn't actually go out of town and decided to see if he could set you up by putting the body in the basement," Quinn said.

"Or it's all a freak coincidence."

"I'm going to vote for the first one. It's probably someone close to you."

He cocked his head. "It could be, but not necessarily."

"Why do you say that?" Quinn asked.

"My secretary, Bridgett Holmes, keeps my schedule. I was supposed to leave Friday around midmorning and come back on Saturday evening. All anyone would have to do is call and ask for me. If the person acted it well enough, she might let the caller know I was out of town and when he or she could get in touch with me."

Quinn's phone rang and he stepped away to answer it.

She frowned at Daniel. "It sounds like your secretary is a little too free with your whereabouts."

"Yeah, well, trust me, that's all about to change."

"Good."

Quinn hung up his phone. "Got some information back on your financials."

Daniel stilled. "And?"

"You don't have any reason to burn down your restaurant."

"No. I don't."

Quinn nodded. "Also, Armstrong was up to his ears in debt. No evidence of gang activity that's been speculated, but he owed a lot of legit people money. If he owed some people who weren't so legit . . ."

"Don't have to be in a gang to be dangerous," Daniel murmured. "But if he needed money because he was scared of retaliation from some bad guys, guess that's a good motive for stealing." He shook his head. "I wish he'd just come to me and told me. I'd have tried to help him."

"But he didn't, unfortunately." Katie pushed a stray strand of hair behind her ear. "Anyone that's good for a suspect?" she asked Quinn.

"Several. We're running them down now." Quinn slid his notebook into his pocket. "I'll let you know what else develops."

"Actually, I may have something else for

you to check out," Daniel said.

Katie lifted a brow and Quinn mirrored her expression. "What's that?" Quinn asked.

"Tim Shepherd."

"The real estate developer?" Quinn said.

"Yes. He's been after me for the last six months to sell him my restaurant on North Lake. He wants to put up some high-rise apartments. He's also offered me double what the land and restaurant are worth."

Quinn let out a low whistle. "Wow."

"Yes."

"And you said no?"

Daniel shrugged. "I don't need the money and I like my restaurant. Or I did before someone burned it down. Now I'm going to rebuild it and continue on with business as usual."

"And you're just now telling me this?"

"It didn't occur to me until now, but when I got home after the fire, Riley said he'd called again. And this time he called the house number. I don't know how he got it, but I didn't give it to him."

"What about your secretary?"

Daniel shook his head. "No, she might let someone know if I was out of town, but she wouldn't give out my home number."

"When did he call?" Katie asked.

"Last night."

118

"Before or after the fire?"

"Before. But with everything that's happened, I haven't had a chance to call him back."

Quinn nodded. "I'll check into it. See if this is a pattern for people who won't sell out to him. If so, then we may have a good break here."

"Thanks, Detective."

"Just call me Quinn. And you're welcome."

Quinn left and Katie turned to Daniel to study him. Silently. Curiously.

"What?" he asked.

"You did three tours as a Marine in Afghanistan and Iraq."

He eyed her warily. "Yes."

"The shooting didn't seem to faze you at all. You slipped right into soldier mode. No PTSD?"

His eyes went dark. "It's not important, is it?"

"Of course it is."

"Why do you want to know?"

She looked away. "Because I do."

"Not a good enough reason."

"You've learned to cope." She finally met his gaze. "I haven't."

He tilted his head and narrowed his eyes, his body tense, alert. "What do you mean you haven't?"

She drew in a deep breath and shook her head. "Nothing." She forced a smile. "Never mind. Like you said, it's not important. I don't want to go back there."

"Go back there? Go back where?" His frown deepened and he studied her. She could feel his gaze piercing, probing, trying to read her.

"Drop it." She shuttered her expression and gave him a tight smile. "I'm hungry now."

He gave a slow nod. "I can do something about that."

[8]

Riley stared at the computer screen. The words blurred and she rubbed her eyes. She checked her phone and grimaced, then shoved the device away and focused back on the screen. Then reached for her phone again. With a groan, she gave up and lowered her forehead to her arms.

Something dropped onto the desk next to her and she looked up to find Olivia nearby and a bag of M&Ms next to the keyboard. "Chocolate," she breathed.

"Katie texted and said you could use some."

"And you just happened to have a bag in your pocket?"

Olivia snickered. "In my purse. It's sort of a joke we've started. Haley's never without some and it's not pretty if she runs out. So we all carry a stash just in case. Katie texted

121

and said she promised you chocolate and I should deliver."

"You guys are simply amazing." Riley opened the bag and poured out a handful. "I think I want to work for you one day if this is how you treat your employees."

Olivia laughed. "We're all equal partners in this business, but yes, we definitely try to take care of one another." Her smile faded. "You okay?"

"Sure. I'm just peachy."

"Worried about your uncle?"

"Yes. A lot. Are you sure he's okay?"

"Katie said he was fine. Didn't he text you?" Olivia's gaze went to the television Riley had turned on only moments ago.

"Yes, a couple of times." She popped several of the pieces of candy in her mouth and savored the chocolaty sweetness. Her attention, however, was on the television. The media still reported from her uncle's restaurant, but the fact that the scrolling marquis stated no one had been hurt allowed her to breathe easier. "But —" she shrugged, then glanced back at the computer and sighed.

Her phone buzzed and she checked the screen. A text from Beth. Her hope deflated. As much as she loved her friend, it wasn't Beth she was so hoping to hear from.

Are you going to church in the morning? Kyle and I can save you a seat.

Probably not. Crazy stuff going on.

I saw the news. Is Daniel okay?

Yes.

Okay. TTYL.

Riley set the phone aside once again and glanced at Olivia. "Do you go to church?"

"Yes. What about you?"

"I sometimes go with my grandmother when she's in town or I go with Beth, my best friend. We all go to Riverland Community Church. They have a pretty good youth group there. But since she's started dating Kyle, I feel kind of like a third wheel, if you know what I mean."

"Yes, I know what you mean. I feel your pain on that one. Not so much anymore now that I've met Wade, but . . . yeah. What about your uncle? Doesn't he go with you?"

"Uncle Daniel doesn't go to church."

"Why not?"

"I think he's mad at God because my parents were killed by a drunk driver and God didn't do anything to stop it."

Olivia grimaced, then nodded. "That's understandable."

"Yeah, but —" She shrugged.

"But you're not mad at him? God, I mean."

Riley sighed. "I was at first. Kind of. But God didn't make the man get drunk, then drive. That man chose to do that. Isn't that the whole purpose of free will?"

Olivia blinked. "Yes, I guess it is."

"I know God could have stopped it but . . . he didn't."

"And you can accept that?"

Riley frowned. "What choice do I have? Unless I want to be angry and bitter my whole life, I have to believe that there's a reason it happened."

"That's mighty mature thinking. It's pretty amazing that you've arrived at that place of peace."

Riley gave a wry smile. "Maybe so. But I didn't get there easily. It helps that I know God's motives are good even when he allows bad things to happen." She ran a hand through her dark hair. "I've had a lot of time to think and grieve, and I'll admit that I sometimes yell at God for letting it happen, but for the most part, I'm at peace with it." She sighed. "And besides, it's what my parents taught me. They loved God with their whole hearts. If I reject him or hate him or whatever, then I'm rejecting them, discounting everything that they lived for. And I just can't do that." Olivia blinked like she was clearing tears from her eyes and Riley shifted. "Sorry, didn't mean to preach."

"No, not at all. I love that you're so free with sharing your heart. It's a beautiful thing."

Riley laughed, feeling self-conscious now. "But I was thinking that if Uncle Daniel is going to have people trying to kill him, he probably needs to work out this whole anger-at-God thing he has going on. Just in case."

"Honey, if your uncle loves God, he's still going to heaven. Even if he happens to die while he's mad at him. God's big enough to shoulder that. And forgive."

Riley sighed. "I know. In my head I know that. But my heart wants him to let go, to find peace with it. I don't want him to die —"

"We're doing everything we can to make sure that he doesn't die."

"I know that too. And I appreciate it."

"What else are you worried about?" Olivia asked.

Riley studied her for a moment. "It's kind of scary how you do that."

"What?"

"Read me so well. Katie can do it too."

Olivia gave her a brief smile. "It's part of our training. Well? Are you going to tell me?"

"Sure, why not?" Riley shrugged. "It's this project for school." She frowned. "Or rather, trying to decide which project I want to do. We have these things called internships. They last for two weeks. I have so many interests, it's hard to choose. The good news is, I've narrowed it down. The bad news is, I've narrowed it down."

Olivia gave a low chuckle. "Narrowed it down to two choices and you're stuck?"

Riley nodded. "Yes. My uncle's friend, Martin, wants me to work with him. Which might be pretty cool because I'm completely fascinated by archaeology, history, and, you know, old stuff, but I also have the choice to go to Mexico to learn about marine biology."

"Those are two pretty amazing opportunities. I can see why you're conflicted. You've got a tough decision."

"Tell me about it."

"What about flying? I hear you're good at that."

Riley bit her lip. "I love to fly. It's like an escape. When I'm in the sky, I'm free, you know? No pressure, no worries, just me and the plane and God." She tilted her head back and closed her eyes for a moment, letting herself remember the feel of being in flight, being in control, and just . . . being. Then she opened her eyes and looked at Olivia. "But I don't want to do that for a job. I want to keep that as something personal and private. My own special thing."

Olivia smiled and sipped her coffee. "I get that. So which do you prefer? Digging in the dirt or swimming in the ocean?"

Riley gave a soft laugh, grateful for the woman's presence. It made it easier to not give in to the worry clamoring inside her. "Good question. Unfortunately, the answer is both."

"When do you have to decide?"

"By tomorrow. If I send in my decision now, I can start with Martin as early as Tuesday. If I choose to go to Mexico, that internship starts later." She groaned, pressed her palms against her eyes, and sighed. "Okay. I can't do this another day." She sat up straight. "I'm going to choose." She hovered the mouse over Mexico and lifted her finger, ready to tap the track pad. Then glanced at her cell phone, thought about her uncle. She shook her head. "I'm going digging in the dirt, I guess." She made the selection and pressed submit. "There. It's done." Her friends would call her crazy for not choosing Mexico. And frankly she wasn't sure she wouldn't agree with them.

"How do you feel?"

She lifted a brow and thought about it. "Relieved."

"Relieved you made a decision or relieved you're going digging?"

"Just relieved."

"Then it was probably the right decision."

"Yeah." She smiled at the woman. "I think it was." At least she hoped so. She'd definitely prayed about it enough. And while her reasons for wanting to stay in town for the internship might not be particularly altruistic, they weren't wrong either. She picked up her phone. "I'm going to text Martin and let him know."

She fired off the text about the same time she heard the garage door start to rise. Olivia slipped from the den and Riley rose to follow the woman to the kitchen door. "That should be Uncle Daniel."

Olivia glanced at her phone. "Yes."

"Katie was supposed to talk to him today about hiring you guys. Do you think she did?"

"Probably."

Uncle Daniel stepped into the kitchen and

stopped when he saw her and Olivia. "Hi, guys."

"Hi," Olivia said.

Katie stepped in behind him and Riley caught her eye. She smiled, but it was tense and tight. Riley saw something drip onto the floor. She homed in on the source, which turned out to be Katie's knee. "Hey, you're bleeding."

Katie looked down. Surprise lifted her brow. "I hadn't noticed."

"I'll get the first aid kit." Riley shook her head. "You people need a keeper."

Katie immediately tuned in to the pain in her knee now that her attention had been drawn to it. How had she missed it on the drive over to Daniel's house? In spite of the throbbing, she bit back a soft chuckle. As tired and on edge as she was, Riley could still make her smile.

It worked on Daniel too. His lips turned up a fraction as his niece headed out of the kitchen.

"A keeper, huh?" Katie asked as she finally gave in to the pain and moved to the table to sit in the nearest chair.

"She's a mother hen at heart. She can't help it."

Katie rolled her pants leg up and examined the gash. A flap of skin rolled to the side and she grimaced. "Ugh."

Daniel grunted. "That looks pretty nasty."

"Thanks."

He knelt in front of her and cupped her calf in his palm. "Looks like you could use a stitch or two." The heat of his hand on the back of her leg distracted her, momentarily silencing her. He looked up. "Did you hear me?"

"Uh, yeah. A stitch or two." She cleared her throat. Really? After inhabiting the dating desert for the past two years, she was going to choose this man to be attracted to? Not smart. "I can do it."

"You're going to stitch it?"

She grimaced. "Well, I could if I had the appropriate tools. In the meantime, I'll just take some antibiotic cream and a Band-Aid."

For a moment he looked suitably impressed, then shook his head. "You've got a hunk of skin hanging off. I'll do it."

"You? You were a detective, not a medic."

"I'm a Marine. I've been on active duty." He scowled. "I've stitched a wound or ten."

Riley returned with the first aid kit and passed it to Daniel. She looked at Katie. "It'll only hurt a little. Trust me, I speak from experience."

"He's stitched you up?"

"Yep, when I dropped the steak knife and it landed in my foot."

Katie winced at the visual. "Ah." She'd wondered about the scar on the teen's foot but had never asked.

Riley grimaced. "I try not to remember about how bad that hurt. But the ER doc said Uncle Daniel did as good a job as he'd seen and just put me on an antibiotic."

"I'm sure he'd do a great job." She gestured to her knee. "But I think I'll just take the bandage. If I decide it needs a stitch, I'll get it looked at later."

"Whatever you want," Daniel said.

What she wanted was some distance. Her feelings for this man were tumbling all over the place and it had her off-kilter. She didn't like being off-kilter. She stayed still and watched him.

He opened the first aid kit and pulled out the box of Band-Aids. He then went to the sink, scrubbed his hands, and returned to clean and close the wound. He covered it with the cream and bandaged it. Blood started to seep through, but she ignored it.

"How's that?"

"Perfect, thanks." Her voice sounded slightly breathless to her. She hoped if anyone noticed, they attributed it to the pain.

He looked doubtful. "You're going to need another bandage before long."

"I'll take care of it."

"Doesn't it hurt?" Riley asked.

"Yes, it definitely does now. I'd rate it a five on a scale of one to ten. Can't believe I didn't notice it until you mentioned it."

"Adrenaline," the teen said wisely. She popped the top on a bottle and shook two pills into her hand. She passed them to Katie. "Ibuprofen. I'll get you some water."

"Don't bother." Katie downed them dry and pulled the damaged pants leg down over the bandage. "Thanks." She stood and winced. "I'm going to head home, but I promise to come back tomorrow and see if I can find someone who might have noticed the person in the car last night. I meant to do that earlier, but I've been a little distracted." She pulled her phone from the clip on her side. "On the way over here, I got a text from Quinn. He said the vehicle that was parked out front belongs to someone named Jake Thomas."

"Jake?" Riley exclaimed.

"That's my neighbor," Daniel said. "He drives a dark blue two-door Jeep Wrangler."

Katie lifted a brow. "And I drive a black one."

"Which would make it impossible to distinguish one from the other at night. But Jake lives next door and always parks it in his driveway, not across the street."

"That wasn't Jake in there last night," Riley said. She frowned. "At least I don't think so. I seriously thought it was you."

Katie reached for the door. "We'll figure it out." She nodded to Olivia. "Thanks for your help."

"My pleasure. I asked Haley if she could cover the rest of the evening if you needed someone because I need to head out. Wade, Amy, and I are taking his boat out on the lake for a late dinner and star-gazing. I promised to be there." Wade was Olivia's fiancé and Amy her soon-to-be stepdaughter. "Charlie can cover some too, but Lizzie is tied up until tomorrow morning. She can help after that."

"Thanks. I'll keep that in mind."

"I assume you're going to be here for the duration?" Olivia asked.

Katie slid a look at Daniel. "I think the jury's still out on that one. I'll get back to you as soon as I know something."

"Gotcha." She looked at Daniel. "Be careful. Don't take unnecessary chances, and accept help when it's offered."

He smiled. "Noted."

Olivia left and Katie watched her slip into her car. She sat there until another vehicle pulled in behind her. Haley Callaghan, formerly with Ireland's G2, the country's national security agency, had come on board with Elite Guardians after she and Olivia had become friends at the bodyguard school. Haley didn't talk much about her past, but every now and then she'd let a little something slip and Katie knew it was painful for her. So Katie didn't ask. The woman was good at what she did and that was all that mattered in the long run.

The fourth member of their team, Maddy McKay, a former special agent with the FBI, was still recovering from an attempt on her life less than three months ago. She'd be ready to return soon, though, and Katie would be glad to have her friend back at work. Until then, they were making do with Charlie, Olivia's brother, and Lizzie as contract help.

Haley got out of her car and headed toward them. "Glad you could make it," Katie said.

Haley's eyes narrowed. "My vacation was last week. I'm ready for something."

Katie led her inside and introduced her to

Daniel and Riley. Daniel looked bemused. "What is it?" Katie asked.

His gaze bounced from Katie to Haley and back to Katie. "Have I hired you and your agency?"

She paused, locked eyes on Riley, then turned back to him. "No, Riley did."

"Riley doesn't have any money."

Riley's face went red. "Uncle Daniel! Thanks a lot."

Katie slid an arm around Riley's shoulders and frowned at the man. "Sometimes the job is about more than money."

"And besides," Riley said, "I do have money. I have the money from my parents' life insurance policies, and if I have to spend every dime of it to make sure nothing happens to you, I'll do it."

The room fell silent. Daniel took two steps toward his niece and wrapped her in a tight hug. When he looked up and met Katie's eyes, the tough sheen that was usually there was gone. In its place was a vulnerability she instinctively knew he didn't show most people.

He cleared his throat. "Guess you're officially hired." He kissed the top of his niece's head. "Keep your money, Princess, I've got this one covered."

[9]

He slammed the door and ordered himself to get a grip. He'd shot him. He knew he had. But Daniel had popped up like he'd been hit by a water balloon, not a bullet.

His hands shook as he poured himself a shot of vodka. Then another. Okay. Whatever. He'd managed to accomplish his goal. The restaurant was closed for now. Daniel's attention would be on the North Lake rebuild. All was good. It didn't matter that Daniel wasn't in the hospital or dead. At least not yet. But his do-gooder bleeding heart had accomplished what personal threats wouldn't. As long as he thought his family or his employees, customers, whoever, were in danger, he'd do whatever it took to keep them safe. Including shutting down his restaurant.

The problem was, now that he had the restaurant closed, how was he going to keep Daniel away from it?

He went to the desk and pulled a clean legal pad from the drawer, flicked the tip of a new pen, and started to write.

MONDAY MORNING

Sunday had passed in a blur of calm. Daniel kept waiting for something to happen, but thankfully, all had been quiet. The eye of the storm? He grimaced. Probably. Now Haley and Katie sat at Daniel's kitchen table to map out a schedule and a plan. Riley was at school with Lizzie keeping an eye on her.

Daniel sat across from Katie and listened to her and Haley talk while he worked on a spare laptop that he'd dug from the recesses of his closet. All for naught. The thing was dead. The whole reason he'd bought the one that had taken the bullet for him Saturday. He pressed the power button and got nothing. He sighed and shut it. "Guess I'm going laptop shopping."

"Hope you had everything backed up," Katie said.

"I did." He pulled out his phone and found the website he wanted. It only took six clicks and he had another computer on the way. To be delivered tomorrow.

Katie's phone buzzed and she snagged it from the table. "Hello?" Her eyes lifted and met his. He raised a brow. "It's Quinn . . . Detective Holcombe," she said. "He wants to know if you're free later this morning."

Daniel sighed. "Sure." He gestured to his dead laptop. "Not like I'm going to be getting anything done here. Has he heard from the arson investigator?"

Katie repeated his question into the phone. She nodded.

"Good," he said. "Tell him to meet me at the site."

She met his gaze. "You want to go out there?"

"Yes."

"You hear that, Quinn?"

"I heard."

She pressed the speaker button so Daniel could participate in the conversation.

"It's not a bad idea, Katie," Quinn said. "Bring him out to the site. I want to hear what you have to say. I want you to take a look at what's left and tell me what you think."

Her lips tightened. "You don't need me. I would probably say the same thing as the arson investigator."

"Nevertheless, I want you to look at it."

Katie sighed. "Quinn, we've been through all of this. You don't need me out there." She took the phone off speaker and held the device to her ear.

Daniel wished she'd left it on speaker. He was curious about her response to Quinn's request. He could hear Quinn's voice, but the words were muffled now. Katie listened, her jaw tight and her face two shades lighter than when she'd answered the phone. "I know I was fine Friday night. Watching the fire didn't bother me much, but . . ." She stopped and listened again, and Daniel's curiosity almost got the best of him. She finally made a sound that was a cross between a sigh and a growl. "All right then. Fine. See you there around 11:30." She hung up with a ferocious frown. "He has to get clearance to go to the site, make sure they're done with it before we go tramping around in it. It shouldn't take him long to find out."

"What did you mean, you were fine watching the fire on Friday night?"

"Nothing."

"Something."

She grimaced. "I had a bad experience three years ago. It's left me . . . with some issues. Quinn seems to think I need to face my fears."

"Do you?"

"Probably."

"Is that why you asked me about the

139

PTSD?"

"Yes. Now I'm done talking about it." She slapped the table and stood. "I'm going to see if your neighbor is home and ask him about his car being on the street Friday night."

Daniel let her drop the subject. "I'll come with you."

She nodded. "Good idea. Jake and the others will probably be more open to talking to me if you're with me."

They exited the house and Daniel led the way next door. "He could have left for work. I don't see his Jeep in the drive today." He walked up the steps and knocked on the door. When no one appeared, he rang the bell. Again, nothing. "Guess he's not here."

They started back down the steps when the door opened. "Daniel?"

Daniel turned back to find his sleepy-looking neighbor staring at him. "You need something?"

"Yeah. Hey, didn't mean to wake you up."

"It's fine. Come on in. It was a late night."

Daniel stepped inside. "Thanks. This is Katie Singleton. She's a friend."

The two shook hands and Jake shut the door. "I was just getting ready to put some coffee on. Can I get you some?"

"I'll pass, but thanks," Daniel said.

"I had three cups this morning," Katie said. "I'd better pass too."

"Good enough." They followed him into the kitchen where he started the brew. "What can I do for you?"

"This is going to seem like a weird question, but do you mind telling me where your Jeep is?"

Jake paused in measuring the grounds, looked at them, and cocked his head, curiosity gleaming in his green eyes. "It's getting detailed. I drove it early this morning, and dude, let me tell you, it had some nasty funky smell in it."

Daniel frowned. "What kind of smell?"

"Just strong. Like my sister's nail polish or something." He finished prepping the coffee and pressed the button. When the coffee started to drip, he turned back to Daniel and Katie.

"Okay," Katie said. "Another weird question. Riley noticed your Jeep parked across the street Friday night. Did you leave it there or did someone else move it?"

"I parked it there. I had my parents and brothers and sisters over earlier. My flight was delayed so they beat me here and took up all the parking spaces. I parked across the street. By the time they left, I was too tired to do anything about it." He crossed his arms. "Why all the questions?"

Daniel scratched his head. "Some things have happened. Suffice it to say, it's been a very strange weekend."

"Oh yeah, hey, I heard about your restaurant burning down. Man, that's a tough break." His expression morphed into confusion. "But that still doesn't explain the questions about my Jeep."

"Someone was sitting in it Friday night, watching my house."

"Whoa. No way. Sitting in *my* Jeep?"

"So I guess it wasn't you."

"No, it wasn't me. But maybe that's where the weird smell came from. Maybe some homeless dude used it to get out of the cold or something."

"Could be. You don't lock your Jeep?"

Jake shrugged. "Sometimes. When I think about it. I don't keep anything of value in there so I don't worry about it."

Daniel shook the man's hand again. "Thanks for your help."

"Don't know how much help I was, but you're welcome."

Daniel walked out of the kitchen to the front door. He opened it for Katie and she slipped through. He followed and shut it behind him. He stood for a moment staring at the spot where Riley had said she'd seen the Jeep.

"What are you thinking?" Katie asked.

"I know most of my neighbors pretty well. I'm just trying to figure who would have been home. I don't have any really nosy neighbors who stay up at all hours of the night peering out their windows. At least not that I've noticed." He rubbed his chin. "And I can't think of anyone who works second or third shift — except for the pilots — and they're usually gone first thing in the morning to make their shift. Occasionally, there's one that leaves extra early or comes in late, but most of the residents in this neighborhood are really nine-to-fivers. Not all are commercial pilots, some just want to live out here so they can fly whenever they want. Like me." His eyes landed on the house three doors down from Jake's and diagonal to the house the Jeep had been parked in front of. "Zachary Drews works from home. He owns Drews Landscaping, but he's got enough people working for him he doesn't go out on jobs much anymore. He sits back and rakes it in."

"Like you do with your restaurants?"

He laughed. "Hardly. I still put in a good forty-hour work-week. Most weeks anyway."

She lifted a brow. "Maybe so, but something tells me you don't have to if you don't want to."

"No. I don't. But I'm a hands-on kind of guy. I need to see and know what's going on on a daily basis. I can't just hang out at home, I'd be bored stiff."

"And you're not bored sitting in an office all week?"

He pursed his lips and cut his gaze to her. "Let's go talk to Mr. Drews."

Unfortunately, while Mr. Drews was home, he hadn't seen anything suspicious that night. Nor had the other neighbors they found at home.

They were heading back to Daniel's house when Katie's phone rang. She answered, listened, then looked at him. "Quinn said the investigator ruled it arson."

Daniel pinched the bridge of his nose, then pressed his thumb and forefinger against his eyes. "So, it's official then."

"Yes. Afraid so."

He pursed his lips and nodded. "Well, can't say I didn't expect it." His phone buzzed, and he checked the text, then groaned. "I can't go out to the site until later after all. I forgot I have a couple of conference calls that will take me until after lunch. And maybe beyond. Could we meet Quinn around four?"

"That should be fine. I'll let Quinn know."

For the rest of the afternoon, Katie was his shadow, but she was a subtle one, making sure she stayed between him and any potential threat. His nerves were tight, his patience wearing thin. If Katie felt the same, she didn't show it.

After the last meeting, he stood up from the chair he'd occupied for the last hour and stretched. "I'm ready when you are."

"I'll drive." She pulled her keys from her pocket and he followed her to the Jeep.

When they pulled up to the restaurant's charred remains twenty minutes after that, Daniel's jaw tightened. He sat still in the passenger seat for a long moment and simply stared. Black wood, soot, destruction. The loss was significant, but not as bad as it could have been. Antiques were valuable and he regretted that they were gone forever, but they could be replaced. And a building could be rebuilt. At least no one had died in the blaze. He was grateful for that.

Katie stayed quiet, seeming to understand his need for a moment. Either that or she was grappling with her own demons. He glanced at her pale features. "If you clench your teeth any tighter, they're going to shatter."

She shot him a startled look, then flushed

but relaxed her jaw. When the quick flash of color faded from her cheeks, she was still pale. Daniel wanted to comfort her but wasn't sure how — or if she would welcome it. He took her hand and squeezed just in case. She pulled in a deep breath and gave him a grateful look.

When Detective Holcombe arrived, Daniel climbed from the Jeep and shut the door. Katie walked around to his side and Quinn did the same. The detective held an iPad in his left hand.

"You okay?" Quinn asked him.

Daniel lifted a brow. Was that concern in the man's voice? For him? "I'm all right."

"And you?" Quinn asked Katie.

"Fine."

Her snapped answer didn't seem to bother him. "Ran the plate on that guy you said assaulted your waitress. In all the excitement I haven't had a chance to pass it on to you."

"You haven't arrested anyone, so I'm going to assume the check came back clean?"

"Yeah. Your guy is Terrance Parker. I did some checking into his background and, like you said, he came back clean. No record, no nothing."

Daniel frowned. "Okay, thanks." He rubbed his chin. "Guys like that usually have a history of that kind of behavior, but I guess everyone has to start somewhere."

"Exactly. I did a little more checking and he and his wife separated about a month ago. She said he had a temper and she was sick of it. Told him to get out."

"Ah. Well, that explains his comment about his marriage being on the rocks. So he could have been acting out a bit with Sarah and then got scared when he got caught," Daniel said.

"Looks like it. Who knows?"

"Let's hope he learned his lesson and will keep his hands to himself in the future."

"We can hope," Quinn said. He turned his focus on the building — or what was left of it. "Let's take a look then."

Together, they approached the area. Quinn stopped just outside the yellow, taped area. "Jarrod Lamb was the incident commander. He sent me his notes." He swiped the screen of the iPad. "Here we go. No bodies found inside or in the surrounding area. No accelerants found inside or out. Jarrod determined that someone turned the gas stove on and simply threw something onto the flame that burned and spread — probably a roll of paper towels. Easy peasy."

"Wait a minute, Detective," Daniel said. "Why didn't the sprinkler system attached to the fire alarm come on?"

"Told you that you could call me Quinn." He read more, then said, "It was disabled."

The muscle in Daniel's jaw began that twitching thing it did when he was exerting extreme self-control. "What do you mean? Disabled how?"

"The water was shut off from outside. The arson investigator said there was very little damage to the system's wires and they were all intact from the inside."

"So the question is, was the actual burglar alarm activated when the fire broke out?"

"It never went off, according to the alarm company."

"Then whoever set the fire knew the code," Daniel said. "Because the last person to leave — the manager — always arms it as he or she walks out the door. So what was it that the arson investigator found that convinced him without a doubt that it was actually arson? Why couldn't it have been an accident?" He glanced at Katie, then back at Quinn. "For example, why couldn't something have fallen on the stove? There were shelves above it. Maybe someone got careless and placed something flammable above it and it fell." No one was supposed to, of course. Only pots and pans were kept on the wire shelf above the stove, but it didn't mean it wasn't possible.

Quinn nodded. "That's a lot of speculation. I'm not comfortable with that. Yes, it could have been an accident, but when you factor in what happened with your other restaurant and the fact that the water was turned off here after everyone was gone — and the fact that the investigator found RDX —"

Katie jerked. "RDX?" Cyclotrimethylenetrinitramine.

"Military-grade explosives." Daniel grimaced and ran a hand through his hair.

Quinn looked at Katie, then Daniel. "I'm thinking it's a stretch to believe this was an accident. And hanging that body in your basement certainly wasn't an accident."

"Okay, it's arson," Daniel said. "The RDX sealed it for me. So now that I've come to terms with that, what else do you need to know?"

Quinn looked at him. "Can you arm and disarm the alarm with your phone?"

"Of course."

"And will it tell you when the system was armed and then shut off?"

"Yes." He pulled up the alarm app on his phone. "Armed at 12:06 a.m. Saturday. Disarmed at 1:32 a.m." He blew out a breath. "So, the person entered the code and shut the system off."

"Exactly. And the fire started shortly after that. And the only alarm that sounded was the fire alarm, not the security alarm. And the person who set the fire wanted to make sure the place burned, so he turned off the water."

"I found Maurice Armstrong hanging in my basement shortly before 1:00 a.m.," Daniel said.

"The suspect then went straight from there to here and set the fire," Katie said.

"Or," Quinn said, "he had help. I requested video from the convenience store across the street." He pointed in the direction of the large QT gas station that took up most of the block. "I was hoping it would have something, but there weren't any cameras aimed in this direction. However, the good news is, I've got something to work with here." He held up the iPad. "I've downloaded the footage from the Elmwood location."

"I'm still on the fact that more than one person could be involved in this," Daniel said. "You think there could be *two* people who want to see me destroyed, out of business, or dead?" He shook his head. "Awesome."

"Could this be related to one of your cases

when you were a CID investigator?" Katie asked.

"Anything's possible." He shot a wry smile at the detective. "I could *speculate* all day."

"Any particular case that stands out as more possible than the others?" Katie asked.

He sighed and pursed his lips. "There are a few. Billy Kendall is the one that instantly comes to mind."

"Who's he?"

"A Marine. He killed his roommate because the young man, Carl, danced with Billy's girlfriend one night when they were at a bar. She asked him and he said yes. When they got back to their room, Billy cut Carl's throat after Carl fell asleep."

"And you investigated the case?" Katie said.

"I did."

"And?" Quinn asked.

"I proved without a doubt he did it and the jury found him guilty. The judge sentenced him to life without possibility of parole." He shook his head. "His brother, Lee Kendall, vowed to get even and I watched my back for a while. I caught him following me a few times. The last time I caught him, I confronted him and I haven't seen him since."

Quinn rubbed his chin. "Sometimes it

takes people a while to plot their revenge. Or maybe after you confronted him, he may have decided he needed help if he was going to take you on. He might have been angry that you made him back down."

"Maybe," Daniel said. "But I've checked up on the guy off and on over the last four years and he's been a model citizen. Haven't looked in on him lately, though, I'll admit."

"I'll see if he's still playing nice." Quinn made a note in his little notebook. "In the meantime, Katie, you want to take a look around?"

She stiffened. "Do I want to? I'm not sure, but I have my gear."

Quinn lifted a brow. "You just happened to have it in your car?"

"No. I put it there last night."

"Huh."

"As much as you've pushed me to come out here, you still didn't expect me to agree, did you? Even after our last little conversation."

"No. But I'm glad you did."

Daniel watched the exchange and was privy to the strong undercurrents. What was going on? "Does this have anything to do with you not wanting to 'go back'?"

She met his gaze. "Everything."

[10]

Katie stood still and stared at the building — or what was left of it. A bomb could have gone off — and actually might have, if the RDX was any indicator — and left the same type of damage she now faced.

She fought the flashes of memory, the smell of burned flesh, and resisted the urge to gag. Instead, she cleared her throat and concentrated on the workers next door. Each person had a job to do to make the land fit to build on. The backhoe operator pulled the stumps from the ground, following the directions of the guy to his side. Others raked and shoveled the dirt aside. The dump truck driver waited patiently to haul off the excess. Each person knew his job. And when the job was done, each one went home and probably didn't take the job home with him. Or her. Even as she stood there watching, workers were picking up lunch coolers and waving goodbye. The sun continued to sink and Quinn and Daniel talked as though she weren't there. Right now, she was fine with that.

It had been three years and she still had issues at the thought of going into the charred area. From a CFI, Certified Fire Investigator, with ATF to Certified Explosive Specialist to bodyguard. She'd done a lot in the last ten years. Each job had had a purpose and she'd had her reasons for moving on. Good reasons. "I promised myself I wouldn't go back," she murmured.

"You mentioned that before," Daniel said. "You want to explain?"

She took a deep breath. "It doesn't matter. Maybe Quinn's right. Maybe instead of avoiding it, I should face it. Maybe once I face it, it'll go away." She shook her head. "Guess we'll find out." She glanced at the setting sun. "And if we're going to do it today, we'd better get busy."

He frowned at her but didn't ask her to elaborate. She walked around to the back of her Jeep and motioned for Quinn to join her. He did. She reached in and pulled out two bags. "Suit up."

He blinked. "Huh?"

"Well, the first rule of fire investigation is, you don't go in alone. You blackmailed me into being here, so you get to participate in

154

the fun. There's a communication system built into the suit. When you pull on the headgear, it'll be activated. Just start talking."

Quinn reached for the bag.

"No. I want to." Daniel took the bag from Quinn before the man could form a response, set it on the ground, and unzipped it. "We're about the same size so I shouldn't have any trouble fitting into the suit."

To Katie's surprise, Quinn didn't protest, and within minutes she and Daniel were ready to enter the area. At that point, the shakes wanted to set in. She refused to let them. *Stay in control, you can do this.*

Standing on the sidelines watching a fire, she was fine. Disarming bombs didn't faze her. Going head-to-head with a killer didn't make her blink. But going into a scene as an investigator was something that made her want to freeze.

She drew in a slow, deep breath. She could do this. She'd done it before. Just not since the incident three years ago. Why had she chosen now to say yes to going in? She could have refused, she *should* have refused. Brushed Quinn off and told him to mind his own business. But she hadn't. Because she really wanted to conquer this thing that controlled a part of her life. She hated it, the fear.

She shoved the thoughts aside and looked at Daniel. "Ready?" she asked.

"Ready." His voice sounded clear in her ears.

"Let's see if we can find that box for Riley then."

Together they ducked under the tape and approached the building. With each step, her heart pounded harder, her breath came faster. Sweat popped out on her forehead and rolled down her temples.

"Help meeeee."

Katie gasped. Stopped. Looked around. Shook her head. No, not here.

"Are you all right?"

She looked into Daniel's eyes. Concern clouded them and she gulped. Nodded. "Fine. I'm fine."

She made it to the front door and even inside what used to be the lobby area of the restaurant. The mess the fire had left behind came to her in stark detail.

"Help me! Get out, Katie! Run! Help meeee!" The voice echoed in her ears again.

She spun, looking for the source. "I can't, I'm sorry!" The words slipped from her without her even realizing her lips had formed them.

"What?" Daniel gripped her upper arm.

"Hey, are you okay?"

"I can't help you! You're dead!" She jerked away from him and placed her hands over the head covering where her ears were. She met Daniel's startled gaze, saw the sudden knowing that glimmered there. She spun and raced out of the building.

"Katie, wait!"

She ignored him and bypassed Quinn, who was saying something.

"Help me, help me, help me . . ."

She ripped the mask off and flung it, reached the edge of the property, and lost what little food she'd eaten that day.

She panted, reached into her pocket, and pulled out the tissues and breath mints she always kept on hand. Humiliated, she felt tears burn in her eyes. Why couldn't she do it? She felt a hand on her shoulder and didn't know which man it was. "Go away," she whispered. "Just . . . go away for a minute."

"Mine is the children," Daniel said. "I hear the children screaming. Crying. They come toward me carrying their body parts. Sometimes it's arms, sometimes it's organs. A beating heart or . . . whatever. One little boy is holding his head. And the head talks to me. They all talk to me. And they're begging me to put them back together so they can be whole and grow up happy." He cleared his throat. "And I throw up too," he whispered. "Every stinking time."

Katie bit back a sob and felt his arm go around her shoulders. It was bulky and awkward in the suit, but she leaned into him. Allowed herself to take comfort from him. He knew. He understood. "But you didn't flinch when the gunfire went off yesterday. Does it still come at you? The PTSD?"

"Sometimes. In my nightmares mostly. Fortunately, when I got out, I played it smart and didn't deny what I was going through. I knew the symptoms and recognized them in myself. I got help as soon as I got back and got out. When Riley's parents were killed, I knew she needed me and she needed me to be whole. I couldn't be waking up in the middle of the night screaming and I sure didn't want to have to be worried I'd accidentally hurt her. I still can get jittery or anxious, but I haven't had a nightmare in over a year." He gave her a quick squeeze. "It comes and goes, but I've learned coping strategies."

"Like when the sniper was shooting."

"Once I realized the bullet got my computer instead of me and I was alive, I started using one of those coping strategies. For some reason as long as I chant 'It's not real' over and over in my head, it works."

"But it was real. Those were real bullets."

He nodded. "Still worked, though."

"Good, I'm glad." She paused for a moment to swipe a stray tear.

"What did you mean when you said Quinn blackmailed you to come out here?" he asked.

She pulled back. "It doesn't matter."

"Tell me."

She hesitated. "He just said that it was my duty as your bodyguard to come to the site with you. That if anything happened, it would be on my shoulders and Riley would never forgive me."

Daniel stiffened. "That jerk."

The ice in his voice surprised her. He started to spin, but she caught his arm. "Now, now, don't do anything rash," she said. "While I appreciate the sentiment, I know Quinn. He thinks he's helping in his own pushy way. He was just really wrong this time."

Daniel hugged her against him even tighter this time. "Pushy nothing. That's pure bullying. I'll hurt him if you want me to," he whispered against her ear.

A watery chuckle actually escaped her lips. "No. If he needs hurting, I can do it."

"Oh. Right. Of course."

The brief moment of humor helped restore her equilibrium a bit. She looked up to find Quinn walking toward them. She turned her back on him for the moment. "But I'd be open to letting you help me."

"With pleasure." The flashing eyes and tone of his voice said he was serious.

"I'm sorry," Quinn said from behind them. "I thought . . ." He sighed. "I thought by asking — pushing — you to come out here, I was helping. I guess I was wrong."

Katie sniffed and swiped her eyes. She pulled away from the only comfort she'd allowed herself in three years and turned to face Quinn. His eyes shimmered with remorse and she could see he was kicking himself for pushing her. In fact, she didn't think she'd ever seen him look so unsure and hesitant. His right hand flipped his cell phone over and over.

"Yes, you were wrong." She glared at him, then let her gaze drop to his hand with the phone. "And are you actually fidgeting?" she asked.

Quinn scowled and clipped his phone to his belt. "Absolutely not."

"Good." She couldn't stand to see Quinn so discombobulated. It was unnerving. Calling him out had reset him. So to speak. She sighed. "And it's okay. I wanted to do this." She shook her head. "The other night when I was able to stand here while the building was burning, I thought, 'Maybe I could do the investigation. Maybe I'm getting better.' And now this." A tremor shuddered through her. "It's disappointing. Frustrating. Maddening. Humiliating."

"It's normal," Daniel grunted.

"Not for me, it's not," she snapped. Then grimaced at her tone. "Sorry."

Daniel shook his head. "No apology necessary. You're stressed and you probably feel like you have ants crawling all over your brain right now."

At her stunned look, he gave her a soft smile. "I know PTSD when I see it."

She knew he did. And somehow that made what happened a little easier to deal with. "I'm still embarrassed."

"Don't be," Quinn said. "No reason to be."

She looked back at the building. A burned, charred shell of the magnificent piece of architecture it used to be. Disappointment and frustration were accurate descriptors, but at the same time they weren't strong enough. She was also heartbroken.

"One day at a time," Daniel said.

"It's been too many days. I'm ready for it

to stop."

"Yeah. I know what you mean."

Quinn rubbed his chin. "Don't sweat it, Katie. You're good at what you do. You don't have to get back to arson."

"Exactly," Daniel said. If his glare had been a laser, Quinn would have been eviscerated. "And people shouldn't push her to do so."

Quinn opened his mouth to respond, then snapped it shut. He gave a short nod. "You're right."

Katie squeezed Daniel's tense arm. "I hate that I'm letting the past win, that it has this much control over me."

"We all have something," Daniel said.

Quinn took his phone back out of its clip and glanced at it. "Let's get out of the cold and take a look at this video footage from the security camera at the Elmwood location. I want to see if you recognize anyone."

"Wait a minute, we have to look for Riley's box," Katie said.

Daniel shook his head. "Not today. Come on."

They piled into Quinn's unmarked car with Daniel volunteering for the backseat. Quinn pulled the video footage up on his laptop, then turned it so they could all see the screen. "This is from your camera. We've analyzed it and it shows a person dressed in black with a hoodie covering his head." The person came on-screen and kept his head low. "He's opening the basement door."

"Wait a minute," Daniel said. He leaned forward. "He used a key."

"Yeah. We noticed that. Keep watching."

Daniel did. Katie stared at the screen. After the door was open, the intruder walked to the side of the building and returned with Armstrong's body over his shoulders carrying him in a fireman's hold. When he arrived back at the door, he used his foot to shove it open. He disappeared inside. Minutes passed and Katie wanted to get out of the vehicle to pace. Instead, she tamped down her racing energy and focused on whatever was coming next.

The figure finally reappeared, only to vanish from camera view almost as fast as she could blink. Just a few short moments later, Katie saw Daniel on the screen as he bolted out the basement door to stand and watch. "That must be when I saw the taillights." Then the on-screen Daniel turned and went back inside.

Where he'd discovered Armstrong's body.

"While we can't see the guy's face and have only an approximation of his height and weight, there is one good thing about the footage," Quinn said.

"What's that?" Daniel said.

Quinn met his eyes in the rearview mirror. "It pretty much clears you as the murderer."

[11]

Katie released a breath and Daniel could tell she was glad to focus on something else. He was too. He was also glad the video showed someone else as the suspect. At least he could put that behind him.

"That guy never looked at the camera," Katie said. "He made sure his face was hidden the whole time. He adjusted his body when he moved back into the building. He was careful about the way he carried Armstrong. Everything."

"Which indicates he knew where the cameras were," Daniel said. He sat back. "But that's not really a big deal. All you have to do is look up and they're right there."

"True," Katie said, "but think about it. This makes it seem more premeditated than spur of the moment, don't you think? I mean, if you kill someone by accident, you

165

react. You're in panic mode, you're not thinking about the cameras — or if you do, it's after the fact. Probably too late to do anything about it because your face is already there. But this guy didn't do that. He never once looked at the cameras."

"Or if it was spur of the moment or an accident or whatever, he actually didn't panic, but took time to think about what to do next," Quinn said. He reached up and turned on the interior light as the sun had set and darkness covered the car.

"Except call the cops. He didn't consider that," Daniel muttered.

Katie nodded. "Which could mean he was up to no good in the first place and Armstrong had really bad timing and stumbled onto the murderer."

Quinn rubbed his eyes. "But what would he be doing at the restaurant?"

"Trying to break in?" Daniel said. "But he didn't have to break in, he had a key."

"I think there's one question we haven't asked," Katie said.

Quinn lifted a brow. "What's that?"

"What was *Armstrong* doing there? You'd fired him a couple of weeks ago. Why would he be there at that time of night?"

Daniel blew out a low breath. "Yes, I'd

like to know that as well."

"Evidence showed that Armstrong was killed right there outside the restaurant. There were signs of a struggle and the crime scene investigators found drops of blood."

"Armstrong's?" Katie asked.

"Probably. His nose was broken. The blood is being tested to see if it matches his. If it doesn't, then they'll run it to see if there's a match in the system."

"So after Armstrong was dead — killed out of sight of the cameras — the killer brought him around to the basement."

"But why hang him? Why not just leave him out of sight of the cameras?" Daniel asked. "Why risk exposing himself?"

Katie shrugged. "He may have been thinking he'd set you up." She studied him. "He's about your size. It's obvious he has access to the building. He may have even known that you didn't go out of town like you'd planned and that you'd be at the restaurant that evening."

"Maybe." He sounded doubtful, and she agreed it was probably a long shot. She looked at Quinn. "Did Francisco say when he'd get to the autopsy?"

"Soon. Tomorrow, I think." Quinn rubbed his chin. "But I'll remind him." He pulled his phone from the clip on his belt and shot the man a text. "Armstrong didn't have any bullet holes, no stab wounds."

"Back the video up," Daniel said. "Pause it right where the killer comes around the corner with Maurice on his shoulder." Quinn did. "There." Daniel pointed. "Look at his neck. I'd bet it was broken."

Quinn zoomed in the screen and Katie saw what Daniel meant. "It's hanging at a very strange angle. Almost rotated to where his chin rests *behind* his shoulder."

"The killer incapacitated him with pain by breaking his nose, then followed up and broke his neck," Katie murmured.

"This guy might be military," Daniel said, not taking his eyes from the screen.

"Someone you served with who has a grudge?" Quinn asked.

Daniel shook his head. "We were a tight-knit unit. We still keep in touch. Those of us who made it back." His eyes flashed with grief, then it was gone. "No one I served with would do this."

The car jolted hard enough to fling Katie against the passenger door. "Hey!" She grabbed the handle. She stared out of the window in horror. It was dark outside, but the streetlights offered enough of a glow that she could see what was going on.

The backhoe driver had driven the machine right into Quinn's unmarked car, and now the vehicle rocked up onto two wheels. Daniel hollered and Quinn let out a string of words she'd never heard him use before. Then the car slammed back down. She grabbed the handle and pulled, but the door wouldn't open.

"My door's crushed!" Daniel yelled from behind her.

"Mine's jammed too," she said. The backhoe had plowed into the passenger side of the vehicle. She looked for the machine and saw it in a blur. "Quinn! Get out while you can!" she cried. "He's coming back for another hit."

But Quinn didn't act fast enough and once again the car shuddered with the impact of the backhoe. And this time it rocked the vehicle up and onto the driver's side. She heard Daniel fall the length of the backseat even as gravity took her crashing into Quinn. He grunted.

The engine of the backhoe roared and the machine came once again to push against the bottom of the car. The vehicle went over onto the top. Windows popped. Metal creaked and groaned, giving a horrid death cry.

In her stunned state, Katie heard screams that filtered through the now-shattered windows. Screams of the workers? No, they were gone for the day. Or were the screams just hers? She managed to catch a breath, even crushed against Quinn like she was. "Quinn! Daniel! Are you okay?"

"He's coming back, hold on," Quinn shouted in her ear.

How did he know? The sound. She heard it now over the roaring in her ears. Another slam. She knocked her head against Quinn's chin. He gave a grunt but wrapped one arm around her waist. "Daniel!"

He didn't answer.

Katie crawled off Quinn and onto the center of the ceiling that now served as the base of the car.

"They're in the car! Stop him!" Shouts from the outside. Who? Did she hear sirens? She desperately hoped so.

Through the broken back window, Katie had a glimpse of the tanklike wheels rolling toward them once again. Panting with a fear that had her sweating, she scooted toward the front seat passenger window and in the side mirror saw what the driver intended. The backhoe's single arm was lowering. Heading straight toward the back of the vehicle. "Quinn, he's going to crush us! Daniel!"

A panic attack threatened, but the desire

170

to live was stronger. She wriggled so she could see between the two upside-down front seats. Daniel lay collapsed up against the window just behind the driver's seat. His eyes were shut and blood ran from a gash on his temple. With adrenaline pumping through her, she reached through the seats and grasped the back of his shirt. "Quinn, help me."

He moved beside her and added his arm, managed to snag Daniel's belt. "Got him. Pull!"

Together they dragged Daniel into the front area of the sedan. He lay almost on top of Quinn in the cramped quarters.

In the side mirror, she caught sight of the backhoe arm dropping, felt the harsh jolt. The screeching crush of metal once again blistered her ears and the back of the car crumpled like a soda can. But the action popped the front windshield and then lifted the front of the car.

Glass rained over her. She ignored it. "We've got to get out now, Quinn."

"Working on it. Go!"

"Daniel —"

"I've got him."

Katie rolled out of what had been the front windshield and onto the ground. She turned back to help Quinn get the still-unconscious Daniel out the window. "Pass him through," she grunted. Her wounded knee protested the weight she had on it, but she ignored the pain and flexed her fingers as she readied herself for Daniel's weight. Quinn heaved him through the opening. She slid both forearms under his armpits. "Hurry, Quinn. If he drops that arm again —"

"I know. You got him?"

"Yes. Give him another shove."

He did and she lost her balance in the tight space between the hood of the car and the ground. She went down, but didn't let go of Daniel. He came with her part of the way, then stopped. Sweat dripped into her eyes.

"I can't get enough leverage," she panted.

Daniel groaned.

"Come on, Daniel, wake up." With half of his weight resting on her, she wiggled to the side, braced her feet on the frame, and repositioned her arms under his armpits.

Quinn gave Daniel another push and she managed to roll with him. He stirred. "Now would be a really good time to wake up." But Daniel didn't open his eyes.

Quinn slid his upper body out of the car onto the ground beside them. "I'll push, you pull." She rolled out from beneath the front hood of the vehicle, ignoring the glass under her. She felt hands on her arm and someone yanked.

She was out from under the hood. She stood and turned back for Daniel, but someone had already pulled him out too. Dizziness hit her hard and she gasped.

Someone screamed, "Get him out!"

She spun to see the arm of the backhoe aimed straight for the exposed undercarriage of Quinn's car.

Sirens sounded close.

"Quinn!"

His hands appeared in the opening and the people who'd stopped to help grabbed for them. They pulled as the arm of the backhoe dropped and slammed into the vehicle.

[12]

Quinn's scream ripped through Daniel's consciousness. His head pounded in time with his heart. Cries echoed in his ears. "Quinn!" Katie's scream mixed with the others. "Get him out, get him out!"

"What happened?" he demanded.

But no one answered.

Sirens closed in. A loud crack brought more yells. A gunshot. Then a body — Katie — fell on top of him and he grunted. Darkness swirled again.

"Daniel?"

"Katie?"

"You're okay?"

He gripped her forearms. Noticed the rock-hard muscles beneath her skin. Then was distracted by the renewed throbbing in his skull. "I'm okay."

She rolled away from him and he squinted to watch her sit up. His vision blurred, doubled, then righted itself. Nausea swept him.

She moved away from him and he reached for her, snagged her wrist. "Wait."

"I need to check on Quinn." Her pale face and ravaged expression didn't bode well.

Someone moved next to him. "Sir? You shouldn't move. Let me take a look at your head."

Daniel squinted. A paramedic. The man dropped to his knees next to him. Daniel ignored him, pushed to his feet, and swayed. The paramedic rose, hands outstretched. Katie slid a hand around his waist and stepped toward the demolished vehicle.

"What happened to Quinn?" Daniel whispered, stumbling after her. Spots danced before his eyes.

"Sir?" The paramedic again.

"Katie? What happened to Quinn?" He wasn't going to let her just walk off. He'd crawl after her. And if the weakness in his legs was any indication, that might be exactly what he'd be doing if she moved much faster.

She stopped and looked up at him. "He's hurt, Daniel. When the arm on the backhoe came down the last time, Quinn was only halfway out. His legs . . ." She shook her head even as she focused on the rescue workers prying the car off the man.

Daniel took a step in Quinn's direction, determined to help him, but his legs gave out. He heard Katie calling him, felt her grip tighten, but this time he couldn't stop the darkness from overtaking him.

Katie caught Daniel as best she could and managed to get him to the ground with only a slight thud instead of him having another hard landing. No doubt he had a concussion. She felt his pulse and found it strong, if a bit fast. She turned to wave the paramedic over and found him already there.

"He's stubborn," the man noted.

"For sure."

"Let's hope that works in his favor." He went to work, checking his vitals. Another paramedic joined him.

Once she was sure Daniel was in good hands and wasn't in any immediate danger, she turned back to find that the workers had extracted Quinn. When she caught sight of his legs, she gasped at the bloody mess and raced to his side. She wrapped her fingers around his hand, but one of the workers caught her arm. "Stand back, please, he's lost a lot of blood and we need to get him stabilized."

Katie moved out of the way and watched

them work. Tears clogged her throat and filled her eyes. "Quinn," she whispered. He was more than a friend and co-worker, he'd become the brother she so desperately missed. "God, let him be okay, please." As much as she wanted to go to him, she knew there was nothing she could do. He needed her to stay out of the way and let the professionals work on him. And Daniel needed her.

She whirled to find Daniel on a stretcher, his eyes open. She raced to his side and grasped his hand. "I'm right behind you, Daniel. All the way to the hospital."

"Quinn?"

"He'll be there too."

Katie was making a mental list of all the people she needed to call. Riley. Quinn's partner, Bree. Quinn's family. His girlfriend, Maddy McKay. "I'll see you at the hospital," she told him. But he was already unconscious again. She bolted toward her Jeep.

Daniel's head buzzed. His dry throat ached. Memories flashed and he gasped. "Katie, Quinn." It didn't sound like his voice. More like a long groan.

"Uncle Daniel?" A soft hand slipped into his.

He forced his eyes open and slowly they

focused on the face in front of him. "Riley?" he whispered.

She nodded and a tear slipped down her cheek to land on his chin. She swiped it away. "Hey."

"What happened?" he croaked.

"You almost got squashed like a bug, from what I hear."

"Awesome." Sarcasm. His go-to coping mechanism. He coughed and winced as his head started to pound again. "Where's Katie?"

"Right here."

Her low voice reached his ears. He turned his head and a wave of nausea swept over him. "I hit my head, didn't I?" He'd had a concussion once before. This felt exactly like the last time.

"Yes, you hit it hard when you fell from one end of the car to the other. You have a slight concussion and that gash on your head, so they're keeping you for observation."

He lifted his hand to feel the bandage. "How's Quinn?"

"In surgery, but he's alive."

Daniel swallowed. Riley pressed a straw to his lips and he took a long draw on the water. "Thanks, hon. Why does he need surgery?"

She blinked. "You don't remember?"

He searched the black hole that had become his brain. "No."

"What do you remember?"

"Watching the video. Then being bounced like a ball in a pinball machine. Then . . . nothing."

"You woke up a couple of times while everything was going on."

"I did?" He frowned, searched his memory. And just got blackness. "I don't remember."

She rubbed her eyes. The action emphasized the dark circles under them. "Quinn wasn't able to get out of the vehicle quite as fast as we did," Katie said. "When the arm of the backhoe came down the last time, it crushed the car and trapped his lower legs. They're broken in several places, but not shattered, and the doctor thinks he can put him back together to be good as new."

Daniel went still as he processed the information. "I'm sorry." He had a flash of seeing a crowd of law enforcement officers gathered around the car. "I'm sorry."

She shook her head. "It's not your fault."

"I feel like it is," he murmured.

"Quinn did what Quinn does. He comes across aloof and haughty, but he's got a protective streak in him that runs a mile long. He made sure you and I got out before he would even consider trying to escape."

"I don't remember, I'm sorry."

"Again, not your fault. You were out cold." He grimaced. "What happened to the guy who was driving the backhoe?"

Katie sighed. "He got away, believe it or not. After the arm dropped, trapping Quinn, everyone mostly focused on rescuing him."

"Who were the people helping?"

"Good Samaritans. People from nearby stores and people driving by."

"Good to know there are those who'll stop to help others," he murmured.

"Yes, unfortunately, one person tried to get the driver of the backhoe and wound up getting shot." The crack he'd heard. "Everyone else scattered and took cover and the guy ran. The cops looked for him but weren't able to locate him. No one got a good look at him since it was dark and he had that stupid ski mask on."

"Unbelievable." He took another sip of the water. "Who has that much luck? And how did he even crank the backhoe? How did he get the keys?"

"It looks like he walked into the trailer they're using as an office and simply took them."

"What? How?"

"When everyone was clocking out and leaving, there was a lot of chaos. He blended."

"Wow. Just . . . wow."

"Yeah. I know."

"Any video?"

"Nothing so far."

He shifted on the bed and gave a grunt of pain. "How's the guy he shot?"

"Also alive. But the bullet caught him in the chest, so it's been touch and go. I asked to be informed if there was any change." She drew in a deep breath. "I'm not going to lie. This guy is clever, he doesn't want to get caught, and he's good at taking advantage of the opportunity when it presents itself."

"What do you mean?"

"He had to have been watching us, following us. He's probably worried about the investigation into the murder and the fire. By watching us, he thinks he will know what we know when we know it. When we were all piled in the car looking at the video footage, he stole a backhoe and turned it into a lethal weapon — and he knew how to drive it."

"Exceedingly well," Daniel grunted. "So no one could give the cops a description?"

"Not that I've heard. I know they're still

interviewing the construction workers." She leaned forward, the concern in her eyes deep. "Daniel, he saw an opportunity to take you out and went for it. That was a massive risk for him to do that. For some reason he was willing to take that risk."

Daniel's eyes rested on Riley. She looked shaken and scared. When she caught him watching her, she lifted her chin. "Don't even say that she shouldn't talk about this stuff in front of me. I need to know what we're up against."

Daniel sighed. "Yeah. I know."

Some of her stiffness eased. "Good. I'm glad we understand that."

He looked at Katie. "So what now?"

"Bree Standish, Quinn's partner, is going to be taking over as lead on the case, and we'll be working with her while Quinn recovers. So for now, we're sort of in wait mode." She lifted a hand and ticked the items off on her fingers. "We're waiting on the results of the autopsy of Mr. Armstrong. We're waiting on reports of witnesses from the incident today. We're waiting to hear about Billy Kendall and if he's still incarcerated. We're just . . . waiting."

Weariness hit him and his head ached.

The sound of movement pulled him from his self-pity. He opened his eyes to see Katie standing. "I'm going to get out of here and let you rest," she said.

"I can't rest. I need to go home. I can't let Riley stay there by herself."

Katie gave a low chuckle. "That's what you hired us for, remember?"

"So you'll be with her tonight?"

"If not me, someone from the agency."

"Or I can just stay here," Riley said, eyeing the window seat that did double duty as a bed for overnight guests.

Daniel started to nod, then thought better of it. "No, go home." He touched his bandage again. "It's just a concussion. And a *slight* one at that. I'll get sprung first thing in the morning — whether they like it or not."

Riley pointed a finger at him. "You do what they say, you hear me?"

Daniel bit the inside of his cheek to keep his lips from lifting. He nodded. "Yes ma'am."

Tears filled Riley's eyes. "I don't want anything to happen to you. Anything *else* to happen."

He reached for her hand, all humor with her bossiness gone, and pulled her down for a hug. "I'm sorry I scared you. Get some sleep, Princess."

"The police are working overtime on this,

Riley," Katie said. "They just need some time, but they'll get this guy."

"Before or after he kills someone else?" Riley muttered.

Daniel sighed and closed his eyes for a moment. "He's not going to kill me, Riley. I'm not going to let him win."

Riley's hand squeezed his. "I hate to tell you, Daniel, but sheer stubbornness won't keep you safe if he's really out to get you." He heard the worry, the fear in her voice. And the desperate need to know he'd be fine.

"I can take care of myself," he said.

She lifted a brow and her eyes raked his wounded, bedridden form. "Yes, I can see that."

He started to protest, then stopped. She might have a point. A knock on the door sent shards of pain through his head. The throbbing in his right temple had increased in intensity and his nausea had returned. A nurse who looked to be in her early forties stepped into the room, holding a syringe.

Daniel tensed. "Is that going to help me or kill me?"

The woman blanched. "Um. Help you? It's morphine."

A man Daniel had never seen before poked his head around the door and found

Katie with his gaze. "She's clear."

Katie nodded, the door shut again, and she turned to Daniel. "That was Charlie. He's guarding your room and checking IDs of everyone who enters."

Daniel almost didn't care who was who at this point. The pounding in his head was going to send him over the edge into crazy if he didn't get some relief. The nurse moved and injected the medicine into his IV. Within seconds, the thundering eased and the escape from the pain was sweet.

His eyes grew heavy, but he caught Katie's hand as she passed by his bed toward the door. She looked down at him.

"Thanks," he whispered.

"Any time."

[13]

MONDAY EVENING
9:00 PM

Riley wasn't sure which way was up right now. Her uncle had almost been killed. *Again.* One of her greatest fears had been close to happening and she wasn't sure how to deal with it. Praying helped, but she had to admit, her faith was wobbling. She might say all the right things, and truthfully, she really did believe them, but . . . it was hard to understand what God was doing. Not that she thought she had to understand everything about God to believe in him, but seriously, hadn't she and her uncle been through enough?

She and Katie had exited the hospital and Katie had handed her off to the woman in the driver's seat. It was Haley Callaghan. Haley drove, keeping her silence, her eyes alert, her body taut, as though ready to spring into action at the slightest provocation.

"So you're the M&M lady."

Haley glanced at her. "What?"

"I owe you a bag. Olivia gave me the one she was keeping for you."

Haley gave a rich throaty laugh that invited others to share in her mirth. "Honey, you're welcome to them. I've got so many people givin' me bags o' those things, I'll never run out."

"I think that's the point." Riley smiled, not just at her comment but at her accent, which she was trying to place.

Haley glanced at her, genuine amusement lighting her pale green eyes.

Riley looked down at her phone and sighed.

"That's the third time you've done that. What is it?" Haley asked.

"Oh. Sorry. It's just . . . well, there's this guy I'm . . . well . . . let's just leave it at that. There's this guy."

"Ah."

The knowing sound made Riley pause. "What does that mean?"

"You like him, he has your number, but he hasn't texted or called you yet."

Riley lifted a brow. "You bodyguard people

are scary." First Katie, then Olivia, and now Haley.

A snicker escaped Haley. At least Riley thought that was what it sounded like. The woman shook her head. "No, we're just well trained." Another pause. "And I was once a teenager too."

"Ah," Riley said.

Haley glanced at her. "What?"

Riley shot her a small grin. "Nothing. I was just seeing if I could sound as wise as you did when you said it."

Laughter escaped Haley and Riley grinned at her.

"I like you," Haley said. "You're different."

Riley's smile faded and she glanced at her phone again. "In some ways maybe. In other ways I'm just like every other red-blooded teenager out there."

"Crushing on a boy who won't give you the time of day and you can't figure out why?"

"Something like that. He's more of a friend that I've known a long time, but has decided other things are more important. Although he did say he wanted to talk." She paused. "And yes, I might have a small crush on him." She slipped the phone into her pocket. "But enough about that. I have another question."

"Lay it on me."

"How am I supposed to do my job if I'm jumping at shadows — and *have* a shadow? Not that I really mind, but . . ."

"What's your job?"

"You mean you don't know?"

"Well, if you were a usual client, yes, I would know that and anything else I could find during me research into you. However, since I've just been brought into this all of a sudden, I'd like to be excused for not having done me homework."

Riley smiled. "You're excused. I'm a nanny for two girls after school every day — except when the mom doesn't need me."

"A nanny, are you? Is that the politically correct term for babysitter these days?"

This time Riley laughed. "Yes, probably. And I like your accent. Irish?"

"You've a good ear."

"Thanks. Your name kind of gives it away, though."

Haley laughed again. "I suppose so."

Riley pulled her phone out again and let another sigh escape. "I should have gone to Mexico," she muttered.

"What?"

"Nothing."

"Hmm."

Riley rolled her eyes. "Yeah."

Daniel woke early Tuesday, relieved to find the obnoxious pounding in his head had eased to a dull ache. He could live with that. A glance at the clock made him groan. Two in the morning and he was wide awake with his brain spinning. Someone had tried — and almost succeeded — in killing him yesterday. Unfortunately, Quinn had gotten in the way. From what Katie had said, Daniel owed the man — and her — his life.

He'd find a way to repay the detective.

After trying to get comfortable and failing, he flipped on the television. At the end of the half-hour comedy rerun, Daniel realized he had no idea what he'd just watched. He picked up the remote to turn the television off when his face appeared in the top right-hand corner of the screen over a wide shot of a blonde reporter standing at the edge of his restaurant property. A RECORDED EARLIER graphic scrolled across the bottom.

"Thank you for joining us for an update on local restaurant owner Daniel Matthews. After Mr. Matthews discovered a body hanging in the basement of his restaurant, A Taste of Yesterday's downtown location, he then learned that his restaurant on North

190

Lake was burning. And now, we've gotten word that he was attacked during a visit to the burned location. A detective was hurt in the attack as well. We're following the story carefully and will have updates as they come in." Quinn's crushed car was in the background, still where it had been left. "Peter, have you been able to talk to Mr. Matthews?"

The scene changed to the outside of the hospital. Daniel groaned. Great.

". . . unable to speak with Mr. Matthews, but speculation is that his former cook, fired by Mr. Matthews only a few short weeks ago, was a member of one of our local gangs. Now, it was originally reported that Mr. Armstrong's death was a suicide, but new information from one of our confidential sources says this isn't so. And that the gang, who believe that Mr. Matthews is responsible for Armstrong's death, is now retaliating for his murder by burning the restaurant."

"What?" Daniel's head nearly exploded as his blood pressure spiked. "The incidents happened within thirty minutes of each other, you moron. There was no time for any gang to find out about his death and retaliate."

He closed his eyes. He was talking to the

TV. He'd well and truly lost it.

The reporter continued. "It's been speculated that all of the incidents are somehow tied to this gang."

"And is Mr. Matthews a part of this gang?" the blonde woman asked.

"That question has come up, of course, but nothing has been found to support that he has any ties to it."

"Other than a dead body and a burned restaurant."

The second reporter, Peter, frowned. "Again, the only connection proven has been Mr. Armstrong's."

"Thanks so much." The blonde came back onto the screen and Daniel flipped the television off. He shut his eyes again and practiced deep breathing exercises he'd learned in his counseling sessions.

By 3:30, Daniel knew he was done staying in the hospital bed.

He swung his legs over the side, placed his feet on the floor, and simply sat for a moment. His head wasn't happy with the movement, but at least he was upright. When he stood, the room tilted slightly. He swayed, then caught his balance, then waited for the mild dizziness to pass.

Once he could move without the possibility of doing a face-plant into the floor, he found his clothes and dressed, ignoring the blood stains on his shirt. By the time he was done, he was ready to crawl back in the bed.

A light tap on the door made him stiffen. When it opened, a young nurse stepped inside. She blinked when she saw him standing there. "Um . . . sir? Shouldn't you be in the bed?"

"Probably." Another figure entered the room behind the nurse. When he caught sight of her, he blinked. "Katie? You're still here?"

"Yes, I'm your night-duty bodyguard." She gave him a slight smile. "Are you trying to pull a middle-of-the-night escape?"

He sank back onto the bed. "Something like that."

She shook her head. "Lie down, Daniel."

He grimaced but eased back onto the pillows. "I can't sleep. I might as well go home."

"In the morning."

He stared at her. "When do you sleep? This hasn't exactly been a restful day for you either."

Another small smile. "I'll sleep when Olivia takes over."

"Oh."

The nurse moved closer, tossing Katie a

grateful look. Then she turned her attention to Daniel. "On the one-to-ten scale, what's your pain level?"

"A four. Maybe a five. But just some ibuprofen, please. No more of the strong stuff."

She lifted a brow but nodded. "I don't know that that's going to do much, but you're the boss."

He shot a glance at Katie. "I think that's debatable."

Katie gave a low laugh. "Funny. Take advantage of the situation and use it to get some rest, Daniel. You're going to need it."

The nurse turned toward the door. "I'll be back with that ibuprofen in just a few minutes."

"Thanks."

She left and he leaned his head back and closed his eyes, fatigue sweeping away his previous burst of restlessness. He felt Katie's hand on his and opened his eyes to find her frowning at him. "What is it?" she asked.

"I want to be doing something. I *need* to be doing something."

She tilted her head slightly as she studied him. "What is it you think you can do?"

"I have skills. I can use them."

"Help with the investigation?"

"Yeah."

She nodded. "You're right. You do have skills. You're not a run-of-the-mill client, so to speak."

"Okay, glad you recognize that."

"And you wouldn't even have us here if it weren't for Riley."

He hesitated a fraction. Was that true? "Yes, I'll agree with that," he said. "Frankly, the idea of hiring a bodyguard service probably wouldn't have occurred to me."

Her lips tilted in that small, mysterious smile she was very adept at. "I can't say that surprises me."

"So. What next?"

She studied him for a moment, then gave a small shrug. "You tell me."

"I want to visit Quinn."

She hesitated, then nodded. "Of course you would want to, but you have to know, he's pretty heavily drugged — and when he's not, he's ornery."

"That's okay."

"Let me text Maddy. I know she's with him right now. If he's awake, she'll be awake."

"All right. Tell her we'll come first thing in the morning." He glanced at the clock again. "Or in a couple of hours."

Katie sent the text and they waited in silence. The nurse came back and handed

Daniel the pills. He swallowed them and finished off the cup of water. Just about when he was ready to give up on Maddy texting back, Katie's phone chimed. She looked at it. "Quinn's awake and being ornery. Let's go."

"Wait a minute. Now? It's just after four in the morning."

"Maddy sounded desperate. We're going."

He gave a light shrug. "All right then, if you say so."

"I'll roll you down there."

Daniel barked a short laugh. "No wheelchair. I'll walk."

"It's a chair or you don't go." It wasn't an argument when she said it, just a simple fact. Daniel knew if he didn't let her roll him, he would not see Quinn. Stubborn woman. "Fine."

Katie gave him a small smile that carried a lot of triumph. He grimaced. She disappeared for a few minutes, and when she returned, she had the chair. He rose from the bed and swayed. Her hand gripped his arm and he waited for the dizziness to pass before he lowered himself into the seat. Once his head quit spinning, he actually didn't feel that bad, but he'd let Katie have her way with this one.

She rolled him out the door and to the

elevator. "He might yell at you."

"I've been yelled at before."

The elevator doors opened and she pushed him in. They rode in silence to the sixth floor and then exited to head down a long hallway. Other than the darkness outside the windows in the hall, one would never know it was the wee hours of the morning. Nurses bustled, phones rang, family members entered and exited the rooms, some looking sleepy and rumpled.

At room 624, she knocked. A few seconds later, the door opened and a woman he'd never seen before stood there looking wan and tired. Maddy.

"Hey, come on in," she said. "He's been awake for about an hour, refusing to take pain meds, so no guarantee you'll leave with your head."

"You look tired," Katie said.

"I am." She looked down at him. "You must be Daniel."

"Yes ma'am."

"Hope you've got a thick skin," she muttered.

Katie motioned him into the room.

Daniel's eyes sought Quinn's. The man wore a deep scowl that pulled his brows together just above the bridge of his nose. His legs were in casts and held in traction by what looked like some form of torture device. Daniel held Quinn's gaze for a few seconds. "Thank you."

The frown eased slightly. "Welcome."

They studied each other for another moment, then Daniel nodded and looked up at Katie. "We can go now."

She raised a brow and looked at Maddy, who raised one back. Katie drew in a breath. "All righty then." She started to turn him toward the door, then paused. With a sigh, she walked over to Quinn, leaned down, and kissed his cheek. "I'm not going to ask how you're doing. I'm getting regular updates from Maddy."

He grunted. "Tell Bree to catch the psycho who did this."

"Already done. Be nice to Maddy, Quinn."

He patted her back and gave her a slight shove toward the door. "Get out of here. You're messing with my beauty sleep."

And then Katie was behind Daniel and pushing him out of the room. Once in the hall she took a deep breath. "Well, that went better than expected."

Before he could speak his thoughts, his phone buzzed. With a fierce frown, he snagged it from his lap and looked at the screen, then brought the device to his ear. "Hello?"

"Mr. Matthews?"

"Yes."

"The alarm at A Taste of Yesterday on Elmwood is going off. Officers are en route."

He jerked. "What? I'll meet them there in fifteen minutes." He hung up.

"So you're going AWOL from the hospital?"

"I am."

She pulled her keys from her pocket. "I'm not sure where we're going, but I guess I'm driving?"

Once Daniel had learned that officers were at the scene, he used his phone to shut off the alarm. Upon arriving at the restaurant, Katie hung back while the officers did their job. She didn't recognize any of them so simply watched and took mental notes while she kept an eye on Daniel and the surrounding area. Police officers cleared the restaurant and Daniel came back to stand beside her.

"You sure you're feeling up to this?"

"No, but it can't be helped."

Streetlights cast a hazy glow over the area, giving it a feeling of darkness, a coldness that only the sunshine could chase away. "There's no sign of anyone having gotten inside and there's nothing to indicate that someone was here," he said.

"So why did the alarm go off?"

"Someone punched in the wrong code."

Katie frowned. "Was the person trying to make a good guess and failed?"

Daniel started to shake his head and seemed to think better of it. "No, whoever it was punched in the right code. As of yesterday. I changed it this morning on my phone while I was feeling sorry for myself. And mad."

She lifted a brow. "Well, that puts things in a different light, doesn't it?"

He held his head and closed his eyes for a brief moment, then looked back at her. "Only a little if you think it narrows the field of suspects. All of my trusted employees have the code — the managers, a few who've been with me awhile, and a couple of delivery guys."

"Delivery guys?"

"Yes." He lifted a hand to his head, then dropped it. His head had to be killing him, but other than the occasional grimace and the lines at the bridge of his nose, nothing else told her he was hurting. He sure wasn't going to complain about it. "They've been delivering here for several years. Sometimes they'll want to make a delivery when the restaurant is closed. We've built the kind of relationship where I don't have to come in and open up. They just use the code."

"For an ex-Marine, you're awfully trusting."

"There's no such thing as an ex-Marine. Once a Marine, always a Marine." He gave her a grim smile. "And yes, I'm trusting. But only when someone's earned it. And now? I'm afraid even those people are suspect." He paused and his eyes roamed the area. She could see the hair on his arms spiked. He rubbed them, then he glanced at her out of the corner of his eye. "Want to go flying tomorrow?"

"Tomorrow?"

"Why? You got something better to do?"

She pursed her lips. "I'm not sure flying with a head injury is a good idea."

He scowled. "Maybe not."

"But speaking of deliveries, my new kitchen cabinets are set to arrive around ten in the morning, and I'm installing them tomorrow."

"Want some company?"

She tilted her head and eyed him. "Sure. If you think your head can handle it."

He turned his gaze back to his restaurant. "It can. I need something to take my mind off this mess. Helping you out will be perfect." He rubbed a hand over the stubble on his chin. He touched his bruised cheek, then his still-bandaged head. He narrowed his eyes, a slow anger burning there. "Yeah. I need a distraction." His gaze caught hers and the anger faded. "I find you to be a good distraction."

Katie caught her breath at his look but didn't ask what he meant. She knew. "Thanks. I think."

So he was ready to acknowledge the mutual attraction. Oh boy. Now what? Uncertainty squirmed through her. Did she want to take a chance on him? Yes, her heart shouted. Her head had other ideas, though, and flashed caution signals.

Daniel walked to the entrance of the restaurant and tested the door. It was locked, but she already knew that. He lifted his nose and sniffed. "You smell that?"

"What?"

"It's faint, but it's there. Smells like that stuff you use to take off fingernail polish."

"The same smell your neighbor claimed he noticed in his Jeep."

"Yes."

She followed his example and tested the air. Sure enough, she caught a faint whiff of it. "Interesting."

"So now we can sort of connect the guy sitting outside in the Jeep to the attempted break-in here," he said.

"There's no proof except our noses, but it's good enough for me." One by one the officers exited the area until it was just Katie and Daniel left to lock up and rearm the alarm. Daniel punched in the code and Katie scanned the area, her nerves tight in the sudden, quiet darkness. "Come on, let's get out of here."

"You feel it too," he murmured. He pressed a hand to the bandage on his head and winced.

"The crickets stopped chirping and the hair on my neck is standing straight up."

"Where do you think he's watching from?"

"I don't know. What do you think?"

"From the graveyard," he said, not looking in that direction. "Probably from behind one of the bigger markers."

"Or that mausoleum."

"Or that."

Katie felt the comforting weight of her weapon snugged up under her left armpit. Her fingers twitched, wanting to have the gun against her palm where it would be ready should she need it. She pulled it out and held it comfortably, the weapon a perfect fit. "Do you see anything?" she asked, keeping her voice low, her gaze on him. He'd moved, subtle and slow, like he planned to get into the Jeep. However, his actions placed her vehicle between them and the graveyard.

"No. Do you?"

"No. It's too dark."

He reached up and pulled the white bandage off, revealing a tan bandage underneath. He tossed it under the car. She knew what he was doing. He didn't want to open the door and have the interior light come on, and he didn't want to wear the bandage. "No sense in giving our guy an easy target to find in the dark."

"Yep. So, are you thinking what I think you're thinking?"

"Probably. How do you feel about going hunting blind?" he murmured.

"Not my favorite thing to do. Are you sure you're up to it?"

"Quit asking me that. I'm up to it."

"Then I'm willing." She paused. "And normally I wouldn't say that to a client, but you're not the typical client."

His white teeth flashed for a brief second in the darkness. "Glad you understand that. Let's go hunting."

[14]

TUESDAY
5:15 AM

Daniel wanted to catch the person causing him so much trouble. And pain. Definitely pain. Wanted it so bad he could taste it. Once again his adrenaline had shifted into overdrive. His head pounded a throbbing rhythm. One he ignored while he focused on the hunt. At least he wasn't dizzy. He could handle just about anything except being dizzy.

He moved easily into the shadows, wishing he had a bulletproof vest on. But he didn't, so he'd have to make sure he didn't get shot. Which brought his thoughts to Riley. For a moment he hesitated.

Katie stopped beside him. "You okay?"

"Yeah."

She gestured to her right. "I'll go this way."

He nodded. "Be careful."

"Of course. Don't shoot me. It would

really ruin my night."

He grunted. "As if." He wasn't insulted though. They both knew he'd only pull the trigger if he knew exactly what he was aiming at. But apparently she dealt with stress the same way he did. Through the use of sarcasm, by taking control when she felt it slipping away, stuffing down her emotions so she could think, not feel. Yeah, they were a lot alike. And right now he didn't have time to figure out if that was a good thing or not.

She took off across the back parking lot toward the retaining wall. Within seconds, she'd scampered over and was behind one of the larger headstones. He no longer could make out her form. Which was good. If he couldn't, hopefully whoever was watching couldn't either. Daniel waited a moment longer to see if he could spot any movement, sense any change in the air.

Katie stayed put and he knew she was listening and waiting as well. When nothing happened, Daniel left the car and headed for the opposite end of the retaining wall. Just beyond it, near a large mausoleum, under the glowing single bulb, he saw a shadow slink past and disappear behind the large oak tree that grew next to a well-manicured hedge.

Satisfaction filled him. He had this guy now. Stealthy and silent, he skirted the wall. Crouching low, he stepped lightly, headed to the tree where he'd seen the figure vanish. He looked to his left and saw Katie's dim shadow, also approaching, quiet and slow. What he wouldn't give for an earpiece to be able to communicate with her right now, even though he knew he wouldn't speak and take a chance on revealing himself. He could tap codes though. He moved closer.

Closer.

His head pounded and a sudden wave of nausea swept over him, but he pressed on. This guy wasn't getting away again.

The sliver of a moon didn't give off much light, but enough that he knew the man was still behind the tree. Daniel's heart pounded a steady beat in spite of the adrenaline rushing through him. He stayed cool, his combat training surfacing. His prey was just ahead. Katie closed in from the other side.

Daniel pulled his weapon, stepped up beside the tree, then slightly past it.

He turned, weapon held straight out and ready.

And froze.

He lifted his gaze and snagged Katie's. She shook her head.

The shadow was gone.

Vanished.

"Where'd he go?" Daniel whispered. He pressed a hand to his head and just stood still for a moment.

"I don't know, but he couldn't have gotten far." She studied the terrain. "He could have used that hedge for cover."

"But if he'd have gone over, I would have seen him."

"Maybe not."

"He was right there and then disappeared. How'd he get over the shrubs and the fence without me spotting him?"

She stared at the area. "What if he didn't go over?"

He looked at her.

"What if he went under?" they said simultaneously.

He blinked. "Of course," he muttered. "I'm not thinking straight."

"At least you can blame it on the concussion."

"I have a *slight* concussion."

"The headache then."

"That works." She gave him a small smile, turned and started walking. Daniel followed, wanting to replay what had just happened in his head. Instead, he focused on what he needed to do for now. Katie slipped up to the hedge and looked over. "Could have climbed the fence, but . . ." She knelt and disappeared into the shrubbery.

"Katie?"

"Over here."

He spun and saw nothing. "Where?"

She popped back into view and stood up, favoring her injured knee while brushing the debris from her clothing. "There's a hole in the fence. Excellent little escape route."

"He knows this area, he knew this would be a good exit," Daniel said.

"And it looks like he's gone. I recommend we get out of here while he's not flinging bullets at us."

Daniel nodded. "Good idea."

They made their way back to her Jeep and he climbed in. His head pounded and he was having a hard time ignoring it. He pressed his fingers to the bridge of his nose and closed his eyes for a moment, wishing the headache away. Unfortunately, it didn't go anywhere.

Katie shut her door and started the vehicle. Within seconds, she'd merged onto I-76 and was headed toward his home. "How's the headache?"

"Fine."

"There's a bottle of Tylenol in the glove

box. You could alternate with the ibuprofen."

He shot her a glance. It rather unnerved him that she could read him so easily. He tried to decide if he wanted to be stubborn and hold out until he got home. Then decided pride was overrated and dug out a couple of the little white pills. He downed them and offered two to her. "For the knee."

She gave a low laugh and took the pills. "Thanks."

He leaned his head back but watched her out of the corner of his eye.

So, okay.

He was attracted to her. She was a strong woman who didn't let her weaknesses hold her back. He liked that about her. Admired that.

She handed him her phone. "Text Haley for me, will you? I don't want to show up at your house unannounced and scare everyone to death."

He did as she requested and set her phone in the cup holder even while he noticed the tension on her face. "What are you thinking?"

"That we're missing something. Something so obvious I'm going to feel stupid when I finally realize what it is." She scowled. "I hate feeling stupid."

"I can't imagine you ever feeling stupid."

She shot him a dry look. "It's happened." She tapped the wheel while she drove. "Okay, so why would someone have that smell? What is it? Acetone?"

"What if it's a woman? Someone who used the stuff before going out to do her dirty work?"

"Could be. If you're around it enough, I would imagine you'd get used to the smell. Wouldn't notice it or think about it being something that might be used to catch him or her."

He nodded. "Or someone uses it for their work?"

"The guy who put my prefinished hardwood floors in used it to clean some dull areas. Worked great." She pulled her phone from the cup holder and handed it to him. "Do you mind sending a text to Olivia, asking her to get someone to research the commercial uses for acetone?"

He did so and then continued to watch her until she pulled into his driveway and parked. "We seem to be doing this a lot. You chauffeuring me around."

She smiled. "I don't mind."

"Katie . . ."

"Yes?" She turned toward him, one hand on the door handle.

"At the risk of sounding like a high schooler, I want to kiss you."

She blinked. "Why?"

He let out a low laugh. "Ouch."

She didn't look away, her steady gaze making him want to squirm. But he didn't. He simply kept his eyes on hers. She slid closer and stopped. Stared at him while he wrestled with the desire to take control of the situation and just kiss her. But he waited, let her decide what the next move would be. A small smile curved her lips just before she pressed them to his. Surprise held him frozen for all of a second — then he kissed her back. The spark he knew was there now flared into an electrical storm. He pulled back and stared at her. "Wow."

She bit her lower lip, then gave him a wicked smile. "In case you didn't notice, I wanted to kiss you too."

"Why?" he mocked with a gentle grin.

She lightly punched his arm. "Because." She turned serious. "You're the first person I've connected with in a really long time on a basis that isn't surface or shallow — other than the ladies I work with — and I don't want to kiss them."

He snorted a surprised laugh. "I'm glad."

She lifted her hand and pressed it against his cheek. He relished the contact. "I think you get me. And I like a lot of things about you. You've got integrity and that's important to me."

His eyes clouded. "It's important to me too."

She dropped her hand. "Why the sudden frown?"

"Because my integrity is being questioned. That bothers me. A lot."

It was her turn to frown. "Quinn said your financials came out clean."

"I know, but the murder of my former cook isn't sitting well with some people. I saw the news in the hospital. They're speculating that Armstrong was part of a gang, that I murdered him, staged it to look like a suicide, and the gang retaliated by burning my restaurant down." He clicked his tongue. "I see why Quinn is against speculation."

Katie shook her head. "That's ridiculous. The timeline doesn't even fit that theory. The media just needs a bone to chew on. Once this is all resolved, they'll move on to a new story."

"Yeah, but I don't have to like it while it's happening."

"True." She sighed. "And we probably should keep things from getting too personal while you're a client."

"I don't know if I like that."

"I don't know if I do either, but I think that's what we need to do."

"Hmm. We'll see."

He punched another sequence on his phone and the garage door rose. She pulled the car in, opened the door, and climbed out.

Daniel did the same. He used the button on the wall to lower the door behind them, then led the way inside. Once he stood in his kitchen, he drew in a deep breath. "What time is it?"

"Six fifteen," Haley said from the other side of the room.

"How's Riley?" Daniel asked.

"Riley is just fine, thank you very much." His niece stepped in front of Haley, then crossed the floor to hug him. "Who's doing this, Uncle Daniel? Who's causing all this trouble?"

He sighed and kissed the top of her head. "Still working on that one."

Riley scowled at him. "Need to work faster. And that Tim Shepherd dude called again. You really need to make time in between getting shot at and hospital stays to call him back."

He thought he heard Katie give a light snort. Haley turned her head, but not before he saw her lips curve in a grin. Riley's sometimes macabre humor was something she'd learned from him. When he'd been in the Marines, among his other coping mechanisms, he'd learned to use dark humor to deal with . . . life. And death. Riley was so much like him. Poor girl. "I'll call him first thing today."

"Thank you. And now that I know you're safe, I'm going to bed. And yes, I'm sleeping in, so yes, that might be construed as playing hooky." She scowled and Daniel sighed.

"You're excused this time," he said. "You can start with Martin on Wednesday. I'll text him, then email the school and let them know."

"Perfect. Thanks."

He watched her leave.

Haley rubbed her eyes. "I think I'm off to bed as well," she said. She looked at Katie. "How's Quinn?"

"Out of surgery, in a room, and being ornery. We actually went to see him. We didn't stay long." She glanced at her phone. "Bree's at the hospital and so is Maddy. Maddy's planning to return to work next week, by the way."

"Good. She said she was ready. So what's the plan for the next twenty-four hours or so?"

"Let's stay here and get some rest. Charlie and Lizzie will be on board in two hours. You go ahead and get some sleep. As soon as they get here, I'll crash. Since Riley's sleeping in, we won't have to worry about an escort to school."

"I think that's a great idea," Daniel said. "There's plenty of room. I'll set some things out for you."

He started down the hall.

Katie placed a hand on his arm. "Daniel, we can handle it. Just point us in the right direction and we'll be fine. You're hurt and you need rest. Go." She gave him a gentle shove.

He gave a careful nod. "I won't argue with you. All the sheets on the beds are clean. Extras are in the closet in the guest bath. Help yourself. If you need something you can't find, just let me know. I don't mind."

"Got it. See you in the morning."

"It is morning."

"Right. See you *later* in the morning."

Daniel took himself and his aching head and body to his master bedroom and shut the door behind him. He stretched out across the bed, shut his eyes, and fell asleep.

[15]

Katie was glad she could sleep just about anywhere. She'd let Haley take the guest room while she waited for Charlie and Lizzie to show. They'd arrived around 8:00 a.m. and Katie had crashed in the oversized, very comfortable recliner. Now her rumbling stomach awakened her.

She lowered the leg rest and stretched.

Coffee? She lifted her nose and sniffed. "Oh please, yes." Yep. She headed for the kitchen while firing off a text to Maddy for an update on Quinn. She followed the blessed aroma that grew stronger with each step into the kitchen where she found Riley watching the dark liquid drip into her cup. "You're an addict too?"

Riley glanced at her from the corner of her eye. "Yes. I'll be human in a few minutes."

"Gotcha."

Riley reached into the cabinet next to her and pulled down another mug. She handed it to Katie, who took it and wished the coffee to drip faster.

Finally, Riley moved and Katie was able to fill her mug.

Neither said another word until they had the caffeine sufficiently flowing through their blood. They sat at the kitchen table and sipped. Finally Riley looked up and sighed. "Sorry. It takes me a few minutes to wake up."

"I understand. Although I think you're too young to poison your system with this stuff."

Riley smiled. "I only drink one or two cups in the morning. The rest of the time it's water." She took another sip of the brew. "Are we having class today?"

Katie blinked. Class. "Oh right. I'll have to think about that one. You won't be going, though, okay?" She rose, filled her mug again, then came back to reclaim her chair. "What day is it?"

Riley choked on a laugh. "Oh my gosh. You and Uncle Daniel need serious help."

"Why?"

"It's Tuesday. Class starts in two hours."

Katie pressed a palm against her forehead

218

and thought. She was on the schedule to teach today. Even though she had planned to be on vacation this week, she hadn't bothered to change her class schedule since she was going to be in town. Circumstances had changed, though. She could either cancel the class or have Olivia teach it. She picked up her phone to send a text and noticed the three missed calls. All from the same number.

"My cabinets."

Riley blinked. "Huh?"

"I'm redoing my kitchen. My new cabinets were supposed to be delivered this morning and in all the craziness I forgot and missed their calls." She'd turned her phone on silent since she knew Haley was on duty. She sighed and dialed her neighbor, a widow, who had made it her mission in life to watch out for Katie. A fact Katie appreciated most of the time. "Hi, Mrs. Worth, how are you today?"

"Fine, dear."

"Did you happen to notice a delivery truck pull up at my house this morning around ten o'clock?"

"Yes indeed."

"I'm on a job and forgot about them. I had my phone on silent and slept through their calls."

"No worries, darling. I let them in with the key you left me. You now have a kitchen full of cabinets waiting to be put up." Which Quinn and Bree and a couple of other handy friends had planned to help her with. Only Quinn was now out of the picture and quite possibly Bree as well, depending on how things were going with her family. "Thank you *so* much. That's a relief."

"My pleasure. I also fed Backdraft for you and cleaned his litter box."

"Mrs. Worth, I simply don't know what I'd do without you. You're the best."

The woman laughed, a hearty chuckle that expressed her pleasure with Katie's sentiment. "You know I don't mind. It's not like I have anything else to do, so I rather enjoy looking after you. Oh, I almost forgot."

"What?"

"While they were delivering your cabinets, there was someone in your backyard. I asked him if he was a friend of yours, and he said no, he was with a landscaping company and you'd asked him to come by to take a look at your yard."

Katie frowned and straightened. "Really? Can you describe him to me?"

"Oh, tall, slender build. He had longish blond hair pulled back in a short ponytail. Lots of grease on that hair, but he smelled good. I liked his cologne. Needed a good shampoo, though. He had on some black-framed glasses that made him look rather nerdy. I wanted to tell him he could probably find a more flattering pair, but I restrained myself."

Katie's frown deepened. It didn't sound like anyone she knew and she certainly hadn't contacted any landscaping company. She planned to do the yardwork herself. One day. "Did you get the name of the landscape company?"

"No, I don't recall seeing it. I just noticed he drove a brown truck."

"Okay. Thanks for letting me know."

"Is there anything else I can do for you, dear?"

"No, Mrs. Worth. Thank you so much. I really appreciate everything. I'll talk to you soon, okay?"

"All right then. Have a good day."

"You too," Katie said and hung up. She stared at the table, thinking. *She* hadn't hired anyone from a landscaping company, but that didn't mean *someone* in her neighborhood hadn't. Could the company have simply gotten the wrong address? If she had the name of the company, she could call them, but . . . she didn't.

"Anything wrong?"

Katie jumped. She'd almost forgotten about Riley, who sat so quietly. "No . . . um . . . at least I don't think so." She smiled. "It's probably nothing." But she'd be keeping a close eye on her home and her weapon even closer. She sent a text to Olivia asking if she could teach the class. Olivia responded with a "sure" and Katie breathed a sigh of relief. Now she could concentrate on keeping Daniel safe.

"Morning."

She turned to find the man standing in the doorway. He had on a black T-shirt and faded blue jeans. His hair was still wet from the shower, his feet were bare, and he just plain looked good. If a bit cranky and tired. She cleared her throat. "I think you mean 'Afternoon,' but how'd you sleep?"

"Not great. How about you?"

"Better than I thought I would. Coffee?"

"Of course." He poured himself a cup, grabbed two more ibuprofen from the bottle on the counter, and settled into the chair beside her. His presence made the room seem smaller, the air thinner. She sucked in a deep breath and couldn't help remembering the kiss. That amazing, toe-curling kiss. "Nightmares?"

He grunted. "Yeah. A few."

Riley frowned at him. "You haven't had a

nightmare in a while."

"I know. I'm sure the recent events have triggered them." His niece chewed her lip and Daniel covered her hand with his. "Now don't go getting all mother-henny on me. I'll be fine."

"Mother-henny?" Riley snorted. "Is that even a . . . thing?"

Daniel scowled at her. "You know what I mean."

She snickered and stood. "I do. But I also have schoolwork that I need to make up, so I'll see you two later." She paused. "I also told my family that I work for that I needed a leave of absence effective immediately. If I need a bodyguard, I don't need to be around the girls. After I explained the situation, their mom agreed. She'd seen the news and had been considering asking that I step down from the job for the time being anyway, so it all worked out."

Daniel grimaced. "Aw, Prin— honey, I'm sorry."

Riley shrugged. "I am too, but it is what it is right now." She rubbed her nose. "You think I'll be all right working with Martin? Not so much that I'll be safe, but that he and the others around him will be?"

"Martin has security on site. I think everyone will be just fine."

She nodded. "Good. I really didn't want to have to make up that internship." She blew out a low breath. "Although I'm considering that I probably should have gone to Mexico instead." Her phone buzzed and she pulled it from the waistband of her pajama bottoms. Her brow lifted and her cheeks reddened. "Then again, maybe not." Without looking back, she left the kitchen and headed toward her room.

Daniel shook his head. "What was that all about?"

"A boy."

"Huh?"

Katie snickered. "Oh me."

"What?"

"Nothing. Look, let's —"

This time it was her phone. "It's Bree."

"Put it on speaker."

Katie placed the device in the middle of the table and pressed the speaker button. "Hi, Bree, what's up and how's Quinn this morning?"

"Hi, Quinn's doing well. He's awake and biting heads off."

Katie let out a relieved sigh. "Oh good."

"Yeah. Maddy's still with him, so I think he's controlling himself a bit more than usual."

"How long does the doc say for the healing process?"

"A couple of months for sure. Physical therapy after that."

She grimaced and saw the flash of guilt cross Daniel's face. "All good stuff. It means he'll recover."

"Indeed." Katie heard papers shuffling in the background. "Okay, we got the autopsy back on Armstrong. He died of a broken neck. Looks like he was knocked out from behind, fell forward, and broke his nose when he crashed into the asphalt. Then someone broke his neck while he was either unconscious or too stunned to fight back."

Katie swallowed and looked at Daniel, who rubbed his eyes and pinched the bridge of his nose. "What else?" he asked.

"We talked to several employees who all knew the code to the restaurant. We also talked to the ones Daniel said had keys. So far they all have pretty airtight alibis. There are a couple we're running down, but so far nothing's causing us too much concern."

"What about past employees?" Katie asked.

Daniel shook his head, then spoke for Bree's benefit. "No, anytime I've had an employee leave, I always get back my key and then change the code to the alarm." He rubbed his chin. "And before you ask, the keys all have the 'Do Not Copy' symbol on them, but that doesn't mean they can't be copied. So if an employee decided to share, it's not impossible that someone who doesn't work for me has a key."

Bree's sigh came through the line. "We'll keep searching, but I'm afraid we're heading for a dead end."

"Anything on Billy Kendall or his brother, Lee?" Katie asked.

"Billy Kendall is still in prison. He's up for probation in a couple of years, so he's not a threat."

"What about his brother?" Katie asked.

"Now he's an interesting character. Lee Kendall was an exemplary employee with a local car dealership. He's a mechanic and well-liked by his co-workers."

"So what's so interesting about that?"

"Every fourth Saturday of the month, he visits Billy in prison. One of Lee's co-workers said that Lee thought Billy got a raw deal and that the sentence was too severe. He said Billy was in a blind rage and didn't know what he was doing."

"So Lee agrees? We should just forgive and forget because his brother didn't know what he was doing? We should let a murderer walk the streets again?" Daniel asked.

"According to the co-worker, Lee wasn't

so sure about everything, but that he felt obligated to visit his brother," Bree answered. "I'm just passing on information. Anyway, also according to said co-worker, Billy has been after Lee to be his 'angel of vengeance' or some such thing."

Katie lifted a brow at Daniel and he frowned. "Meaning, Billy wants Lee to take me out. Yeah, I kind of figured that out after I confronted him when he was harassing me, remember?"

"Yes, but he doesn't just want you dead, he wants to destroy you and everything you hold dear." She paused.

"I see. What else?" Daniel asked.

"I went to visit Billy in prison. I asked to see his cell and one of the guards took me back there. Billy is quite the accomplished artist. He's good. I mean seriously good."

"Okay," Katie said. "And?"

"He's got the walls papered with drawings of avenging angels. There's one with a knife stabbed into the throat of a man that looks a whole lot like you, Daniel."

Daniel leaned back in his chair. "Nice."

"Isn't it?"

"So pick up Lee and question him," Katie said.

"Well, we would if we could find him. He hasn't been to work since the day before the fire and no one's been able to make contact with him. We've checked his apartment that he shares with another mechanic, but the man said he hasn't seen him either. He said he was getting ready to report him missing when we showed up."

This time it was Katie's turn to draw in a deep breath. "Okay then. Sounds like we might have a real winner here."

"Sounds like. We'll keep looking for him and you two keep looking over your shoulders."

Katie disconnected the call and took another sip of her coffee. "What are your plans for the day?"

"To survive it."

"Hmm. I like that plan. Anything else?"

"I need to catch up on some paperwork with the restaurant. I think I'm going to shut myself in my office and work. As long as I know Riley's all right, I'll be able to get some work done."

"Didn't look like she was planning on going anywhere. I did get Olivia to take the self-defense class so she may want to do that."

He sighed. "I'll ask her. What are your plans?"

"I'm going to visit Quinn."

"He won't appreciate you seeing him in

his weakened state. He couldn't wait for us to get out of his room last night."

"I know."

"Give him my best."

"Of course."

[16]

WEDNESDAY MORNING

Tuesday afternoon had been productive, and Daniel felt satisfied with the work he'd accomplished, although his concentration level hadn't been up to par. His headache had eased, though, so that was a relief.

He had his new computer and had needed to get some more things done today. If he'd tried to work with Katie in the room, he was afraid he'd be too distracted. So he shut himself away in his office and it worked. He was able to concentrate and get everything loaded from his backup drive onto the new device.

No one had bombed his house or set fire to his car or done anything to any of his other restaurants. Could the person be finished tormenting him?

He grimaced. He had a feeling the answer was no. But *what* did the person *want*? What was the point with all of the craziness? Who would benefit with him dead? The only people who came to mind were Riley and his mother. They would inherit everything. But he was certain neither of them were behind the attempts on his life. He stood and gazed out of the window. He'd awakened early with these thoughts refusing to leave him alone. Even a swim hadn't helped much.

His mind kept circling back to the question. *Why* had Armstrong been at the restaurant that night?

He had no answer. The man's daughter hadn't known, and Armstrong's mother hadn't even realized her son wasn't home. And none of the employees had been forthcoming with any information as to why the man would have been there.

And now Daniel had a nagging headache, sore muscles and joints. And he hadn't seen Katie since she'd walked out of his house yesterday afternoon to go visit Quinn.

Haley had arrived just before Katie left and had been there ever since. She stayed tense. Alert. Ready for action if the moment called for it. And he appreciated it. Admired her for it.

"You would make a good Marine," he told her.

A smile creased her cheeks. A real one, not one of those fake ones people used when they thought they were supposed to be amused with something they really didn't find funny. "Thanks."

His phone pinged and he glanced at it. A text from Riley, who'd left with Lizzie at the crack of dawn.

At the dig. Martin hasn't shown up yet. People are wondering where he is. Can you check on him?

You call him?

Yes. Like ten times. No answer, just voice mail.

I'll try him. Stay near your phone.

Daniel frowned and dialed Martin's number. It rang four times, then went to voice mail. "Martin, you okay? Riley said you haven't shown up to the dig yet. Call me."

He texted Riley.

I'm headed to Martin's house. Will let you know what I know when I know it.

The knock on his door brought his head up. At the motion, dizziness spun his head for a brief second, and he gritted his teeth while he waited for it to pass. Haley walked on silent feet to check who was on the other side. "It's Katie."

His heart thudded and he grunted. Those two little words had shifted his entire mood. For the better.

Haley let Katie in. When she stepped inside, she took off her coat and hung it on the rack to her right. "I wish it would snow later."

"Riley would love that."

"Not so much if she has to work the dig site in it. But it's October. I can't remember the last time it snowed in October. She's probably safe."

He smiled. "True."

Haley picked up her coat and bag. "I'm off for a bit of shuteye then. Call if you need me."

"Thanks. You're off for the rest of the day. We'll trade out tomorrow morning."

233

"Lovely. Bye, Daniel. Behave yourself."

"I'll do my best."

Haley pulled the door shut behind her and that left Daniel staring at the woman who'd just blasted into his life and knocked his feet out from under him. "Put your coat back on, will you?"

She paused. "Okay. What's up?"

"I need to make a house call. Riley texted and said Martin hasn't shown up at the dig. He's not answering his phone and no one at the university has heard from him."

Katie slipped her arms back into the heavy coat, then waited on him to get his. "Are you sure you're up for this?"

"Yes. I've got a hard head. I get a bit dizzy if I turn too fast and I still have a slight headache. I've had worse."

He grabbed his keys and she reached for his hand and closed her fingers around his. Her hands were still cold from the chill outside. "I'll drive."

He sighed, then gave in. "Sure." Why fight her? "You're a control freak, you know that?" He shoved his keys into his pocket and she led the way outside. He climbed into her Jeep and she slid into the driver's side and twisted the key. The vehicle rumbled to life and they rolled out of the driveway.

"I'm not a control freak."

"Yes. You are."

She shot him a sideways glance. "Maybe a little."

"A lot."

"And you're stubborn."

"I would agree with that."

She huffed and shook her head, but he could see the small smile playing around the corners of her lips. "Do you mind giving me directions?"

"Head toward the university. He lives on Joshua Street."

She followed his directions. He noticed her eyes bouncing from mirror to mirror. "We're not being followed."

"I know."

"Not very talkative this morning, are you?"

"No, not very."

"In a bad mood?"

"No."

"How's Quinn?"

"Cranky. Ornery. Rude."

"Sounds like he's on the road to recovery."

She laughed. "Yes. That's for sure." She drove in silence for the next few minutes.

"Are you sure you're okay? You seem . . . off."

She pursed her lips and glanced at him.

"And you're perceptive. But yes, I promise I'm all right. I'm just . . . reflective, I guess is the word."

"About?"

She lifted a shoulder. "Family stuff. Trying to figure out some things."

"Like what?"

"Like how to let go of the past." Her smile was sad this time. She pulled to a stop in front of Martin's home and lifted a brow. "And we'll save that topic for later."

"Right."

They climbed from the Jeep. Daniel walked up the front steps and knocked on Martin's front door. Katie stood quietly by his side, her eyes scanning the area. He knew she was making sure they hadn't been followed or were targets for someone with a sniper rifle. Not that she would be able to see a sniper, but Daniel had to admit it felt good having someone have his back. He just hated the reasons for it.

Martin's house sat on about two acres of prime property. He'd built the small mansion for his last wife but said he'd made sure he'd incorporated enough things about it that he liked in case the marriage didn't last.

And it hadn't. But Martin loved the house and he'd fought tooth and nail to keep it.

Daniel knocked again. "Martin, you home?"

The door flew open. His friend stood in the entryway, disheveled and — frantic? His hair stood on end and he'd misbuttoned his shirt. "What are you doing here? Who is she and why'd you bring her with you?"

Daniel frowned. "Riley called. You were supposed to meet her at the dig this morning to start her internship. This is Katie Singleton, she's a friend. Now what's going on?" He ignored the question about the reason for Katie's presence.

His friend ran a hand through his already spiked hair. "I can't believe this."

"What?"

"It's gone. It's lost. No. Someone stole it."

"Stole wh— ah . . . the coin." Daniel and Katie stepped inside his friend's home. Daniel's eyes landed on the living area to his left and he blinked. "Have you called the police? Someone did a number on this place." Martin wasn't the neatest person in the world, but having a weekly housekeeper meant his home was usually spotless. The cushions had been pulled off the sofa, the chairs overturned, a lamp lay on the floor. "Were you here when this happened? Are you okay?"

Martin slumped onto the edge of the cushionless sofa. "No, I haven't called the police."

"Why?"

"I . . . I didn't think about it. All I could think of was finding the coin." He threw his hands up. "But it's gone. And I have the media coming to my dig tomorrow. And now I have nothing to show for it." Tears welled in his eyes and Daniel felt his breath leave his lungs. His friend just couldn't catch a break. Martin's hands shook and he wiped his face. "Unbelievable. Just . . ." He shook his head. "This is it. After everything I've worked so hard for, after everything I've done . . . I'm . . . done. My life is over."

"No, it's not. You're going to cancel the media, get back in the dig, and find something else."

Martin laughed. Almost hysterically. Then he buried his face in his hands and blew out a sigh. "Yes, I'll cancel the media. I'll definitely cancel the media."

"And report this to the police," Katie said. She pulled out her phone.

"No," Martin said. "No police."

"What? Why not?" She stopped mid-call.

Martin stood and drew in a deep breath. "If word gets out about this, all eyes will be on the dig, and while that was the original intention when I had the coin, I don't want or need that right now." He looked at Daniel. "You're right. I'll keep searching the site. There's bound to be something else there. Another coin, something."

"Wait a minute," Katie said. "I'm assuming this is a pretty important coin. A coin that someone was willing to break into your house and steal. So you're just going to let whoever did this get away with it?"

He held out his hands in a beseeching gesture. "I don't know what else to do. I don't want the media involved yet."

"You're bringing my headache back, Martin," Daniel muttered. "Who else knew about the coin?"

"No one. Just you and me."

Daniel pursed his lips. "Well, someone else knew about it. What about the other workers at the dig?"

"No. I didn't tell them. I was there late one night when I found it. The only person I've shown it to is you. At the restaurant." His eyes darkened. "You told someone."

"What?" Daniel reared back. "Are you crazy? You know me better than that." Daniel held his friend's gaze and Martin's shoulders slumped.

"I know. You're right." He sighed and rubbed his eyes. "I'm sorry. I'm just a little frazzled right now."

"I'll say. Have you searched the house?"

"Yes, every square inch."

"Well, so much for preserving evidence," Katie murmured.

"I wasn't thinking of preserving evidence," Martin said. "I had to find the coin."

"Are you sure whoever did this found it?" she asked.

"Of course they found it," Martin said. "Look at this place!"

"Right. Well, where did you keep it? If you'd put it in your safe-deposit box, it would still be there."

"My pocket. I decided not to put it in the safe-deposit box because I . . . I was keeping it as my lucky piece and now it's gone." He looked shell-shocked and Daniel felt a shot of compassion for his friend even as he wanted to berate him for his stupidity.

Katie shot a look at Daniel, then slid her gaze back to Martin. "If it was in your pocket, how did the person steal it?"

"I don't know," he shouted. "All I know is that it was in my pocket yesterday and now it's nowhere to be found — and my house has been turned upside down." He rubbed a hand down his cheek. "Let me think. Let me think. I took it out of my pocket and put it in my bedside table drawer. Now it's not there. No one else has been in my house for three days. It's gone. Stolen." He looked like he might cry again.

"You need to get yourself together, Martin. Then you need to call your team and let them know what's going on. Understand?"

Martin groaned. "Yes, yes, of course." He looked at Katie. "I'm not usually so scattered and unprofessional. I'm sorry."

"It's understandable."

Martin reached for his cell phone. He eyed Daniel and Katie. "No one can know about this, you understand? Don't tell anyone."

"We'll keep it quiet, Martin, chill," Daniel said. "Now get yourself together and get to the site. You've got a team waiting for you."

Martin ran a hand over his face and sighed. "Yeah. Okay. Thanks." He shook his head.

Daniel's eyes fell on an item on the end table. He picked it up. "A pattern for a dress? Have you taken up sewing now?"

Martin rolled his eyes. "No, it's for Sarah. I found it online and ordered it for her. There's a market for these 1860s dresses, and she asked me to help her start selling them. Since you're being so generous and still paying them while the restaurant is closed, she's got some time to sew." He used a forefinger to push the glasses back onto the bridge of his nose. "She's become a friend." He snatched the pattern from Daniel's fingers and flung it back onto the end table. "So anyway, have you figured out who's trying to put you out of business?"

Daniel looked at Katie. "No, but we're working on it."

"Hope you catch the guy. Now get out of here, I've got to get to the site. There's got to be something else where that coin was. There has to be."

Daniel clapped his friend on the shoulder. "I have no doubt that if there's something there, you'll find it."

"You know the way out. Thanks for talking me off the ledge."

Daniel wasn't quite so sure the man was actually *off* the ledge, but maybe he wasn't quite as close to going over as he had been. Whichever the case, there was nothing more he could do at this point. He placed a hand on the small of Katie's back and escorted her to the door. Once outside, she took over the role of protector, her gaze traveling to and fro until they were both safe inside her Jeep. She cranked the engine and turned on the heater. "Stay here for a second, will you?"

"Why?"

"I want to take a look at something."

She got back out of the vehicle and he watched her until she got back in. "What are you thinking?"

"Just an idea."

"You want to share?"

"Martin's home is in a nice area. Fairly short driveway, backs up to that wooded area, and is enclosed with a huge privacy fence. At least that's what I could see from the windows from inside. When I went around to the side of the house, there was no way I could get into the back. He's got the gate padlocked. I don't even think I could climb over if I tried. Not without a ladder or standing on someone's shoulder."

He frowned. "Yes. All of that sounds right."

"But the front . . ." She waved a hand toward it. "This road is pretty busy. It's an older section of town. There are three businesses just across the street here."

He nodded and figured he knew where she was going with her line of thinking. "Cameras?"

"Couldn't hurt to check with the businesses. If they have one pointed to a street view, it might catch the front of Martin's house."

"I think it's a great idea."

"I'll call Bree." She pulled her phone from the clip and pressed a speed-dial number. Daniel listened as she talked. So pretty, so smart, so . . . off-limits? Maybe.

Then again . . .

She hung up.

He looked at her. "So. You want some help putting up cabinets?"

[17]

4:00 PM

Riley swiped the sweat from her forehead and gently shoved the trowel into the dirt, lifted and dumped the load into the plastic sieve. She picked up the sieve, and the dirt ran through the small holes, leaving some larger rocks at the top. Who would have thought she'd get so hot in forty-degree temps? She'd already discarded her heavy coat. Next to go was the sweater.

"How's it going, kid?"

She looked up to see Martin standing at the edge of the grid. His head blocked the sun, allowing her to look into his eyes. "Going okay, I guess. I marked off this area like you said and am working the grid to check every little bit of dirt."

"Good, good job." His eyes moved from her to a few of the other workers. "Everyone treating you well?"

"Sure. They're all really nice. Are you okay? Uncle Daniel just said you'd had a personal emergency."

"Yes, I'm fine. Well, not exactly fine, but I'm dealing with it. Thanks." He looked over her shoulder. "I see you have your watchdog over there."

Riley rolled her eyes. "Her name is Lizzie and she's not a watchdog. You know what's going on with Uncle Daniel. He just wants to make sure it doesn't spill over onto me — or anyone else I'm around."

He held up a hand. "I know. I know. I'm not complaining. If she's here to keep you safe, I'm all for it."

"Good."

"We have security as well, so everything should be fine."

"I think so."

"Okay, well, let me know if you need anything else. I'm going to be working in another area, but I'll come back and check on you in a bit."

"That's cool." Riley stuck the trowel in the dirt again. "Thanks, Martin."

"You bet, kid."

He walked off and another person took his place. She gasped. "Steve. What are you doing here?" Oh great. She probably had dirt on her face. She looked at her hands.

She definitely had dirt under her fingernails. Great. Just great. She pasted a smile on her lips and hoped her deodorant was working.

He hopped into the shallow hole in the ground and knelt beside her. "I decided to see what you were up to."

She shook her head. "You know what I'm up to. The same thing you should be up to."

"My internship doesn't start until tomorrow."

"How did you get past security?"

"She let me in."

Riley looked over to see Lizzie smiling at her. Great. So not only were these lady bodyguards practically psychic, they communicated with each other as well. Had it been Olivia or Katie or Haley?

Probably Haley.

Steve swiped a hand across his chin. "You're not answering your phone."

She patted her back pocket and pulled it out. "Oh. Sorry. I had it on silent instead of vibrate."

"So you going to answer my text or not?"

She read it, then looked up. "You serious? You really want to eat pizza with me? In public?"

He frowned, then sighed. "Of course I do."

"What happened to Sherry Lane?"

He flushed and dropped his gaze. "I'm

not interested in her."

"You were."

He gave a slow nod. "Yes. I was." He ran his hands through the dirt. "I was, but she's . . ."

"What?"

"Not you."

Okay, that was . . . interesting.

"Not me how?"

"Just . . ." He shrugged. "You and I can talk, Riley. With Sherry, she's all about appearances and into the latest fads and shopping." He looked away and brushed some dirt away from the front of his shirt, then looked back up at her. "I like hanging out with you better. So . . . you interested?"

Riley bit her lip on her immediate answer, then tilted her head and studied him. "I might be."

A slow smile curved his lips. "Might be?"

She laughed. "Okay. It sounds like fun." Then she frowned. "But . . ."

"Uh-oh."

"Yeah, there's an 'uh-oh.' " She drew in a deep breath. "Look, you don't live under a rock. I know you've heard about my uncle's troubles with his restaurant."

"Yep."

"And that doesn't bother you? That some people believe he's capable of something like that?"

"No. I mean yes. Yes, it bothers me that people would think that about him when he's done nothing but good for this city and community, not because I believe he's guilty." He shifted on the red dirt, not seeming to care that his jeans would never be the same. He took her hand. "Look, Riley. We've been friends a long time. The fact that we . . . grew apart . . . is my fault. Mostly."

"I'll say." She paused. "And wait a minute. Mostly?"

"You're the one who moved away."

She gave a short laugh. "My parents were missionaries. The fact that they wanted me on the mission field with them was kind of beyond my control."

He rubbed his head. "I know. This isn't going like I'd hoped." He bit his lip, then sighed. "I'll admit I made some stupid decisions."

"Yes. I'll agree with that."

He grimaced. "I'm not proud of them, but I did learn some things."

She studied him. "Like?"

"Like real friends are what's important. I'm really sorry for pushing you away, Riley."

She was sorry too, but not quite so sure she was ready to put her heart back out there for him to stomp on again. "What about your football buddies? Thought they had you convinced I wasn't cool enough to hang out with. That I was, what was the word? Oh yeah, *boring.*"

His face went red. "You heard that conversation."

"I heard it."

"I'm sorry."

"You didn't defend me."

"I know." He dropped his chin to his chest. "I'm a jerk, I admit it." Another sigh slipped from him. "As for the guys, I mean, we're a team, on and off the field, but I won't let them dictate to me anymore. My life is my life. It's time I started living like it."

"And you want to hang out with me."

"Yeah, I really do."

"You don't think I'm boring?"

He groaned. "No, I don't think you're boring. And I don't care what the guys think."

"Ready to start thinking for yourself again, huh?"

"More than ready. You don't let anything faze you or hold you back." He paused. Then licked his lips. "I was at the funeral."

"You were? I didn't see you."

His lips twisted. "I know. I was too

ashamed to speak to you. But I watched you and I could see that their deaths nearly crushed you."

"Yes." She cleared her throat against the sudden lump that had formed. "It did. You should have said something."

"I don't know how you've held it together, but you've stayed strong. You didn't let it break you."

"God got me through it." She looked away, then back. "He's still getting me through it. And I won't keep quiet about my faith even if it makes your football buddies uncomfortable."

"It's not all of them, just a select few."

"The few that influenced you."

"Yes. But I like your faith, I admire it. I even believe the same and I'm tired of denying it. You're strong and will talk about God to anyone. That's just one of the things I like about you. Admire about you. I want to be like that too."

She frowned. "Don't put me on a pedestal, Steve. I'll fall off. Trust me, I can wear a mask just like anybody else."

He stilled. "What do you mean?"

"I mean, you really hurt me, Steve. We've been best friends since kindergarten. As corny as it sounds, every time you passed me in the hall and wouldn't speak, every time you looked like you might sit at my table at lunch, then bypassed me, it hurt. I might have stayed cool on the outside, but I was crying on the inside." Well, now she'd done it. So much for not putting her heart back out there for him to stomp on. Nothing like opening up and being vulnerable.

He swallowed hard and nodded. "I know." He let the dirt trail through his fingers.

"Why did you take so long to text me?"

He sighed, then looked her in the eye. "Because I had to make sure I wasn't going to hurt you anymore. And as hard as you tried to hide it, I still saw it in your eyes." He pinched the bridge of his nose. "I had to make sure I was ready to stand up to my football buddies if need be."

"And you're ready for that?"

"I just said I was." He nodded. "Look, Riles, we're getting ready to go to college. All this, high school football, being the popular kid, it's fun, I'll admit it. But —" he ran a hand through the dirt and let it filter through his fingers — "I've been doing a lot of thinking and I realized I had to decide what kind of man I'm going to be. I can either care what other people think so much that I let it dictate my decisions or I can think for myself. Watching you stand up for what you believe in, it's made a differ-

ence. I've already told you what I decided."
He trailed a dirty finger down her cheek.
"I'm glad you stayed in Columbia instead
of going to Mexico."

She swallowed and did her best to ignore
the flip-flop of her heart. She smiled. "I am
too." *I think.* No way was she going to tell
him the *reason* she chose to stay.

Steve smiled back, then stepped out of the
dig site. "I've got to go. I'll call you later.
Okay?"

"Sure. See you later."

He walked toward the gated exit and Riley met Lizzie's gaze. The woman lifted a
hand in a salute and Riley shook her head.
But she couldn't help sending Lizzie a
thumbs-up. She was pretty sure she heard a
snicker in response. Riley clamped her lips
together to hold back her smile and stuck
the shovel in the dirt again.

Katie stood back, hands on her hips, and
stared at her kitchen. "I'd say that's an
improvement." She swiped an arm across
her forehead, then reached for her water
bottle. In six hours, she, Daniel, Charlie,
Wade, Olivia, and two friends Charlie had
talked into helping had completely trans-
formed the room. Haley had come in to
help with cleanup. "Impressive. You guys

are amazing. I can't thank you enough for helping put this together."

Daniel had done more blueprint reading and offering instructions than actual physical work, and Katie had arranged it that way on purpose. She wasn't going to let his stubbornness cause him to have a setback with his head injury.

And she was satisfied with the results. They made a good team. The stainless steel appliances gleamed under the new fluorescent light. Her new stools sat tucked under the bar, and the dining area held her most recent online purchase — the square table that would seat eight comfortably. She smoothed a hand over the stove that was still warm from its test run. "Now, I just have to learn to cook."

Charlie shook his head. "You and Olivia are two of a kind."

"Hey," Olivia said, "I've learned how to do a few dishes."

"That's true. Popping a can of tuna does take some special skill."

She punched her brother in the arm and Katie laughed. "I can do a little better than that," Olivia said.

Katie shook her head. "So now that I have this beautiful new kitchen, dinner is on me at Cantina's." She looked at Daniel. "But not tonight. When all of this is over. Deal?"

"Deal."

Daniel and Wade walked to the sunporch and Katie wondered what they were talking about. Before she could go be nosy, Olivia slipped up beside her. "It's nice, Katie."

"Yeah."

"Good idea getting Daniel to help you out. It kept him in one place and didn't give anyone a chance to get at him."

Katie let out a short laugh. "Well, I'd like to take credit for that, but he volunteered. Said he needed something to keep his mind off of everything and I was happy to have his help. How's Riley?"

"Lizzie said it's been quiet. Riley's a great kid and easy to look out for." Olivia's phone buzzed and she glanced at the screen. "It's a text from Maddy." She pressed the button to pull up the message. "She says Quinn's had a pretty good day, even though he's being his usual temperamental self."

"Good, glad he's feeling all right."

A slight smile curved Olivia's lips. "Yes, it sounds like it." Another buzz. "She also says that the second set of X-rays they did are consistent with the first ones. They look good and his legs should heal well. They were broken below the knee and he's got some serious tissue and muscle damage.

He's looking at a couple of months' recovery, but they're saying that when he walks again, he'll be considered a 'walking miracle.' "

"Cute. His birthday is eight weeks away, you know."

"No, I didn't." Olivia looked up from her phone. "Are you thinking of doing something special for him?"

"Something."

"Count Wade and me in."

"Thanks."

The men walked back into the kitchen. "So which room is next?" Daniel asked. "Sunroom looks great, but your den is a mess."

"Then that's the one we'll tackle."

"We?"

"Why not?"

He laughed. "Okay, I'm in."

She saw him pull a couple of pills from his pocket and down them. "Head hurting?"

"A little."

Now that she looked closer, she could see he was pale. "Come on, let's get you home. Lizzie's with Riley and will spend the night. Haley's on duty tonight with you."

He frowned and nodded. "All right."

"Why the frown?"

"Nothing." He looked at Haley. "I'm

ready when you are."

Haley nodded. "Let me just get my stuff out of the sunroom." She disappeared around the corner.

"Wade and I are out of here too," Olivia said. She turned to Charlie. "Will you make sure Haley and Daniel get home?"

"Of course."

Once the door had shut on everyone, Katie drew in a deep breath and released Backdraft from her bedroom where he'd spent the majority of the day. After appeasing his indignation with an extra can of food, she headed for a hot shower.

Thirty minutes later she shut the shower off before she depleted the hot water supply, her aching muscles eased. The guys had done most of the heavy lifting, but she'd definitely done her share. As she dressed, she couldn't stop thinking about the fire at the restaurant, the images that it evoked, the fear that it resurrected. Even now, it was like she had to come at the memory sideways instead of head on.

It had been Thanksgiving Day three years ago when a bomb had gone off in the two-story apartment building. An evicted tenant hadn't taken it so well and had returned with vicious intent. Katie had been a part of the bomb squad. Paul, her brother, had been the arson investigator. She'd arrived at the scene just as the last ambulance was pulling away. A family of five had perished in the fire. Scores of others had been wounded. And she and Paul had gone in —

She gritted her teeth and forced the memories away. This was her downtime, her off-work time. She should put it to good use. She spent the next few hours unpacking boxes with dishes and setting her kitchen up. By the time she finished, the memories were safely tucked away and she had a new resolve to learn to cook. Later.

She glanced at the clock. 11:00. Wow, she hadn't noticed the passing hours and she was starving. In spite of the late hour, she microwaved some leftover Chinese and carried it into the sunroom where she settled into her favorite chair and curled her feet beneath her. Backdraft joined her and she gave him a piece of shrimp which he proceeded to devour.

She picked up the remote and aimed it at the television. Then stopped. She'd caught a flicker of something outside the sunroom. A whisper of light and motion. A change in the shadows. Trees surrounded her at the back of the house. The passing car lights on the road at the bottom of the hill flickered through the trees, but that was all she could see of civilization from her sunroom. Which was one of the selling features of the house for her. She set her plate on the end table, flipped the lamp off, and plunged herself into darkness.

[18]

Daniel stood at the window overlooking the pool. He couldn't sleep and frankly wondered if he would ever be able to get more than four hours without being knocked unconscious by a concussion or narcotics. The dreams haunted him tonight, but he refused to let them set him back. He knew they were due to the circumstances he now found himself in. Once the mystery of who wanted to kill him was solved and he was no longer a target, the dreams would lessen in intensity once again. He hoped.

So. What to do? He reviewed the incidents of the last few days, silently flipping through the events in chronological order. Trying to figure out who could be behind them. The most obvious choices were Lee Kendall or Tim Shepherd, the real estate developer. Truthfully, he had trouble picturing either person having the skills to do what had been done. Lee was a rather small man with a slight build. He'd have had to take Armstrong by surprise in order to get the best of him. Armstrong shouldn't have had any trouble defending himself against Lee. Then again, he'd seen stranger things. Tim Shepherd was a larger man, easily two hundred pounds or more. However, he wouldn't dirty his hands by taking on Armstrong himself. Daniel wouldn't put it past the man to hire someone.

He closed his eyes against the never-ending headache and thought about praying. Would God listen to him? Yes, he would. Daniel knew without a doubt that as soon as he could lay aside the anger in his heart, the betrayal he felt, God would welcome him back with open arms. Actually, he knew God would welcome him any way he wanted to come back. With anger, with betrayal, with whatever he had. God was big enough to deal with it. So why couldn't he just let him? "Why did they have to die, God? Why did you do that to my family? To Riley?" He whispered the words and waited to feel . . . something. When nothing earth — or soul — shattering happened, he sighed.

"You okay?"

He spun to find Haley in the door of the sunroom. "Yeah."

"Can't sleep though, huh?"

"Nope."

"Want to talk about it?"

"Not really." Not with her anyway. She was nice enough, pleasant company, but she wasn't Katie. The person he seemed to find himself more willing to open up to. More willing to talk with about what went on in his mind. "Tell me about Katie."

She lifted a brow and he turned back to the peaceful scene of his pool. "What do you want to know?"

Daniel had to admit he liked to hear Haley talk, simply for her accent. He smiled. He liked to hear Katie talk because he was interested in what she had to say. "Anything. Is she seeing anyone?"

"No, not that she's shared with us. An' besides, if she were, she wouldn't be kissin' you in the car."

He blinked. "You saw that, huh?"

"I did."

He lifted a shoulder in a slight shrug. "I like her. I'm . . . attracted to her."

"Hmm. Yes, I can tell."

He glanced at the clock and wondered if Katie were sleeping or if she was finding it as hard to relax as he was. Fatigue dragged at him, but every time he closed his eyes, he saw things he'd rather forget. "She's not like anyone I've ever met before." He kept his voice low and his gaze on the clear aqua water. It was heated. He could work off some of his restlessness. Try to wear himself out to the point that he passed out from sheer exhaustion. But then his defenses would be down and he couldn't afford that right now.

"She's definitely one of a kind. And . . . she likes you too."

"I know," he said. Haley laughed. A light sound that brightened the room and made him smile. "What about you?" he asked and turned to face her.

"Me?"

"Anyone special in your life?"

And just like that, the sunshine vanished and the storm clouds moved in. "No," she said. "No one a'tall." Her cool, clipped words effectively shut him out. "But I'll tell you this about Katie. She's had it rough the last few years."

"I gathered that."

"She'll tell you when she's ready."

"I figured that too."

Haley's chill evaporated. "You're a smooth one, aren't you? You know when to be patient." She nodded as though answering the question for herself. "You'll do all right with her then."

"She doesn't open up easily."

"No. She'll have to trust you first."

He nodded. "I'm okay with that."

"Good." She shook her head. "I don't know what God was doing when he put us all together."

"What do you mean?"

"The four of us. Katie, me, Maddy, and Olivia. We all were rather broken when we met. Together, we've made a good team. We've helped each other heal and grow."

"In what way?"

"Once we came to trust one another and started talking, it was better than any expensive therapist." She gave him a tight smile. "But enough o' that." She pulled her weapon from her holster. "I'm going to check the perimeter."

"And I'm going to try to sleep." *Try* being the operative word.

Haley slipped out of the house and Daniel waited until he heard the chime of the alarm and the snick of the lock before he headed to his bedroom.

Riley stared at herself on the screen of her phone. She was just a little box in the corner. Steve's face took up most of the space. "So what did you want to talk about?"

"I don't know. I really enjoyed seeing you today and we didn't get to talk long enough. I thought FaceTiming would be a good idea."

Riley yawned. "It's really late."

"I know, but I couldn't talk any earlier. I was studying with the guys."

"Is that what you call it?"

He grinned, a sheepish smile that revealed two deep dimples in each cheek. Her stomach flipped and she relished his laughter. "Of course."

"Who won?"

He blinked. "What?"

"Who won? The Panthers or the Cowboys?" His jaw dropped. Now it was Riley's turn to laugh. "Why does that shock you so bad? I know how much you love the Panthers. You never miss a game."

"Well . . ." He cleared his throat. "We might have had it playing in the background."

"Sure."

"And the Panthers won."

"Ah." Another yawn overtook her.

"I'll let you go. You obviously need to go to sleep. We're still on for pizza, right?"

"Sure."

"See you tomorrow?"

"If you come by the site."

"I'll do my best. Bye."

"Bye, Steve."

Riley disconnected the call. A slight smile wanted to curve her lips, but did she dare let it? Did she want to get her heart entangled with Steve right before she went to college? She'd be eighteen on Christmas Day. She was graduating in May and planned to go to college and major in education. She already spoke Spanish like a native and looked forward to returning to the country her parents had loved and ministered in. So . . . romance? Her heart wanted to do it, to throw caution to the wind and just have fun. After all, she had her whole life ahead of her to be serious and do ministry, right? Why shouldn't she just be a normal teen for a season?

Something to think about.

Then again, she'd never been "normal." Her mother had often shaken her head over Riley's maturity and wondered where it had come from. "You don't think like a fifteen-year-old."

Riley figured it was just the way God made her, and she couldn't explain it either. So would she be trying to be someone else if she flirted a little? All of her friends were dating someone. And she had no one. At least not until Steve started showing some interest.

She snuggled down against the pillow and sighed. "Brain, you can shut off now," she murmured. "I'm done for the day."

She heard a footstep outside her bedroom door and sat up. When the footsteps retreated, she figured it was her uncle just checking on her. She slipped out from beneath the covers and went to her door. When she opened it, she caught a glimpse of his back as he disappeared into the den area. She heard the door open, then shut. She hurried into the den to find Haley, hands on her hips, frown on her lips. "Where's he going?"

"To see Katie."

"At this time of night?"

"Yep."

"And is anyone going with him?"

"No, he said he didn't want anyone, that he needed to be alone a bit."

Riley stomped her foot, anger flaring. Then hurt. "Fine. Let him be alone then. I'm going to bed."

"He'll be okay, Riley." Haley's soft voice stopped her, but she didn't turn. "He's a big boy. He can take care of himself. Plus, he has us whether he likes it or not."

"What do you mean?"

"I mean I checked his car for him and he

has a tracking device on it that I can read."

She turned. She couldn't let the woman keep talking to her back. "I have a tracking device too. As long as he has his phone on him, I know where he is. But really, what good is a tracking device if someone runs him off the road and puts a bullet in him before anyone else can get to him?"

"You hang around with your uncle's military buddies quite a bit, don't you?"

"A bit. Not lately because of all that's going on, but yes, they're here on a regular basis."

"I can tell." Haley sighed. "Seriously, though. Your uncle is not our usual client. He's smart, he's trained, and he's got a natural instinct when it comes to self-preservation. He could actually hire himself out as a bodyguard if you think about it. He has all the requirements. He'll be all right."

Riley refused to let her shoulders slump. "Those are the right words, Haley, but you and I know he's not invincible."

"Trust him."

"What?"

"Trust him that he knows what he's doing and that he loves you enough not to do anything stupid."

Riley looked at the door. "That's the problem. In my opinion, he just did."

Katie quick-stepped through her house. The front porch light was off. The inside lights were off. She might be able to manage getting outside without being seen. Especially if the possible intruder was still at the back of her house. She opened the front door and slipped out onto the porch. She armed her alarm system, then shut and locked the door behind her and hurried down the dark steps. She slid behind the large pine tree next to the porch railing and waited.

Listened.

She wasn't sure how much time passed, but she stayed there for what seemed like endless minutes. Five? Seven? Ten? At least. She'd learned early on, one of the most important factors with any job she took was that patience almost always paid off.

So as long as her back was covered and she could see what was in front of her, she could wait in her position for a very long time.

Just as she was ready to believe the intruder had left and she was going to head back inside, she thought she heard the soft crunch of footsteps to her right. He was coming from the back. Her blood pounded faster and she stayed still, breathing shallow breaths through her nose.

Then the footsteps stopped.

Did he know she was there? Could he sense her presence like she did his? Had he seen her come out of the house? There was a bit of light from the moon, so it was possible he'd seen her movement. But she'd been almost certain he'd been at the back of the house and hadn't seen her slip out the front. She waited longer, wondering if she reached for her phone to call for some backup if he would hear her. Sense her motion.

Then the footsteps receded, so quiet she barely heard them. He headed for the cover of the trees that lined the land between her house and her neighbor's. She started after him when headlights coming up her drive caught her attention.

She paused, unsure whether to go after the person to her left or confront the person coming up her drive this late at night. Was he friend or foe?

Daniel pulled the vehicle to a stop and cut the engine when he saw the figure standing in the middle of her drive. Katie? He climbed out of the truck. Her body language shouted she was in hunter mode.

"Daniel?" she whispered. "What are you doing here?"

"I wanted to talk." He took the cue from her and kept his voice low. "What are you doing outside?"

"Someone was snooping around. He headed toward my neighbor's house when you pulled in." She took off toward the edge of the woods, gun held ready for use. Daniel followed her. She broke through the tree line into her neighbor's yard. She glanced right, then left. Then lowered her weapon.

"Snooping? You're sure?" he asked. She shot him an annoyed look. He held up a hand. "Sorry. Looks like he managed to get away."

"Yes, I think your headlights scared him off."

"Or the fact that you were going after him."

"Maybe."

"Whatever the reason, he's not here now." He blew out a breath and watched it fog in the night air.

"That we know of. Let's get inside," she said. "No sense standing here inviting someone to use us for target practice." The distant sound of a car engine starting made her pause.

"You think that's him?"

"Could be. No way to know, is there? Where's Haley?" She led the way to the front door and opened it. She punched the alarm code on the keypad, then rearmed it after she shut the door behind them.

"I left her with Riley," he said.

"Well, if you were any other client, I'd fuss at you for taking the risk." She led the way into the den. "It's not much yet, but at least I have a couch."

He sat on it. "I didn't feel like it was much of a risk to ride over."

"It's late. What were you going to do if I was asleep?"

"Wake you up."

She lifted a brow. "Really? This must be important."

He sighed. "Probably not."

"Hmm. I guess we'll find out. But before we talk, I want to walk through my backyard and see if I can find anything to indicate who was out there."

"Aren't you going to call it in?"

"I'll let Bree know. But there's no point in having officers come out here tonight. The guy's gone. For now."

"Exactly. But what if he comes back?"

"Then I'll worry about it at that point. For now, I'm just going to watch my back and hope I scared him off tonight." She

272

motioned him to follow her. "I'm going to go out into the backyard and the woods beyond where he could have been waiting and watching. Upstairs in the bonus room, there's a perfect view of my yard. Will you go up there and watch the woods behind my house?"

"How are you going to see? There's no way you should use a light."

"Give me more credit than that," she chided gently. "I've got night vision goggles. I'm going to check the area first, then if it's all clear, I'm going to let you turn on the floodlights so I can check the yard area."

"Which will make you an easy target. Let the officers come out here and do it."

She drew in a deep breath. "He's not after me. He's after you. I'll be fine. As long as you'll watch my back from up above."

"You must have some doubts if you want me up there watching. Either that, or you're trying to be clever about keeping me in the house."

"Not trying to be clever. I want your eyes on the woods. This guy was at the back of my house. He came around the front and then disappeared into my neighborhood. I heard a car drive off. It might have been him, it might not have. He could very easily double back and hide out in the trees."

He hesitated, then nodded. "I'll watch."

"Thanks. I have an earpiece you can use so we can at least communicate with each other." She led him back to the spare bedroom and got him fitted with the earpiece. She pushed hers in her left ear. "Stay here and we'll test them."

Katie walked out of the room and down the hall. "Can you hear me?" she whispered.

"Loud and clear." His deep voice rumbled through the wireless listening device and she had to admit she really liked the sound of it. She really liked him.

She cleared her throat. "Great." She went back to the spare room. "That'll work. Now come this way." She took him upstairs and he followed her into the dark bonus room, but she didn't turn on the light. She led him to the window where he planted himself, then withdrew his weapon from his shoulder holster. She didn't ask questions, just raised the window slightly. She handed him a pair of night vision goggles. Then kept a pair for herself.

"Be careful," he said. "If I see anything, I'll yell."

"And I'll duck."

"Perfect."

She left him and made her way back down

the stairs, taking a moment to stop back by her spare bedroom and don a Kevlar vest and grab her mag light. She added an extra gun to her defense, then headed for the back door.

Her nerves twitched. She felt antsy, like she was waiting for something to happen. It was like when Paul used to sneak her into the horror movies and she'd scream her lungs out when the monster jumped right at the camera — and Paul would laugh his head off. She felt like she was waiting for the monster in the dark to leap out at her. She shuddered. Only this monster was far more deadly than the on-screen one. She patted the vest.

Might as well not take any chances. While Daniel appeared to be the target, she couldn't come up with a reasonable explanation for who might have been snooping around her home.

Daniel stood at his post, weapon ready, eyes scanning. He had his phone dialed to 911 and ready to simply press send if he needed to. He did wonder about her motives in sending him to the window, but had to admit she was right in the fact he had an excellent view of the backyard. Her very dark backyard. He pulled the goggles over his eyes, adjusted them one eye at a time to his eyesight, and then took a good look at the green-hued landscape.

"I can't see you, Katie. Where are you?"

"I'm turning the alarm off and exiting the back door."

"The backyard is clear and I don't see any movement in the woods beyond."

"Good. I'm coming out."

And then there she was. She made her way across the short expanse of the yard and to the back where she merged into the tree line. The goggles were good. He could see her form clearly. If anyone tried to sneak up behind her, Daniel would know. Or if anyone came from either yard to her right or left, he'd know. He could hear her slow, even breathing. "Anything?"

"Not yet." Her voice was low.

If it were his home, he'd be doing the same thing, but he chafed at being confined to the window. Did he dare insist on joining her? No. She was right. He was more helpful where he was. From his position, he could see what she couldn't. She walked to the edge of her yard, her head bent. He knew she was scanning the ground. She stayed right at the edge, and he figured she knew that if someone was watching her house, he'd want to be far enough back to keep from being seen, but close enough to the edge to have a good view. About midway, she knelt. "You found something," he said.

"Yes."

"What is it?"

"From where I'm positioned, I can see straight through the trees and into my sun-porch. It's a good place to sit and watch. He's gone, but he was definitely here."

Daniel's gut tightened. He hated to think of her being in danger. Because she was looking out for him, she'd attracted the attention of a murderer. "The backyard is still clear. Did he leave anything to use as evidence?"

"No, just what I think is a knee impression. No shoeprints, no cigarette butts, no fast-food wrappers or receipts. Nothing."

"Couldn't get that lucky."

"Nope. But I know he was here." A sigh reached him. "I'm heading back for the house. Meet you in the den?"

"Sure thing."

He'd meet her in the den, but he'd watch her back until she entered the house.

When he heard the back door shut and the alarm rearmed, he pulled the goggles from his head, closed the window, and made his way downstairs. He found her in the den, shedding her vest. "You've got some serious equipment."

She smiled. "Compliments of the mayor." She settled herself on the sofa, leaned forward, and clasped her hands in front of her. "So, what's on your mind?"

"You."

[19]

She blinked. "Me."

He gave her a slow smile. "Yes. I can't get that kiss off my mind. Therefore, you're right there, front and center all the time."

Katie felt the heat leak into her cheeks and she had to look away for a moment. Not because she was embarrassed but because she understood. She gathered her thoughts and looked back at him, his intense green eyes bored into hers. "How long have we known each other?" she asked him.

"A little over a year?"

"Hmm. We've known *about* each other that long. I wouldn't say we've *known* each other that long."

"True. We've known each other in passing, I would say."

She studied him. "And I probably know more about you than you do me, thanks to Riley. So. What do you want to know, Daniel?"

"Everything. But start with what happened three years ago."

"*That's* what you came over for? It couldn't wait?"

"No. It couldn't." He closed his eyes and raked a hand through his hair.

"The nightmares. You're avoiding them."

"Yeah. So talk to me. So I don't have to think — or sleep and dream."

Katie took a deep breath. She didn't talk about that time. Ever. The only people she'd talked to about the incident were those in law enforcement who needed to know the details right after it happened and then her three best friends. The ladies she worked with at Elite Guardians. She hadn't even had to testify in court because the man who'd set the bombs had killed himself.

"Three years ago, there was an explosion at an apartment building. A tenant was evicted and he was bitter about it. Downstairs in the basement where the laundry room was, he set off a bomb. It was a simple, homemade thing that he probably got the recipe for off the internet. It went off right under Paulo and Maria Lopez's apartment. It happened about eleven o'clock at night. Paulo and Maria and their three children, ages two months, three, and eight, were killed."

He closed his eyes. "It's the children that get me."

"Yes. I was working with ATF at the time as a CFI."

"Certified Fire Investigator."

"Right. I had a dual role there. I was also a Certified Explosive Specialist. And so was my brother, Paul."

"Your brother?"

She nodded. "He was five years older than me, and I thought he was perfect. I wanted to do everything he did." She grimaced. "Only I wanted to do it better, to prove to him that I had what it takes to be worthy of his respect."

"Why did you feel compelled to earn his respect?"

"I don't know. My parents were gone a lot. They both traveled with their jobs. Paul was there for me and my younger sister. He was the one I wanted to please, the one I wanted to make proud."

"And was he? Proud of you?"

She felt her lips tug upward. "Oh yeah. I was bragging rights in the department. He took full credit for having taught me any-thing I did that was worthy of recognition." The smile slid off. "But that day, I wasn't there as the bomb investigator, I was there as the CFI. Usually, the explosives investigator goes in first to clear the building, but because of my training in that area, I went ahead and went in with Paul." She closed her eyes and saw those last moments with him. "I was so proud of myself. Too proud really. Cocky. Arrogant in some ways."

"You?"

"Oh yes. Guys aren't the only ones who can be that way, you know. Paul and I scoured the building, but it was a mess. The bomb in the basement had done its job. Paul had a dog, Jojo. She was an amazing animal."

"A bomb detection dog?"

"Yes. Or Accelerant and Explosives Detection Canine if you want to get technical. Anyway, at the top of the set of stairs that hadn't been destroyed from the first bomb, the dog alerted us to another bomb. It had five seconds left on the timer. The man had set the bombs to go off exactly one hour apart." Her throat wanted to close. "Paul shoved me down the stairs and threw himself on the bomb. It went off as I hit bottom. I continued to roll down the next set of steps while the debris rained down on me. I don't know how I wasn't buried, but somehow I managed to crawl out. Paul and Jojo didn't."

Daniel stared at her, horror written in his

eyes. "He had on a suit, I'm sure, but . . ."

She shook her head. "He had on some protective wear, but he couldn't wear a full-body blast suit, not in that building. And neither could I."

"Too hot."

"Too hot, too cumbersome. And it wouldn't have kept him from dying that day anyway."

"No, not even the suit would have protected him. That's — wow." He looked away as though absorbing a blow. She knew how he felt.

"Yes."

He looked back at her and locked his gaze on hers. "He sacrificed his life for yours."

Tears gathered. She forced them back. "Yes. And now every time I see a fire or try to investigate one or whatever, I hear him. He's crying out to me to help him . . . and I can't." The last two words slipped through gritted teeth. She rose. "Excuse me a second. I want to check on . . . things." She checked the windows, the front door, the back door, the sunporch. There was no indication that anyone was on her property. In the kitchen, she drew in a steadying breath and let it out slowly through her pursed lips.

His hands landed on her shoulders with a

283

gentle grip. "It wasn't your fault."

She let out a hiccupping laugh. "Well, tell that to my family."

"They blame you?"

"They do."

"Why?"

She shrugged, but his hands remained. "Because they didn't want me to be a cop in the first place. And they felt like if I hadn't been there, Paul could have gotten out. Or at least not been killed. He surely wouldn't have thrown himself on the bomb."

A sigh slipped from him. "Man."

"Yeah. But I . . . can't imagine doing anything else. I may not be with ATF any longer. I may not walk into danger every day and defuse bombs, but my heart is law enforcement, helping people, catching the bad guys. It's my calling. If I'm not doing that, then . . . I'm nothing," she whispered.

He spun her to face him and her breath hitched. She thought he might kiss her again, but he didn't. Instead he drew her to him, pressed her head against his chest, and simply held her. "You're not nothing, Katie. You're amazing. And I understand exactly what you mean about law enforcement being a calling. I really do."

She swallowed and thought about pulling away. But she couldn't. It felt good to be held, to know that he didn't blame her for what had happened. It was bad enough that she blamed herself.

She closed her eyes and sighed and let the comfort of his presence wash over her.

When she finally got herself somewhat together emotionally, she pulled away and ran a hand down her face. She glanced out the window over the sink into the darkness beyond. As much as she couldn't help it, she wondered if her intruder had returned. If he sat outside and watched even now. "You'd better go."

"I know. I don't want to, but I will."

She gave him a light shove toward the door. "Yes, you will." She frowned. "But not until we check your car."

"I'll check it."

"Well, I'll help."

He nodded. "Fine."

"Stay here while I get my mirror."

She walked to the spare bedroom once more, grabbed the item, and then followed him out the door.

Daniel didn't waste time. He took the mirror from her and she held the light while he checked his vehicle. He started at the front and worked his way down the passenger's side, then along the back bumper. "All clear here." He moved up the driver's side and paused. "Shine that a little closer, will you?"

She did. "What have you got?"

"I think while we were so focused on the backyard, your visitor was in the front creating some havoc."

"Like?"

"Take a look at the chassis under the driver's seat." He handed her the mirror and she gave him the light. He heard her indrawn breath when she saw what he was talking about.

"Yeah." She backed up and motioned for him to do the same.

"Okay, get on the phone and let's get the cops out here." He rubbed a hand down his face. "Bomb squad too."

"Definitely." She studied the car again. "I'm going to use my landline. I'm not taking a chance on using my cell. Cut yours off too, will you?"

He did. "I want to keep an eye on the vehicle. I know it's late and unlikely anyone would be coming to your home, but I don't want anyone coming close to that car. And if you've got curious neighbors —"

"Do it from inside the front door. You're a sitting duck out here in the open."

He shot her a stiff smile. "That was the plan I had too."

"Sorry, adrenaline is a little high right now."

"I know."

She ran in and Daniel followed behind her. Once behind the protection of the door, he watched the car. The fact that the car hadn't blown up when he'd started checking it comforted him. Slightly. He heard Katie on the phone in the kitchen. Heard her report the bomb.

When she hung up, she turned back to face him. "They're on the way. Told them to be discreet so they're coming in with no lights or sirens. They'll start evacuating the neighbors." From the window, she looked at the car. "Physically, it's a relatively small bomb, but I don't know what's in it or what kind of reach it will have. Or if someone's going to push a button and have it go off if I approach it again." She paused. "Although I'm guessing since it didn't explode while we were checking, we might be all right."

"You're a mind reader."

"How's that?"

"I was just thinking the same thing."

She rubbed her forehead. "You know what else I'm thinking?"

"What?"

"Why did he have that bomb on him?"

Daniel frowned. "He didn't follow me. He

was here before I got here."

"Which means he originally intended to put the bomb somewhere on my property?"

The implications hit him. "Which means you're now a target as well."

She huffed a small breath. "Maybe. Or he was planning on putting that bomb on your vehicle at some point anyway and just took advantage of the opportunity?"

He shook his head. "Carrying a bomb around hoping for the opportunity? How stupid is that?"

"Some people are just stupid."

"Don't I know it." He shrugged. "The only one with the answer to all the questions isn't available to ask." He scowled, then looked at the neighbors on either side. "You have a good amount of distance between your property and theirs, but still . . . you think we should evacuate them now?"

She hesitated. "Not yet. I don't want to leave you alone and we can't take a chance someone will come on the property. Generally, we'd want at least five hundred feet between us and that bomb, but I won't leave it and take a chance someone wants to be a night owl on a stroll." She shot him a wry look. "And I don't suppose it would do me any good to order you away from it." He snorted and she rolled her eyes. "That's what I thought. We'll let the experts handle the evacuation."

"Thought you were the expert."

Her jaw tightened. "Not anymore."

They stood in silence just inside her front door. Waiting.

The first cruiser rolled up approximately six minutes later, followed by a large truck that stopped behind it. It helped to have a bomb squad close by. There had been times when she'd had to wait an hour or more. Katie opened the door and walked onto the front porch. When the driver exited the vehicle, she flashed her badge and pointed to the SUV. "On the chassis, under the driver's seat."

He turned and consulted with someone inside the large truck. Then he turned back to her while more police cruisers pulled up and were motioned to a stop well away from Daniel's car. "We're going to park across the street and work it from there. You can get in and be safe while we take care of this."

Katie and Daniel climbed into the back of the truck and the driver made his way slowly down the street. "There's not a great spot that's far enough away but close enough to do what we need to do," Katie heard him say.

"Do your best," was the response from the man seated next to him.

The best they could do was about a football field in length away from the bomb. The man in the passenger seat turned and his eyes found Katie's. "Now we can take care of the introductions."

"I'm Katie Singleton." She flashed her badge and he nodded. "This is Daniel Matthews, my client. It's his vehicle with the device strapped to it."

"I'm Jack Sinclair, lead on this." Jack held out a hand and she shook it.

"Do you mind filling me in?" she said.

"Who are you with?"

Katie held his gaze. "The mayor."

"Ah yes, Elite Guardians, isn't it?"

"It is."

He nodded. "Heard of you." He shot her a smile. "All good things. So, you found the bomb?"

"My client and I did."

"Good job." He spoke into the radio he held and looked up at her. "We've got uniformed police officers setting up a perimeter and going door to door to evacuate the homes. No telling what's in that bomb and how far it'll send debris."

Katie nodded. She knew a few curious

onlookers would ignore the order and could only hope that the bomb didn't go off. Daniel sat next to her, eyes glued on the screens. Floodlights illuminated Daniel's vehicle.

The team worked quickly getting the robot prepped and on the way. Within seconds it was rolling toward Daniel's SUV. Katie watched the bomb squad member at the controls expertly maneuver the robot.

It stopped next to the SUV and a camera slid out to disappear underneath. Pictures immediately popped up on one screen, and another member started his analysis of them. The camera withdrew. Next, the operator clicked and sent another order to the robot. "All right, Rocky," he murmured. "Time for the X-rays." The robot seemed to follow the order as the X-ray machine slid under. The computer screens lit up with other pictures and Katie got her first look at the inside of the bomb.

"C4," she whispered.

Jack raised a brow in her direction. "Looks like."

"It's enough to turn that vehicle into its own bomb. It'll send pieces all over the place."

"Indeed."

"And it's rigged to go off when he opens the driver's door, isn't it?" she said.

The man raised a brow again, higher this time. "Yes. How'd you know?"

"I've had some training and I saw the wires leading from it to the bottom of the door when we found it. So what are you going to do?"

"Unrig it." He started to pull on the head-protection gear.

"C4 contains RDX," Daniel muttered. "Bet he used that in the other one too."

Jack stopped, lowered the protective helmet. "Other one?" Jack's gaze bounced between her and Daniel.

"This isn't our first rodeo with an explosive," Katie said. "The same person who did this might also be responsible for Daniel's restaurant burning down."

Jack drew in a deep breath. "Ah yes, I thought I recognized you."

Daniel grimaced and kept his gaze on the action around his vehicle.

"Well, Rocky's waiting on me."

"Rocky's not going to defuse it?"

Jack shook his head and climbed out the back of the van. He opened a storage compartment on the side and started pulling out gear. "Not this one. It's going to take a steady pair of hands."

Once he had all but his headgear on, Jack pointed to the computer. "Let me take a look at the X-rays one more time, Goose."

Goose tapped a few keys. "It's a cylinder-shaped device," Jack said. "The detonator is right there at the top. Screws?"

"Yes."

"Great."

Katie knew what he was thinking. He wouldn't be wearing the hand protection very long if he had to use a screwdriver. The robot was equipped with the ability to use a screwdriver, but the location of the device was such that it was going to take human intervention.

Jack pulled his head protection back on and headed toward Daniel's SUV. Katie watched him from the safety of the van. Her fingers curled into fists at her sides. He strode confidently, but she knew what he was feeling. His heart was thudding inside his chest and sweat was probably running down his back and pooling in his armpits. She started to perspire just thinking about it. At least it wasn't a hundred degrees outside.

Jack reached the vehicle and the tension in the bomb truck went up tenfold.

Katie stared at the screen. She could do it. She could defuse it as well as the man now kneeling at the side of the vehicle. She'd use a rolling board and slide herself under to get a good look at the device. She'd disrupt the detonator, remove the bomb, and place it into the total containment vessel. And all would be well.

Which was exactly what Jack Sinclair was doing.

Within minutes, he had the bomb released from the undercarriage of the vehicle. He slid out from under and motioned for the robot. The robot rolled over to Jack and he placed the device into the metal container. The robot then moved to the containment vessel and gently inserted the metal container in the black hole. The door closed and the bomb was sealed.

Katie let out a breath. Everyone in the truck cheered. She shot a glance at Daniel and saw him watching the containment vessel roll into the back of the large truck that had delivered it. Now it would be whisked away and detonated in a safe area.

Unfortunately, it didn't look like she and Daniel had anything they could remotely consider a safe area. She kept her silence while law enforcement vacated the property. Now it was about four in the morning and Katie could feel an adrenaline crash headed her way.

"I'm done with this," Daniel said. He stood staring at his bomb-free vehicle.

"What do you mean?"

"I mean I'm done letting him come after you and me. It's time to go on the offensive."

"How do you plan to do that?"

"He wants me? Fine. I'm going to make it easy to get to me." He shot her a glance. "And Riley doesn't need to know about any of this. Got it?"

"I think that's a mistake, Daniel."

"Why?"

"She needs to know the danger — and she'll have your head if she sees it on the news." She pointed to a news van parked just beyond the police line.

Daniel groaned. "Great."

[20]

Riley slid the hangar door open and walked to the front of the plane. She ran a hand down the side and closed her eyes, picturing herself headed for the clouds.

"You're going to be late."

She spun to find Daniel leaning against the back of the plane. "Just a little and Martin won't care. In fact, he's so preoccupied, he probably won't even notice."

Her uncle eyed her for a moment, then nodded to the plane. "You thinking of taking her up?"

"Yes. Maybe after school or on Saturday."

"Why don't you do Saturday? I'll take her up and give her a test run, make sure everything's ready for you."

"You know I'll do my own preflight check."

He smiled. "I know. But I also know

someone who'd like to go for a ride."

"Let me guess. Katie?"

"Um-hmm."

"Thought so." She nodded. "Sure, I can wait until Saturday. That might actually work better. I have an essay I need to turn in by midnight tomorrow anyway."

"I'll see if Katie wants to go up this afternoon."

"Cool. Was she all right last night?" He raised his brow and Riley rolled her eyes. "You left around 11:30 and didn't come back in until around 4:00 this morning."

He frowned. "What were you doing up so late?"

She shrugged.

"Riley?"

All smiles gone, she lifted weary eyes to his. "Look, Daniel, you took off in the middle of the night without telling me anything and you didn't take anyone with you. Not a bodyguard, not a friend, no one. If someone wasn't trying to kill you, I wouldn't think twice about it. But someone is."

"And you were worried."

"Of course I was worried. You promised you wouldn't do anything stupid." Was he really that dense? If she hadn't been tracking his phone with the app he'd provided so she could always find him, she would have been a basket case. But she'd watched the app that had put his location at Katie's home and then she'd tracked his progress all the way back in the wee hours of the morning. "Why did you do that?"

"It wasn't stupid, Riley. And I needed to talk to her."

"It couldn't have waited?"

He sighed. "I . . . don't know if it could have waited or not. Maybe. I thought you were asleep and wouldn't know whether I was there or not."

"You thought wrong." They fell silent for a moment. "You like her a lot, don't you?" she asked.

Riley watched his face. He thought he was so good at hiding his feelings, and in some ways he was, but she had learned to read him pretty well over the last eighteen months.

He glanced back at the plane. "Yeah. I do."

"You have a lot in common."

This time he looked her in the eye. "What do you mean?"

She pressed her lips together, then blew out a small breath. "You've both lost a brother you cared about," she said. He lifted a brow. "One day when we were eating lunch, I asked her if she had any brothers or sisters. She told me she had one of each but that her brother, Paul, had died. It seemed to make her really sad, so I didn't ask her any more questions."

"Yeah."

"Also, you both have a lot of hurt in your past that you need to deal with. I think you're probably good for each other in that you can help each other do that. Deal with it, I mean." She waved a hand. "Ignore me. I'm not making any sense."

He sighed and pulled her in for a hug. "Actually, you make more sense than most adults I know. Thanks."

Surprised, she squeezed him around the middle. "Sure." She paused.

"What?" he asked.

"What?" she countered.

"I can tell you want to say something else."

She sighed and leaned back. "Forgive God. It's not his fault."

When he didn't move or say anything, she figured maybe she'd pushed him too far. Then she felt a gentle kiss on her head. "I love you, Riley."

"I love you too, Uncle Daniel. Which is why I want you to be safe. But we've already had that discussion."

He cupped her face. "I really can take care of myself."

"Yes, I know. In a face-to-face, hand-to-hand fight, I believe you can beat just about anyone, but if someone's got a bead on your back, then you're just as vulnerable as the next person."

"Bead on my back?"

She grimaced. "Well, I've hung around you and your buddies enough to pick up the lingo. And you know what I mean."

He nodded. "I know. But I'll tell you, I won't be bullied, Riles. I won't take unnecessary chances, but I won't be bullied — or run scared." His jaw tightened, but he didn't look away from her.

She held his gaze for a long while. "Something else happened last night, didn't it?"

He hesitated and she thought he might be trying to decide what to say. He finally nodded. "Someone put a bomb under my car while I was at Katie's house. That's why I was so late getting home."

She froze. Then nodded. She could see the anger in his eyes. Not at her, but at the person who was putting them through the craziness. "What are you going to do?"

"Fight back."

"How?"

"I'm not sure yet, but I need you to understand that sometimes staying safe isn't always the best choice."

She swallowed and glanced away. "I'm not sure I want to hear what you're going to say."

He placed a finger under her chin and forced her eyes to meet his again. "You know me, Riley. You've known me for a long time. Have I ever run away from a fight?"

"No, you never have. At least not that I know about." She sighed. "You fight for what you believe in. You stand up for yourself and for those who can't." She stepped back and crossed her arms. "Believe it or not, I do understand. It's not in your nature to allow yourself to be bullied. Or anyone else for that matter. I know you need to fight back, just do it smart. Make sure you have backup."

"Yes. Smart. That's the key, isn't it? And I was smart last night, I promise. I know how to watch my back and I know how to take care of myself. You've got to trust me to do that."

"That's what she said," Riley murmured.

"Who?"

"Haley."

"She's pretty smart, you should listen to her." He glanced at his phone. "Now go before you're too late. I look forward to the ride this weekend."

"Could I invite a friend?"

He hesitated. "Maybe not this time."

She heard the unspoken words. He didn't want her to bring a friend, because in spite of his words of not being bullied, he wasn't comfortable enough putting someone else in the line of fire. She got that. Didn't like it, but got it. "Okay. And I'm going to grab pizza with Steve after school today."

"Steve? Little Stevie Patterson from kindergarten?"

Riley resisted the urge to roll her eyes. "Yes. Little Stevie. Only don't call him that if you see him. Please?"

"Of course not." He shot her a wounded look and she almost laughed. "I thought he was being a bit of a jerk."

"Yes. He was."

"He's not being a jerk anymore?"

"No, at least not the last couple of times I've talked to him." She pulled her hair up into a ponytail, slid the ever-present hair tie from her wrist, and wrapped it around the black strands. "I don't know. I guess I'm going to find out."

"Let me know if I need to beat him up."

This time she gave in to the eye roll. "Ugh. Really?"

"No. Not really." He kissed her forehead. "I just don't want to see you get hurt."

"I know. See you later."

"Later, gator."

"I'm not saying it."

"Yes you are. Later, gator."

"Bye."

"After 'while, crocodile."

"Stop, I'm not five." She put her hands over her ears and turned to leave when she spotted Katie standing in the hangar doorway. "He's being obnoxious."

"I see that." A smile played around her lips. "Lizzie's going to hang out with you today."

Riley dropped her hands from her ears. "That's cool. I like her."

Katie smiled. "She likes you too. And she has a fascination with archaeology, so you're like her dream assignment."

Riley laughed. "Glad I could help her out there." She looked back at Daniel. "Could we do something after I get home from the dig and eat pizza with Steve?"

"What's that?"

"I want to go to the restaurant site and look for Mom's box."

Daniel hesitated. "I tell you what, I'll go out there today while you're at school and see if I can find it. Okay?"

Riley nodded. "Sure. I don't care who finds it, I just want it found."

Daniel looked at Katie. "Do you think you

can go?"

Katie drew in a deep breath. Then nodded. "Yes."

"Thanks." Riley walked out of the hangar and found Lizzie standing near her car. "Ready?"

"I'm ready."

Riley looked back over her shoulder and saw Daniel smiling down at Katie. And Katie was smiling right back. Yes, Daniel liked her. And Katie liked him. Riley sucked in a deep breath, then let it out slowly.

"Lord, just let them live long enough for all that like to turn into something a little more permanent. Please?" she muttered.

"Sorry," Lizzie said, "I didn't catch that."

Riley shook her head. "Nothing." The only ears she needed to hear her words already had.

Back in the house, Katie listened absently as Daniel discussed options with the insurance company. The claims adjuster had already been out to look over the damage. She knew Daniel had received three estimates on what it would cost to rebuild the North Lake restaurant. He'd already decided to go with the middle estimate. He'd said it was pretty close to what he'd calculated. He figured the lower bid was just an attempt to undercut the competition and in the end they'd wind up going over budget.

She thought he was probably right. Her phone rang and she glanced at the screen. Bree. She stepped into the den area so she wouldn't disturb Daniel. "Hello?"

"Hi, Katie, how's it going?"

"It's going. How's your sister?"

"On her way to rehab. Finally."

"Ouch. I'm sorry."

"It's time." Bree cleared her throat. "I've got some information for you."

"About?"

"A couple of things. The first is Tim Shepherd, the real estate developer."

"Anything make your radar blip?"

"Quite possibly."

Katie took a seat on the couch and got comfortable. This sounded interesting. "Tell me about him."

"He's in his midfifties and a millionaire several times over. He's shrewd and can sniff out a deal almost before it's been thought of."

"But?" Katie glanced into the kitchen to see Daniel pacing back and forth in front of the bar. He looked agitated.

"There was one incident about two years ago," Bree said. "Shepherd was after a small business owner named Joseph Bryant to sell and the man refused. Said it had been his father-in-law's restaurant and he wasn't selling it. A month later, the business burned to the ground."

"Let me guess. Arson?"

"Yes."

"Any charges brought against Shepherd?" Katie said.

"No, nothing could be proven and he didn't wind up with the property. The insurance paid out and Bryant ended up selling the land to someone else. Said he suspected Shepherd was behind it and there was no way he was letting him have the property, he didn't care how much Shepherd offered."

"Oh boy. I'm sure that went over well," Katie murmured.

"According to employees, Shepherd was furious. Apparently, he's quite well-known for his temper and had a full-on tantrum right there in his office for everyone to hear."

Katie stood and walked over to the mantel to study the two pictures Daniel had there. One was of a handsome couple she assumed were his brother and sister-in-law. The other was of Riley about three years ago, holding a huge fish in front of a sailboat. Daniel was helping her hold it. The big grins on both of their faces touched her. "What was the cause of the fire? How did the arsonist set it?"

"Gasoline and a match."

"So he didn't even try to hide it, cover it up and make it look like an accident," Katie said.

"Nope. Found the gas cans on site. No prints meant the arsonist used gloves. There were no *working* security cameras within the vicinity, so . . ." A sigh filtered through the line. "The investigation never led to a viable suspect. Although one of the detectives I talked to who worked the case said he really thought that the owner did it."

"Any reason why?"

"A search of Bryant's financial records showed a possible motive, but it wasn't strong. He wasn't desperate, hadn't missed any payments on anything, but he didn't have any savings and they were living paycheck to paycheck. But again, nothing was ever proven."

"But if that were the case," Katie said, "why not just sell to Shepherd? Why go to the trouble of doing something illegal when he could have just sold and probably made more money to begin with?"

"Exactly."

"No wonder Shepherd was ticked. Did he try to get the other person to sell out?"

Katie paced to the window and looked out. "No, he finally left it alone and moved on. The thing that really supported Bryant's version was the documentation he had on Shepherd's phone calls. The man or someone from his business called every day for two months to try and talk Bryant into selling."

"Harassment."

"At the very least."

"Did anyone ever say anything threatening?"

"No, nothing that was proven. So Shepherd moved on and bought up that building downtown where the children's store used to be. He put a sandwich shop in there and rakes in the big bucks."

"But it does kind of make you wonder, doesn't it? If he decided he wanted Daniel's property, why not try arson again? After all, it almost worked last time. True, he didn't get the property he wanted, but he didn't get caught either."

"I know," Bree said. "Good point."

"What was the second thing?"

"I went by the businesses near Martin Sheehan's house and asked about their cameras. Out of the three, one wasn't working, the other two had inside and outside footage. I've watched them both and never saw anyone other than the guy fitting your description of Martin going into his house."

"No one."

"Nope."

"Okay then." Katie sighed. "Thanks."

"Do you want to tell me what you're looking for?"

"Just . . . I don't know. Someone lurking on the street, sneaking in through the window, something."

"Did something happen?"

"Yes, but he didn't want to report it to the police for various reasons that sort of made sense. In a weird way."

"Ooookay."

Katie laughed. "I'll keep you updated. You keep an eye on Shepherd."

"We're going to."

"Good," Katie said. She saw Daniel hang up and rake a hand through his hair. "Because I've got my eyes on someone else."

Bree snickered. "It wouldn't be that good-looking restaurant owner, would it?"

"Hmm . . . I'll never tell." She hung up on Bree's laughter.

Daniel walked into the den and sat opposite her. "Everything all right?"

She filled him in on what Bree said about the real estate developer and Daniel let out a low whistle.

"So Shepherd could actually be behind this."

"It's possible. Bree and a couple of other detectives are digging even deeper, checking him out."

Daniel rubbed his eyes. "It doesn't really make sense, though. If Shepherd's after the land, why kill someone at the other place?"

"Could be simple coincidence. Perhaps Shepherd had planned all along to burn the restaurant down and that was his focus. It just so happened that same night, someone else was trying to break into the restaurant where *you* were, possibly with the intent of robbing it, stumbled across Armstrong, and killed him."

Daniel narrowed his eyes. "And was desperate to cover up the murder so they tried to make it look like a suicide. Then ran when I came down the stairs. It's a plausible explanation."

"I thought so."

"But you don't believe that."

"No, not really. Although I really can't tell you *why* I don't believe it." She tapped her lip. "Probably because of the security footage that shows the killer being so careful about not exposing his face to the camera."

He nodded. "And the fact that someone

came back and used the old code to try to get in."

"Yes, that too. It just doesn't add up to be some random coincidence thing. I still say there's some connection between the two events." She stood and walked to the mantel, picked up the picture of his brother and sister-in-law. "They're a beautiful couple."

"Yes."

"I know you miss them."

"Desperately."

She placed the photo back in its spot. "And I need to tell you something else."

"What?" Wariness entered his eyes.

"Bree was also able to get ahold of some video footage of Martin's house at the time he said someone broke in. There's no indication there was a burglary."

He pursed his lips and sat back. "So what are you saying?"

"I'm saying I'm not sure the coin was stolen by anyone."

"So you think Martin lost it and is trying to shift the blame by saying someone stole it?" He frowned. "That doesn't even make sense. I mean, if the coin were insured, then maybe that might be a little more plausible, but it wasn't."

"How do you know?" Daniel stared at her and Katie sighed. "I know he's your friend,

Daniel, and I'm not saying that's what he's doing. I'm just trying to look at all the facts and the evidence and come to a logical conclusion."

He nodded. "I don't think he'd do something like that. And besides, you saw his house, it was a mess."

"I know." She frowned. "A mess he could have created himself looking for the coin."

"No. No way."

"I hope you'll at least consider it a possibility."

He ran a hand over his hair. "After all the crazy stuff that's gone on lately —" he shook his head — "I guess we have to."

She drew in a deep breath. "I'm going back out to the site of the North Lake restaurant," she said. "Charlie said he'd come hang out with you for a while, keep an eye on things."

"What? Why?"

"Because you need someone to watch your back and I won't be here."

"Not that. Why are you going back to the restaurant site?"

"I need to."

"Ah."

She didn't bother to pretend she didn't understand what that "Ah" meant. "You sound like Haley, but yeah."

"Going back and facing your fears?"

"Something like that. I'll look for the box while I'm there."

"I'll come with you."

"No. This is something I need to do alone. I don't want . . . can't have . . . an audience."

He frowned. "I know exactly how you feel, but you don't need to be alone. Shouldn't be alone. You need support."

"I *want* to be alone. Seriously, I'll be fine."

He crossed his arms. "I'll sit in the car."

She sighed. "No you won't."

"Yes I will."

She studied him. "Promise?"

"Maybe."

She gave an exasperated huff. "Daniel . . ."

"Fine, fine. I will. I promise."

"Even if I look like I'm . . . in distress?"

"I can't promise that."

Another sigh slipped from her. "Then you can't come."

"Try and stop me."

[21]

Katie pulled to a stop at the edge of the restaurant's parking lot. The yellow tape had been cleaned up, but the restaurant still stood, an empty, charred shell of its former glory. What a waste. "It's a mess, isn't it?"

"Yes."

She heard the anger beneath that one word. A shadow to her right caught her attention, but when she focused on the area, she saw nothing that alarmed her. "All right, I'm going to get suited up. You stay here. I know we weren't followed, but buzz me if anything seems . . . off."

He captured her hand before she could exit the vehicle. "Get me the headgear from the other suit."

"Why?"

"So I'll be able to hear you."

She swallowed and nodded. "Thanks."

She climbed from the Jeep and pulled the suits from the back. She handed Daniel the headgear and he slipped it over his head. Once she was ready, she walked toward the remains. Her blood rushed a little faster, her heart pounded a bit harder. She ignored the adrenaline surge and continued to put one foot in front of the other. Normally she'd never leave a client alone, and frankly, she didn't like doing it now, but he'd insisted and she wasn't his keeper. A bodyguard, yes. She could recommend the best thing for him to do — such as stay home — but if he ignored her, then there wasn't much she could do about it. The fact that he was trained to defend himself helped her feel a bit better, but not much. She drew in a deep breath. The memories crowded her mind, each one fighting for the dominant position. She let them come.

Paul.

How she missed him. By shoving away all thoughts of him, including the gut-wrenching pain of losing him, she'd locked away the good memories too. She wanted to remember him. And she didn't want to. She was such a mess.

But for now, she breathed deep and let him slide into the forefront of her mind. They'd shared a passion for law enforcement. He'd been so proud of her in spite of his reticence. When her pulse slowed, she moved closer. She made it to the front door and then into what had been the lobby area. Sweat broke out on her forehead.

"Help meeeee!"

"It's not real," she whispered. "It's not real."

"That's right," Daniel said in her ear. "It's not real."

Her pulse slowed.

Another step. And another. A shiver swept through her, but she hadn't thrown up yet. Progress? Maybe.

She walked into the front entrance. Dark and dank. She held her breath, then let it out slowly. Paul's image came to life in her mind's eye as she just stood there, letting the smells, sounds, the *feel* of the place wash over her.

And she remembered Paul. The way he looked that last day, confident and strong, his adrenaline buzzing. She thought about how he loved solving the mysteries of the fires. They presented him with a challenge that he couldn't resist. And he'd been good. He'd taught her, helped train her, and she'd been good too. Until she'd been unable to go back into an arson scene after his death.

A shadow to her left jerked her from her thoughts. She spun but saw nothing. "Daniel?"

316

"What?"

"Are you inside?"

"No. Why?"

This time the rush of adrenaline had nothing to do with the arson scene. And everything to do with going into protection mode. "Daniel? I'm taking the headgear off for a second." She pulled it off, then stripped off the suit. She slid her weapon from the holster and gripped it tight. Listened. Still nothing. Had she imagined the movement? "Who's there?"

No answer.

She stepped toward the shadow, her focus now on finding out if someone was in the building. What was left of it anyway. A scrape, a scuffle. A grunt. Just ahead.

Moving as quickly as she could, she did her best not to step on anything that might give way beneath her weight. Katie pulled her phone out of the clip on her belt and dialed Daniel's number with one hand while keeping her eyes on the area the noise had come from. The weight of her weapon against her palm offered comfort. She heard the footsteps clearly now and hurried to catch up. Three steps forward and blinding pain shot up from her ankle. She lost her balance and her knees hit the floor. Pain raced up from her previously injured knee and she couldn't stop the gasp that escaped. Clamping her lips together, she stayed still in case the person decided to turn around and come investigate.

"Katie? Are you there? What's going on? Why did you take your headgear off?"

Belatedly she realized she'd dialed Daniel's number but had never spoken to him. She lifted the phone to her ear. "Shh . . . someone's in here," she whispered.

"I'm on the way."

"No, go around back. See if he heads out the door." She pulled herself to her feet, using the column to keep her balance. The large column wobbled and charred debris rained down. She pulled her hand away and hurried — limped — after the fleeing figure. The footsteps stopped. Katie drew to a halt as well. She wanted to find out where Daniel was but didn't dare speak a word. She lightly tapped the phone with her nail. An answering tap came back to her. He was there. Waiting. Staying silent.

She hovered behind another column, hoping it would offer some form of protection in case the person decided to start flinging bullets.

More footsteps.

"I'm coming out the back, don't shoot me," she murmured.

"I'm actually inside. Didn't see anyone come out."

"Then he's still inside." She saw Daniel moving toward her, the phone pressed against his ear.

When he saw her, he hung up. He held his weapon in his other hand. "You all right?"

"Yes."

He looked behind them. "He could have easily disappeared into one of the buildings across the street if he managed to crawl out of a window."

She grimaced. "Yes, he could have." And probably had.

A low creak reached her ears and she grabbed Daniel's arm while her gaze scanned the ceiling. "You hear that?"

"Yes, I don't like it."

"We need to get out."

"Go for the back exit, it's closer."

She let him take the lead, doing her best to ignore the throbbing, stinging pain in her knee. Another groan and more debris fell from the ceiling. Then a loud crack shot through the air and the building rumbled.

"Go!"

The last column just ahead went down. She felt Daniel's arm go around her waist and he hauled her in the opposite direction just as the ceiling crashed behind her.

Daniel kept a tight grip on Katie. He coughed at the lungful of air he'd just inhaled. She wheezed right along with him. "You okay?" he gasped.

"Yes. You?"

He stood, still just inside the building. "He pushed that column over."

"No kidding." She coughed again. "Did the whole place come down?"

"No, just that section. We're okay right now." His heart pounded. Yet another close call.

She pulled away from him and walked toward the exit. "I'm assuming the person left, but let's not take any chances he's waiting to pick us off as we leave."

"Good idea."

She continued to wade through the rubble, choosing her steps carefully. Daniel stayed behind her, watching. With the sun shining through the holes in the roof, he could see pretty well and he noticed her favoring her left leg.

At the exit, she stopped and gripped her weapon. "You go right, I'll go left," she whispered.

He nodded.

She put her back to his. "Now."

They rounded the doorway, him to the right, her to the left. "Clear," he said and spun.

"Clear." She lowered her gun.

A rumble caught his attention. "You hear that?"

"A car engine?"

"Sounds like. But there are a lot of cars around here. Could be any engine."

"Yeah."

Tires squealed and then nothing but the sound of the men working next door, the traffic in the street, and a plane passing by overhead. Daniel shoved his weapon in his shoulder holster and trotted over to find the nearest worker who might have had a view of the back exit of the restaurant. "Hey, excuse me."

"Yeah?" The man in his early twenties turned from the bucket of cement he'd been mixing. "Help you?"

"Did you see a guy come out of that restaurant over there?"

The worker looked in the direction he pointed, then turned back. "Nope. Sorry."

Daniel grimaced. "It's okay." He moved to the next, then the next, and all gave him the same answer. They hadn't seen anyone.

Katie had followed him quietly, alert and vigilant, but had let him do the talking.

321

"Guess that's that then." She turned and headed for the car. Blood dripped with each step.

His hand on her arm stopped her forward momentum. "You're hurt."

She felt a wetness trickle down her shin and looked down. Blood flowed from the wound in her knee. No wonder it was pulsing with pain. "Great. You don't have any Band-Aids on you, do you?"

"Busted that knee open again, did you?"

"Looks like."

"Well, at least you didn't throw up."

She blinked. Then gave a short laugh. "No, I didn't. When I realized someone else was in there, I forgot about everything except going after him."

"Whatever works."

She scanned the buildings on the other side of the street and shook her head. "He's a slippery one. He's either hiding in one of the buildings or he drove off."

"Wonder what he was doing here?"

"If it's the guy who burned the place down . . . gloating?"

Daniel's jaw tightened. "Maybe."

"Or maybe it was just a vagrant we scared off."

"A vagrant?"

"Maybe. He could have been looking for anything of value that might have gotten left behind."

"I suppose, but I doubt it. Someone pushed that column over on purpose."

He had a point. At the car, she opened a tackle box in the back and pulled out a first aid kit.

"Girl Scout, huh?" he asked as he settled into the passenger seat and rubbed his hands together.

She smiled. "Once upon a time." She found what she needed and examined her wound. It looked a little red and angry, so she slathered on the antibiotic cream and bandaged it once again.

He opened the passenger door and climbed out. "Let's find that box and get out of here."

She looked around. If someone had a rifle, they were sitting ducks. But businesses were busy, traffic was heavy on the street behind her. Then again, that hadn't stopped him from stealing a backhoe with numerous witnesses all around him.

"I'll look while you get back in the car and wait," Katie said. "We already know he's not shy about shooting at you."

"I could wait in the car, but what if our intruder comes after you?"

She scowled. "I'll shoot him in the leg and make sure he doesn't get away again."

"I'm not waiting in the car. Let's look."

"Riley's going to be mad at you if you get yourself shot."

"I know, but I really want to find this for her." He glanced around. "And besides, whoever was here is gone now."

"Doesn't mean he won't double back," she muttered. "At least we'll be inside looking. Will make us harder to hit, I guess."

He ignored her and found the rakes he'd brought. Together, for the next hour, they used the rakes to sweep inside the site, being careful to avoid the shaky columns. Daniel pulled out dining utensils and other soot-covered items. They hadn't wanted to spend too much time inside the building — or what had once been the inside — and had moved outside to continue the search.

Katie's phone rang and she propped the rake on the side of the building to answer it.

"Hey, it's Bree."

"Hey, what's up?"

"I talked to Tim Shepherd."

"Really? Did he have anything interesting to say?"

"He did. When I asked him if he burned down Bryant's restaurant, the man actually laughed. Said there was no way I was going to pin that on him. And that he didn't do it. Said the man burned it down himself and blamed him."

Katie frowned. "Why would he do that?"

"He said he can't prove it, but Bryant's father-in-law owned the business and forbade it to be sold. Turns out Bryant never wanted to be in the restaurant business but couldn't sell it without his wife filing for divorce."

"No way."

"Way."

"Who told you that?"

"Bryant's wife. She didn't say he burned it down, but she said she refused to allow him to sell it."

"So he burned it down himself, blamed Shepherd, even had proof of Shepherd's harassment, and gets the insurance payoff, gets out of the restaurant business, and his wife has no reason to divorce him."

"That's a good summary."

"Wow." Katie ran a hand through her hair and shivered. Now that she wasn't moving, she was starting to get cold. "So you don't think Shepherd's behind all of the threats against Daniel?"

"It's not looking like it."

"Okay. Thanks for keeping me in the loop."

"Welcome."

She hung up and thought about that new development and all she could come up with was, "Interesting."

"Did you find it?"

Katie spun to find Lizzie and Riley walking toward them. She met them near the front entrance. "Hey, what's going on?" she asked.

"One of the workers at the dig sliced his hand open. Martin told me I could take off since he had to get the guy to the hospital and wouldn't be there to supervise," Riley said. "Lizzie and I went to get something to eat, then decided to come here."

Katie paused. "When did that happen? The guy at the dig getting hurt."

"About an hour ago."

"I see." She looked around. "You guys don't need to be around here. It's really not that safe." She escorted them away from the building and off to the side. "How did you know we were here?"

Riley held up her phone. "Daniel's app."

Daniel stepped up beside Katie. She lifted a brow at him. He shrugged. "I downloaded an app on her phone. She can find me anytime she wants to."

"He can track my location with the app on his phone. I simply told him if he could know where I was, then I wanted to be able to do the same."

Daniel swiped a hand across his cheek, leaving a trail of soot. "I don't do that because I don't trust you, Princess, you know that."

"I know."

Katie suspected Riley truly did know that. With everything Daniel had seen in his career in the Marines and law enforcement, he was super protective. He saw it as an extra to ensure his niece's safety. She admired the fact that he was willing to allow her the same access to his location as well. For Riley, after losing her parents, knowing she could find Daniel anytime she needed him had to be a huge comfort.

Riley walked forward, placed her hands on her hips, and looked at the blackened area. Anger tightened the girl's pretty features. "I really hope they catch the person who did this."

"So do I, Princess, so do I," Daniel said.

"So? Did you find it?"

"No."

Riley sighed. Katie turned to Lizzie. "Someone was here snooping around."

"You think it was the guy who burned the

place down?"

Katie shook her head. "Who knows? I couldn't move fast enough to catch him." She saw Riley stoop down and pick something up, study it, then stand. The slump of her shoulders said it wasn't what she was looking for.

"Hey, Riley?" Daniel called. "Let's go. I don't think we're going to find it. Not today anyway."

Riley glanced over her shoulder at her uncle, then gave a slow nod. She trotted over to him. "Maybe when they start clearing the place out, it'll show up." Her phone buzzed. She looked at it. "That's Martin. He said he's back from the hospital and I can come back to the dig site so I don't lose any more hours if I want to. I guess I'll go back."

"Have you found anything interesting?"

Her eyes lit up. "I haven't, but one of the other workers found something. He found a Confederate Leech & Rigdon .36 caliber percussion revolver with original matching holster. It says CSA on it and everything."

"Confederate States of America," Daniel murmured. "When did he find that?"

"Just this morning. Right after I got there. You should have seen Martin. He went nuts, he was so excited. He was dancing and shouting. It was funny."

Daniel gave her a genuine smile. "That's amazing. I'm happy for Martin."

"He stood there and looked it up online and one sold at an auction last year for around fifteen grand."

Daniel let out a low whistle. "Wow, that's impressive. I guess Martin is ready for the press to come in now?"

"Yes, they're supposed to do an interview with him this afternoon. He scheduled it right then. If you think he was hyper before, you haven't seen anything yet."

"I hope he put it somewhere safe," Katie murmured.

Riley lifted her shoulder in a shrug. "I don't know what he did with it, but it's off-site now. He's got a few other things he's found, some bullets, and smaller items, but this is big."

Katie nodded to Lizzie. "You take her back to the site. Daniel and I'll be heading back to his place."

"Sure thing."

Lizzie and Riley climbed into her car and Katie blew out a low breath. "I'm disappointed we didn't find the box."

"I am too." He placed his hands on his hips and looked around again. "I don't understand it. It was on the counter by the register."

"The force of the water could have knocked it a good distance away. It could be anywhere. Buried under anything. We have a lot more space to search before covering the whole restaurant."

"I know."

"We can keep looking if you want."

"No." He shook his head. "I wanted to take you flying."

"What? What about your head?"

"It's fine. Down to a dull ache and I don't have any vision issues. It was a *slight* concussion, remember?"

"All right then, I'd love to go. But I think I still want to talk to Tim Shepherd at some point. I want to see him face-to-face."

"All right, we can fit that into the schedule. But first things first."

"You want to go to the press conference."

He shot her a funny look. "Am I that easy to read?"

She laughed. "Easy like a large-print book."

He shook his head. "We'll go up after?"

"Or another time."

"Well, Riley wants to take the plane up Saturday. I need to give it a good going-over and a test run before she gets in the pilot seat."

"You're a good uncle."

He smiled. "I try. Now let's go cheer while Martin has his big moment."

[22]

The ride back to the dig site took just under twenty minutes. They crossed the long Gervais Street Bridge covering the Congaree River. Once they reached the end, Daniel spotted the news vans already there. They pulled in next to one, and he figured everyone was down the embankment. He and Katie exited the vehicle and she gave the area the once-over, seemed satisfied, and followed him down to the crowd.

The archaeological site buzzed with activity. Team members barely held on to their excitement. He and Katie walked toward the area where Martin stood. On the bank of the river, he'd created a makeshift stage and stood in the middle of it, a portable microphone in his right hand. A box sat at his feet. Daniel also noticed the security. Uniformed officers patrolled and he hoped whoever was after him would be deterred by their presence.

Thunder rolled overhead and Daniel glanced at the darkening sky, then looked back at Martin. There was no way his friend was the one who was trying to kill him. What reason would he have? There was simply no motive. And why would he claim the coin had been stolen if it was just lost? Denial?

Martin lifted the microphone. "Well, folks, I'm excited you're here. Thank you so much for coming out. I'm going to get right to it since it looks like we're in for a downpour. First, let me start by saying that I'm very grateful to the university and private donors for helping to fund this site. When I was putting this together, I had a pretty good idea there were some artifacts in this area thanks to the research my colleagues and I have done. I had no way of knowing the things we would come across, but we're very excited with what we've found. As you know, when Sherman made his march across Columbia back in 1865, he left a trail of destruction in his path. We also knew he threw weapons into this very river. While some excavating has been done in the river, I thought it might be wise to look along the banks area. And sure enough, we've made some fabulous discoveries. We've got some on display there under the tent to your left.

Feel free to browse when we're finished here." He bent down and opened the box. "Now, I want to show you our most recent find." He reached in the box and pulled out a gun and holster. "This is a Confederate Leech & Rigdon .36 caliber percussion revolver. And yes, this is the original holster. Both pieces were found right here."

Oohs and aahs filled the air. Flashes lit up around them. Reporters shouted questions. And thunder rolled overhead once again. Daniel grasped Katie's hand and he smiled at her. "Now, we can go flying." He glanced at the sky. "We might be able to beat the storm, but I'm guessing we'll probably have to wait it out. That being said, while we're waiting, I can get everything ready and do the preflight check."

She nodded. "I just want to check on Quinn, all right?"

"Of course."

He led the way back to the car and listened to her talk to Maddy about Quinn, but couldn't hear Maddy's response. They climbed into her Jeep while lightning flashed in the distance and another boom of thunder rolled across the even darker sky. She hung up and stared out the window. He let her think for a few minutes before he caved to his curiosity.

"How's Quinn doing?"

"He's about the same, according to Maddy."

"Glad he's healing."

"Yes, he'll heal." She frowned.

"What is it?"

"I just hope he doesn't run Maddy off in the process. She said he's giving everyone a hard time."

"That bad?"

"She hasn't given specifics, but I hear the weariness in her voice. Along with an anger that's going to be unleashed on his head if he doesn't stop being such a pain. She said he's acting like a two-year-old."

"Men can do that."

"No kidding."

"Which means there's something mental going on with him."

"I know."

He gave her a slight smile. "What's his story?"

She shook her head. "I'm not sure. I'm not even sure Maddy knows the whole thing."

Her phone buzzed again and she checked the screen. "It's Bree." She tapped the speakerphone. "What's up?"

"Hey, I've got an update on Lee Kendall. We tracked him down."

"Where?"

"He's in Florida attending his aunt's funeral."

Katie pursed her lips and Daniel caught her gaze. "So I guess he's not the one causing all my trouble."

"Doesn't sound like it. He's been there for the past week."

"And he just dropped everything and left? No notice to his boss or friends?"

"He told his boss, who forgot to mention it to the guys he worked with. The boss went on vacation and didn't get my messages until late last night."

"Okay then. Weird that he didn't tell his roommate or at least leave him a message."

"I know. You just never can tell about some people or why they think the way they do."

"That's the truth. Thanks, Bree."

"Of course." Katie hung up and looked at Daniel. "Well, our list of suspects just got one name shorter."

"And you're still looking at Martin as one?"

"I am. I'm sorry, but I am." She tapped the screen of her phone.

"What are you doing?"

"Googling acetone use in archaeology."

■ ■ ■ ■

Riley flipped the coin through her fingers while the thunder rolled above her. She glanced at the sky and figured they wouldn't be staying at the dig much longer. Martin had given them the choice to stay or go, and she'd stayed simply so she could log the hours. Most of the students had left and she knew she wouldn't be far behind. But for now, she focused her attention back on the coin and wondered how much it was worth. Dated 1804, it was old for sure.

Lizzie stood to the side, watching, taking everything in. She was alert and always vigilant, but Riley could tell she really enjoyed the activity. She didn't find it boring like one of the workers who'd thrown a trowel down in disgust and said she was going to change her major.

Riley shoved the coin back into her pocket and shook her head. She'd eventually give the coin to Martin and see if he wanted it, but she wanted to show it to her uncle before she had to give it up. He'd get a kick out of her finding such an old coin on his property.

"Hey, hey! Look at this!"

It sounded like Carol calling out. "What

did you find?" She moved closer, along with the others, excited to see what she might have found.

Riley felt a raindrop on her cheek and brushed it away. She watched Carol scrape away another layer of dirt and reach into the earth to pull out an item. "What is it?"

"A cannonball," Carol said. She pulled it up and someone handed her a measuring tape. She noted it in her small book, then snapped several pictures with her phone. "Where's Martin?"

"He left right after the press conference," Riley said. Thunder cracked and she jumped. "Okay, I'm taking off before we get soaked."

Lightning flashed. "Or electrocuted," Carol muttered.

Riley fell in behind Carol and Lizzie brought up the rear as they all ran for the covered area.

[23]

FRIDAY

Katie was disappointed with the delay in the flight Daniel had planned for them. Yesterday the weather had just been too bad. And while today brought more rain and thunderstorms, it also brought more excitement. Daphne was almost here.

As much as Katie loved her job — and spending time with Daniel even though he was a client — she was looking forward to some girl time. She knew Daniel and Riley were in good hands. They'd doubled up on the security and she knew they didn't plan to leave the house. So. She had nothing to worry about on that end.

On this end, however, to say she was nervous was an understatement. It had been a long time since she and Daphne had spent time together. And while it was long over-due, the butterflies in her stomach wouldn't settle down.

The doorbell rang and she froze. Backdraft hopped from her lap and disappeared into her bedroom. "Thanks for the support, friend." He never looked back. She was on her own.

She smoothed her hands down her jeans and went to the door. She looked out and saw her sister standing there.

Katie opened the door. Daphne's gaze met hers. Then she grinned, stepped forward, and wrapped Katie in a hug. And Katie's nerves fled. "Hey, I'm so glad you're here."

Daphne stepped back. "And I'm glad to be here."

"Come on in."

Once inside, Daphne's gaze widened. "This is beautiful."

"I'm getting there. I haven't done much in here."

"But the kitchen is amazing." She left her suitcase by the door and walked into the kitchen.

"Thanks. Some friends and I put it together just this week."

"You've got some good friends."

"Yes." Katie smiled. "Yes, I do." She grabbed her sister's hand and pulled her toward the sofa. "Give me your coat and have a seat."

Once they were settled, Daphne gave her

another hug. "I've missed you."

"I've missed you too." She looked down. "How are Mom and Dad?"

"They're good. They miss you too." Daphne gave a light laugh that sounded forced. "Sounds like everyone is missing everyone."

"Hmm."

"They do, I promise."

"They blame me for Paul's death, Daph," she said softly. "It hurts to talk to them."

Her sister drew in a deep breath. "I think they're moving past blame, Katie. They love you. Not talking to you, not seeing you? It's taken its toll. Call them."

Katie looked into Daphne's eyes. "I'll think about it. Hard."

"Good. Not the answer I was looking for, but we'll come back to that later." She took a deep breath. "So, tell me about your work. A bodyguard. It sounds like an incredibly exciting and dangerous profession."

Katie looked into her sister's happy, innocent eyes. "Exciting? Dangerous? Hmm. Not usually." She smiled. "But I do get to meet some really cool people." She stood. "Now, I'm starved. Where do you want to go eat?"

"What? You didn't cook for me?"

Katie gave her sister's shoulder a gentle

shove. "Still a comedian, I see. No, I didn't cook, but you're welcome to try out the new kitchen." She headed to the closet to get her coat.

Daphne stood and grabbed her purse and coat. "Let's go. It's on you."

Katie laughed and followed Daphne out the door.

Katie drove with one eye on the rearview mirror. She knew Charlie was back there and appreciated his vigilance. Ten minutes later, she pulled into the parking lot of Alodia's on North Lake Drive, not too far from the charred remains of Daniel's restaurant. Once inside, she and Daphne were seated and spent the next few minutes deciding on their food choices.

"I'll take the chicken parmesan," Daphne said and handed the menu to the waitress.

"And I'll do the blackened Mahi," Katie said. The waitress left and Katie turned to Daphne. "So, how's the hospital treating you?"

Daphne shrugged. "It's a job. I love the people I work with and most of the patients, so I won't complain." She sipped her water. "Tell me what's going on with you."

So Katie filled her in on less dangerous aspects of her life. She knew Charlie continued to keep watch, and it felt good to relax and enjoy the time with her sister as they discussed funny moments from their childhood.

When Daphne brought up their brother again, Katie wanted to change the subject, but Daphne wouldn't let her. "Call Mom and Dad, okay?"

"I said I would."

"No you didn't. You said you'd think about it."

Katie sighed, then nodded. "Okay, all right. I'll call them."

"When?"

"Soon. I will."

Her sister refused to let go of Katie's gaze. Finally, she must have been satisfied with what she saw there, because she smiled and nodded. "Okay then."

Their time together passed too quickly, and soon it was Saturday morning and she was waving goodbye as Daphne drove down the drive and out of sight.

"Looks like you had a good time with your sister."

She turned to see Charlie standing at the edge of the porch. "We did. And because you were here keeping watch, I was able to really enjoy it and not worry about someone snooping around or whatever. Thanks."

"Anytime." He shot her a small smirk.

"And as you know, things have been quiet with Daniel and Riley."

She flushed. "Guilty as charged." She'd checked in on a regular basis when she could get a moment to send a text or make a phone call. "Go home and get some rest, you've earned it."

"What are you going to do?"

She sighed. "Call my parents."

Daniel finished the preflight check and filed his flight plan — although he didn't necessarily need one to fly where they were going, but he liked being on the radar at all times and it made Riley feel better when she wanted to know exactly where he was. He put two water bottles within reach. Riley's plans had changed, which worked in his favor. She was working this weekend and back at the dig site with Martin and Lizzie, leaving Daniel free to spend a few uninterrupted hours with Katie. Hours that didn't include dodging bullets or being crushed like a bug.

Katie stepped into the hangar. "Where are we going?"

"Feel like a visit to the beach?"

"The beach? In October?" Thunder rolled in with the clouds. "It's going to rain."

"Just for a bit. We'll get up there and

outrun it. I'd planned to be in the air before now, but we still have time."

"You're sure?"

"Of course." He paused. "I wouldn't take you up if I thought there was any risk."

She hesitated, then nodded. "Okay. Why not?"

"Once the rain passes, it's supposed to be in the mid-forties. Practically a heat wave in October."

"A heat wave, huh? And what about your head?"

"It's barely aching."

"Liar."

"Okay, so it still hurts a little, but I've taken the ibuprofen like a good boy and I really want to do this. Please?" He took her hand in his. "Riley said the beach is one of your favorite places."

"She's absolutely right."

"I want to share that with you."

"Today."

"Today."

A slow smile lifted the corner of her lips. "Okay, let's go."

While he finished the last-minute preparations, he watched her from the corner of his eye. "How was the visit with your sister?"

"It went well. She's a great girl. I hate that I let things . . . lapse like I did."

"She doesn't blame you for Paul's death anymore?"

"No, she doesn't."

He stopped what he was doing and took her hand in his. "I'm glad."

Her lips curved further and her eyes looked lighter. Like she'd had a heavy burden removed from her shoulders.

"Then let's celebrate."

"By flying."

"Yep." He checked the fuel one more time. He'd already topped off the tanks and all looked good to him.

"Are you ready?"

"I am."

He loved her excitement. Now that he'd convinced her to go, she was all in. Another thing he liked about her.

He'd already loaded the supplies he wanted to take with him earlier. All that was left was to hop in and take off. He opened the plane's doors. She watched as they rose. "They look like an extra pair of wings."

A knock sounded on the hangar service door. "Daniel? You got a minute?" a voice called from outside the hangar.

"Who's that?" Katie asked, her hand already resting on her weapon.

"Martin." Daniel walked over to the door and opened it.

From the corner of his eye he saw Katie relax. A fraction. At least she moved her hand from her gun. Martin stepped inside and he shut the door.

"Hey, I thought you were reveling in your fame back at the site. I drove past and saw news vans still out there."

Martin ran a hand through his hair and shook the water droplets loose. "They've been there since Thursday's press conference, expecting us to pull something else amazing out of the ground. I took off when I could, but I left instructions with my assistant what to have Riley and the other two interns do." He glanced behind him and out the window. "But the weather is getting ready to be ugly yet again and I think she'll probably send them all home."

"It's not going to last long. What do you need?"

"Advice."

"What's wrong now?"

His friend truly looked frazzled. "That coin," Martin said. "I can't think, I can't sleep, I can't eat. That coin was going to send me to the top of the archaeology news reports. I was going to be on magazines. I was going to be famous."

Was that really all that was important to

347

Martin? "Dude, there's more to life than fame."

Martin let out a rough chuckle. "I know, I know. It's not really about that, it's just that I had it all within my hands and now it's like fate has just snatched it away."

"But you found that gun and the holster. You just had an amazing press conference. What's the problem?"

Martin's eyes gleamed for a moment at the reminder. "Yes. I know. All that's wonderful, truly great. But that coin . . ."

"Why don't we move inside the house?" Katie said.

Daniel led the way to the back of the hangar and through the door that led into his mudroom. Martin followed him and Katie pulled up the rear.

Once inside the den, Martin perched on the seat of the wingback chair nearest the fireplace. Daniel dropped into the recliner, and Katie hovered near the window, going back and forth from it to the door.

"What is it you think I can do, Martin?"

Martin wiped a hand down his face. He drew in a deep breath. "I . . . ah . . . need money. I'm getting ready to lose my house." His gaze flicked toward Katie, then back to Daniel.

Daniel straightened. "Katie, you mind giving us a minute?"

Katie cleared her throat. "Of course not. I'll just go check the perimeter of the property. I'll be right back."

Once she left, Martin rubbed his palms down his dusty jeans. "I've put everything into this dig. Can you give me enough to cover my house payment for this month?"

Daniel stared. Stunned. Shocked. Two words that accurately described his state of mind at the moment. "But your tenure at the school, your salary —"

"They let me go."

His voice was so low Daniel almost missed what he said. "What? Why? Even after this find?"

"I didn't find it fast enough. I'm the low man on the totem pole." Martin stood and paced from one end of the room to the other. "I didn't have tenure. I didn't write enough articles or pull in enough research grants. There are no private investors. I'm funding this dig, Daniel, I've put my entire life savings and more into this project and I'm broke. I just need enough to get through this. Now that we've had the press conference and people know what's there, I think I can get investors. It's time that I don't have. I need to make a payment on my house or I'm going under."

Daniel sighed. "Stay here." He walked into his office, pulled his checkbook from the drawer, and wrote a check that should cover his friend's house payment for the next three months. When he returned to the den, he found Martin back in the chair with his face in his hands.

"Here," Daniel said. He held the check out toward Martin.

Martin looked up and his eyes widened when he saw the amount. "I don't need that much. I feel sure after our find that the university will offer me my position back."

"Well, until then. We can consider this a loan."

"I'll pay you back, you know I will."

"Of course. I'm not worried about it."

Martin stood, nodded. "Thanks, Daniel."

"Don't mention it."

Martin glanced toward the area where Katie had been. "I interrupted something, didn't I?"

"I'm just taking Katie flying. I'll call in the delayed flight plan and we'll be good."

"Then I'm out of here." He walked toward the door. "Oh, and Riley's doing great. She hasn't found anything of worth yet, but she's got what it takes to be an archaeologist."

"Patience?"

"And a good old-fashioned dose of stub-born."

"Well, she comes by that naturally." Daniel stopped at the door. "Hey, do you ever use acetone at the dig site?"

"Sure, sometimes. Why?"

"What is it used for?"

"It's a solvent and it's one of the key ingredients in the stuff that's used to conserve artifacts. I can be more detailed if you want, but that's the basics."

"The basics are fine. Thanks."

Martin shot him a troubled look but said nothing more. His phone buzzed and he looked down. Gasped.

"What is it?"

"Ah. Nothing. Just a text that I need to address. I'll see you later." Daniel saw his friend out as Katie slipped inside. He shut the door. "That was weird," he said.

"Does Martin have anything to gain with you out of the way?"

Daniel lifted a brow. "What? No."

"He's not in your will?"

"No, just Riley and my mother."

"But he needed money."

"Yes." Daniel frowned. "And before you ask, the answer is no. He's never asked me for money before. That was a first."

"It probably won't be the last time."

Daniel's frown deepened. "He's good for it."

Katie pursed her lips. "Hmm."

"You don't believe me?"

"I believe you believe it. But if he's asked you, chances are he's asked others as well."

Daniel rubbed the back of his neck. "You don't know him like I do. But I guess time will tell." He shrugged. "And if he doesn't ever pay it back, I'm not going to hold it against him."

"What if he comes back for more?"

Daniel sighed. "I'll cross that bridge when we come to it."

She tilted her head. "I heard you ask him about the acetone."

"Yes. It does make me think, but it doesn't convince me it's Martin who's behind all the trouble."

Katie let it go. "How's the insurance settlement coming?"

"All the paperwork has been filed. I'm just waiting on the check."

She tapped her lip and he moved closer to lift her chin. "What is it? I can see your brain clicking along at warp speed."

For a moment she could only stare. The memory of the kiss swept over her and she almost closed the gap between them. But she didn't. *He's a client, remember?* She stepped back. "Do you mind if I check Martin out a little more closely?"

Disappointment flashed in his eyes, then he glanced at the door where his friend had just left. "No. I don't mind. Martin has nothing to gain if I die. In fact, if I die, he's got no one to borrow money from. He has no reason to want me dead."

"Good point."

"Thank you."

"I still think we should check him out."

"Fine. You won't find anything."

She narrowed her eyes. "Why? You already did a background check on him?"

He laughed. "No, I didn't have to. The school did."

"Ah. For the internship."

"Yes." His eyes widened and then he closed them on a groan.

"What?"

"The internship. Martin's not employed by the university anymore."

Understanding hit her. "Oh no. Poor Riley."

"Yeah. If he's not employed, Riley won't get the credit for the internship."

"And Martin could be sued for misleading the school — and everyone else." He sighed. "Even if he's not involved in something more sinister, this is a big mess-up for him. Do the check."

"Thanks, I will."

She sent a text to Olivia asking her to get things moving on it. Olivia shot a reply back affirming she'd take care of it.

Also, Haley and Maddy on another assignment. L staying with R. All is fine there. I'll take over for you tonight at 8:00.

Got it. Thanks.

"So, are we finally ready to get in the air?"

In the hangar, Katie hauled herself into the front of the single-engine plane, settled into the passenger seat, and pulled on the harness.

Daniel climbed into the pilot's seat and did the same. "Have you ever flown in a private plane?"

"Yes, a few times, but never one this small and never in the front seat." She stared at the display in front of her.

"Small? It's a four-seater. It's not small." She laughed and Daniel looked at the array of screens, knobs, and buttons in front of him and tried to imagine it through her eyes. "Looks crazy, doesn't it?" He handed her a set of headphones.

"I hope you know what to do with all of it," she said as she fastened her seat belt and slipped the headset on her head.

He laughed. "Of course." He pulled on his headset and went to work. He pointed. "Here's our weather display. It does look like we may have to wait." He adjusted his headphones. "N125MK, a Cirrus SR22, requesting IFR flight plan Columbia to Charleston."

"Hold for release," came the response.

He looked at Katie. "Well, I don't have to say this often —" he shot her a grin to let her know he was kidding — "but I was wrong. We're not going to be able to outrun the weather after all, but it's just an area thunderstorm and is slated to pass in about twenty minutes."

"It's fine. I don't mind waiting." Her phone rang. "It will give me time to take care of this. Hello?" She listened and glanced at him from the corner of her eye. "Uh-huh. Really? Wasn't expecting that. Okay, thanks."

"What was that about?"

"That was Olivia. She talked to the worker from the dig who was hurt, and he said Martin was with him the entire time and even drove him home."

Relief filled him. Followed by another thought. "Well, he could have had help."

"Yes. But we know the person at the North Lake restaurant definitely wasn't Martin."

"Unless the worker is lying."

"I don't think so. Olivia also called the hospital and talked to several of the staff who worked that day. They all agreed that Martin was there the entire time."

"Okay then. That's good. Right?"

"Unless he had someone working for him." She tilted her head and stared out the window for a moment. "So we know it wasn't Martin. That's good news."

"Yes. And while we could have been hurt by the column, it doesn't necessarily have to be the same person causing us grief. It could have simply been someone who was trespassing and just didn't want to get caught."

"True." She sighed. "We may never know."

"But," he held up a finger, "we know it wasn't Martin."

"Yes."

The radio crackled. He listened, then gave her a thumbs-up. "We're released for departure."

They sped down the runway just outside his house and then swooped into the air.

"This is great." Her voice came through the headphones. "What beach are we going to?"

"A buddy of mine I served with in Iraq has a runway in his subdivision like I do. He also backs up to a private beach in Charleston. We're going to land in his front yard, then walk down to the beach."

"Sounds lovely."

"I thought so."

She pointed to a screen. "What's this?"

"These are PFDs — Primary Flight Displays. They provide information such as airspeed, altitude, and heading."

"And these?"

"MFDs — Multi-Function Displays. Here we can see what the engine is doing —" he pointed at the instruments — "this is the weather radar, and so on. This also makes sure we don't have a midair collision or get too close to the ground without warning."

"Yes, let's avoid all that. How long is the flight?"

"Just under thirty minutes."

"Parachutes?"

He smiled. "Yes. Under each seat and the plane even has one. But we won't need them."

For the next fifteen minutes or so, she entertained herself by looking out of the window and commenting on different landmarks. He found himself smiling and feeling the weight of the last week start to lift. He needed this. Not having to worry if someone was going to shoot at him or hurt someone close to him.

Yes, Riley was still at the dig site, but no one had gone after her or bothered her. Whether that was due to the bodyguards or the fact that the person after Daniel didn't need Riley for any reason, he wasn't sure. And didn't care as long as Riley was left alone. He knew Lizzie would call if there were any concerns and he was grateful for a silent phone. "So tell me about your family."

"I've already told you about them. What else do you want to know?"

"All I know is that they blame you for your brother's death."

She sighed. "All right. My sister, Daphne, is an ER nurse. She works at the hospital and is incredibly passionate about her job."

"When's the last time you saw her before this weekend?"

"On her birthday. In January." He whipped his head around to stare and she shrugged. "I told you, my family and I are . . . estranged. My mother calls on all of the important dates like my birthday,

358

but . . ." She sighed. "I promised my sister I'd call my parents, though, and . . . check in."

"Have you?"

She grimaced. "I tried. I dialed the number and hung up."

"I think you actually have to talk to them to make progress."

She pursed her lips and shot him a sideways look. "It's just too stressful. It's like I can actually feel the blame rolling off of them. And I'm just not going to put myself through that anymore."

"I can't say I blame you." He paused. "But you promised, right?"

"Yes. I did."

"Then . . ."

"I know. I will."

"When?"

"Soon."

The plane jerked and he gripped the control wheel. Katie raised a brow. He gave a low grunt and leveled the craft back out. Only to have it jerk again. This time he frowned.

"What's wrong?"

"Not sure."

The wheel pulled from his hand and the plane dipped. He heard Katie's gasp. He grabbed the wheel and pulled the plane level, but it jerked and twitched and his concern ratcheted up a notch. "What the —"

"Daniel?"

"I'm having a hard time keeping the plane level." He checked the reading on the panel. "Something's wrong with the elevator."

"Okay. So what does that mean?" He could hear the controlled fear in her voice, but he didn't have time to look at her.

"It means we need to land and we need to land now."

"Are we going to crash?"

"No way." At least he hoped not. "But now might be a great time to send up some prayers."

[24]

The plane pitched forward again and Katie grabbed the dash. "Hang on. If worse comes to worse, we've got a parachute, remember?"

"Parachute?" She shot him a look of sheer terror.

"There's one built in on the plane. I'd need to take it up to a higher altitude though to release it." And then the chute could drag them out into the ocean and he'd have no more control over anything. "But I don't need to do that. I can land us, just hang on."

It was taking all of his strength and skill to keep the plane level, adjusting the trim as he flew.

"Mayday, this is N125MK, a Cirrus SR22. I have an emergency and need to land."

Silence.

Finally, "This is Charleston Approach. I see you on the radar. There's no place where you can immediately land."

Daniel adjusted the trim and power again, pulled the control wheel, and continued to descend. "You don't understand. I either find a place to land or we're going to crash. I have no control over the elevator. I'm using power and trim to land. Got it?"

Silence. Then, "Got it." The radio crackled. He was getting out of range. "I'm looking. The only place . . . on . . . beach."

"Which beach?"

"Cape . . . a . . . beach that's about five miles long."

"Which beach?"

Nothing but static. He switched frequencies. "Mayday. I have an emergency. I need to land."

More silence on the radio. His head pounded and his eyes blurred. He blinked and the instrument panel swam back into focus.

He looked out of the window. "I'm going down on that beach right there."

"Which one?"

"The long one." He spoke into the microphone again. "Mayday, I've got an emergency, can you hear me?" He gave his coordinates. "I'm going down on the beach." He shot a glance at Katie. "You see any people down there?" he asked.

She craned her neck. "No, but that doesn't mean they're not there."

"Hopefully they'll move. I think that's Cape Island. If so . . . what's today?" He adjusted the stick, then the trim and power once more. The plane lowered and stayed level, with the nose slightly up.

"Um . . . Saturday. I think."

"Saturday. Cape Island." He moved the throttle and then returned his hand to the stick. "The ferry that brings the tourists over only operates on Tuesday, Thursday, Friday, and Saturday."

"And you know this why?"

"Field trip with my mother when I was in high school. I see the beach area." Daniel continued the battle with the plane. "I can't hold it much longer. We're going to be on the beach," he said into the headset. "Hopefully, the chilly weather is keeping people away."

He grunted and worked the trim more, keeping the nose of the plane up. Katie remained silent, but he caught a glimpse of her white-knuckled fingers gripping the armrest. The aircraft bucked and jerked and Katie watched him, eyes wide, lips tight. "It'll be all right," he said. "Just hang on. It won't be the smoothest landing I've ever made."

"Just as long as we're in one piece at the end of it."

"That's the plan." He tried the radio once more and got no one. Too low to the ground to get a radio signal and no one else in the vicinity. Great.

He only had one shot at this. The beach came closer. He had the wheels down. Using the parachute that came with the plane wouldn't work this close to the ground. He had stayed low on purpose to allow Katie to see the ground, follow the route, enjoy the view. Now he was going to have to land with a faulty elevator. No flaps, as they might induce more pitching moments that he had no time to countermand. He worked the trim, kept the nose slightly tilted to the sky, and made a beeline to the beach. Only the nose began to tilt down and he wasn't exactly sure how much trim and power to apply to lift it. "Ease the seat back."

"What?"

"The seat has a power button, move it back now. Fast."

She did and the plane leveled back out, the nose slightly up once again. He'd had her shift the seat in order to change the center of gravity for the plane.

The wheels touched down. Bounced. He pulled the control stick, then pushed it forward slightly. Adjusted the throttle. He hit the hard-packed sand once again and pressed the brakes. The plane bounced and shook but slowed. And finally came to a stop in the middle of the beach with the waves lapping the wheels. And not a soul in sight.

Daniel took a deep breath and closed his eyes for a brief prayer of thanks.

He opened the doors and got out, his legs shaky, muscles tight, as he landed on the sand. Katie crawled over to the pilot's side and he helped her down.

She stepped into the circle of his arms and clasped him around his waist. "You did it."

He held her close, relishing the feeling of being alive — and having her in his arms. "Yes. I did, but I shouldn't have had to."

She let go of him and he missed her. "What happened?" she asked. "You did the preflight check and, knowing you, you were careful."

"Of course I was. I don't know what happened, but I'm going to find out."

[25]

Riley stared at the empty spot in the hangar. He'd taken the plane up. She smiled and figured Katie was with him.

"Hey, what's going on?"

She turned. Haley and Steve walked up. "Where's Lizzie?"

"She had something she had to take care of," Haley said. "Hope you don't mind me subbing."

"Not at all."

"What are you doing?" Steve asked.

"Well, I was going to check the plane out, but I guess Uncle Daniel beat me to it."

"Yes, he took Katie up," Haley said. "She texted me about an hour ago."

"I was supposed to be at the dig site today, but Martin sent everyone home, so I thought I'd go flying. Did she say when they'd be back?" Riley asked.

"In a couple of hours."

Riley punched in her uncle's number and

hit the button to FaceTime with him. It rang four times. He finally answered. "What's up, Princess?"

"You took the plane. Steve's here and I was going to show it to him, maybe go up." She held up a hand. "And before you ask, his parents said it was okay."

Daniel gave her a smile, but she thought he looked . . . weird.

She frowned. "You okay?"

"We're fine. We just had a little emergency landing. It's going to take us a bit to get back to you."

Her adrenaline surged, but since she was looking at him, they must be all right. "What happened?"

"I'm not exactly sure. I'm getting ready to figure that out." He cleared his throat. "How's the dig going?"

"It's going fine." She gave a small laugh. "Although I seem to have better luck finding artifacts in other places than the dig."

"What do you mean?"

She dug into her pocket and pulled out the coin. "This. I found it the other day when we were at the restaurant site."

"A coin?"

"Yes. It's rare too. I looked it up. I meant to show it to you this weekend, but everything was quiet and you were locked in your office working so I didn't want to disturb you."

"Aw, Riley, you know you can come talk to me anytime you need to."

"I know I can. Don't be going all guilty on me. Anyway, this coin is cool and really old. It has 1804 on it, but it wasn't actually minted until sometime in the 1830s. There were only fifteen ever minted. Isn't that crazy?"

Another strange look crossed his face. "And you say you found that at the restaurant on North Lake?"

"Yes, why?"

"Have you told anyone else about it?"

"I texted Martin a little while ago and asked him if he'd ever seen one before."

"What did he say?"

"He hasn't answered me yet."

"Let me talk to Lizzie."

"She's not here. Just Haley." She glanced over her shoulder to see Haley talking on her cell phone. "What's wrong, Uncle Daniel?"

"I'm not sure. I have my suspicions, but I —" He sighed and rubbed his head. "Let me talk to Haley real quick."

"Haley?"

Haley looked up, phone pressed to her ear. "I've got to go. I'll call you back." She ended the call. "What is it?"

"Uncle Daniel. He wants to talk to you."

Haley walked toward her.

"Riley? Riley, you here?" Martin's voice came from outside the hangar.

Haley's hand went to her weapon.

"It's Martin," Riley said.

"Don't trust him," Daniel said. His urgent tone took her aback.

"What?"

"Riley, listen to me."

"Riley?" Martin called again.

Haley kept her hand on her weapon. She'd heard Daniel's plea.

"Riley, look at me." She did and saw Daniel's frown and the . . . fear . . . in his eyes. "Don't go anywhere or do anything with him. Understand? And don't give him that coin. If he knows you have it, he won't need you, understand?"

"But —"

"Do you understand?" he yelled.

She flinched. He'd never talked to her in that tone before, but she thought it was more than anger in his voice. She heard fear. For her.

"There you are." She turned to find Martin standing in the hangar doorway.

"Hey, Uncle Daniel, I've got to go. Martin is here."

"Riley, remember what I said. Tell Martin I've got the coin and I'm taking good care of it."

"Okay." Now she was a little freaked. "Hi, Martin, I thought you were taking the rest of the day off."

"Where's the coin? Why does Daniel have it?" Martin blurted.

"What?"

"The coin you texted me about. The one I lost."

"It's *yours*?" Why hadn't Daniel just said so?

"Yes, yes. Where is it?"

"In a safe place." Obviously Daniel didn't want Martin to know that she had the coin, so she kept her mouth shut about the fact that it was in her pocket.

"Where?" he yelled.

Riley flinched and Haley stepped forward, a frown on her face. "Tone it down a notch, will you?" She held out her hands. "I need to pat you down."

"What?" Martin's eyes flared.

Haley stared him down. "Do you have any weapons on you?"

"Of course not, I'm sorry. I just . . . I've been looking for that coin everywhere. I've been frantic trying to find it."

"I thought someone stole it," Haley said.

370

She moved toward him and Martin back-pedaled.

"Well, yes. I thought so, but maybe I just lost it. Where is Daniel and when is he going to be back?"

Riley frowned at him. "*You* lost it? But I found it at the restaurant site. The one that burned down. Why would you have lost it out there?" She was so confused. And she thought she was beginning to understand and that frightened her.

Martin froze for a brief second, then let out a low laugh. "I mean I didn't. I guess the person who stole it must have dropped it out there."

Riley studied him. He seemed nervous. "You're not making any sense, Martin. Either someone stole it or they didn't. Either you lost it or you didn't." He didn't say anything for a moment. In fact, he seemed to be searching for words. "No one stole the coin, did they, Martin?" she whispered. Fear clutched her. They had to get away from him. This was why her uncle didn't want her to give Martin the coin. Martin was the one. *Oh God, help us.*

He laughed again, a sound she'd never heard him make. "Of course they did. Someone did. Just ask your uncle. He saw my place. It was torn apart."

"What were you doing out at the site?" she asked as she took a step back. She bumped into Steve, who reached up to grip her upper arms.

Haley stepped forward. "Riley, why don't you and Steve head inside? I'd like to talk to Martin here."

Riley let her gaze dart back and forth between Martin and Haley. How could she signal to Haley that Martin was dangerous? Haley's hand hadn't left her weapon. She didn't have to signal her. "Okay."

Martin turned to head outside. Haley followed him.

Like lightning, Martin swung around, gun in hand. Riley didn't even have time to scream before the crack of the weapon rang through the hangar and Haley fell to the ground.

Katie heard the shot and froze. Daniel went white. "Riley! Riley! Answer me!" He paced in front of the plane, holding the phone.

"What happened?"

"I think Martin shot her."

"Who?" Katie grabbed him and forced him to stop so she could look over his shoulder. He was still staring at the screen.

"Riley, run!" Katie heard Haley's cry, saw

the screen shake. Riley ran, Steve beside her.

"Riley! Stop!" Martin yelled. His face flashed on the screen, then was gone. She heard him yell again, followed by a thud. Then Riley's breathing as she and Steve ran. Then the screen went blank.

Katie's heart thudded. "Haley . . . ," she whispered. "He shot her."

Daniel dialed 911. "My niece is at home with an intruder. A shot was fired and a person injured." He gave the address. "Get someone over there now, please. And send an ambulance. The intruder's name is Martin Sheehan, he's a family friend. Or was." He hung up and looked at Katie. "We don't have time to wait for help."

"What are we going to do?"

"I'm going to have to get this plane back in the air."

"Can you do that?"

"I don't know yet. I know what's wrong with it, so I should be able to make the repair." He went to the front of the plane and opened it up. "Can you see if you can get Riley back on the phone?"

"Of course."

She took his phone and hit send, watching his face transform into deep lines of worry for Riley and the others. He hauled himself back inside, and when he returned, he held a large tool box.

He set the box on the ground and slapped a hand against the side of the plane. "I shouldn't have left her."

"We cleared Martin. We checked him out and he came back clean."

"I should have known. Somehow I should have sensed it. If he hurts her, I'll hunt him down and make him regret we ever crossed paths." His low voice left no doubt he was serious.

"It's not going to come to that."

Riley's phone rang four times, then went to voice mail. Katie had to admit she was scared. "I'm not going to call her again. If she's hiding and her phone rings —"

He slapped the wheel. "You're right."

She couldn't stop the chill that raced through her. What would Martin do if he caught them? He was now a hunted man, trapped, with no way out. The cops knew who he was. Then again . . .

"Do you think he realizes you were still on the phone when he fired that shot?"

He gave a brief pause before resuming his work under the inspection cover. "I don't know. I know he heard me say I had the coin, but I'm not sure about the rest of it."

Katie continued to call Haley while he

went to work. Concern for her friend pounded through her. Was she hurt? She'd heard her yell for Riley to run. Did that mean if she'd been shot, it wasn't bad?

Daniel grunted, pulled back, and shut the cover, tightening the screws he'd released in order to open it. "Someone messed with the bolts on the elevator control. I just had to tighten them." He tossed the tools back into the box and picked it up. "Let's go."

Riley raced across her neighbor's backyard. Haley had tripped Martin and given her and Steve time to get away. She felt horrible leaving the wounded woman, but if she allowed Martin to capture her, she wouldn't be able to call for help for Haley. She gripped her phone but couldn't stop to call 911. Not yet. How much had Daniel heard? She'd left it on FaceTime, but she wasn't sure when it had cut off. If he'd heard the shot, he would have already called. She just didn't know. And she and Steve had to get away. She'd pulled him into this, now she had to get him out.

But how?

"Riley!" Martin's voice echoed behind them.

Her breath caught again. *Oh God, help us!* "In here," she whispered. Her neighbor had left his hangar open.

"It's too obvious and there won't be a place to hide," Steve said.

"Well, we sure can't stand out here in the open. We'll find something. Come on." She led the way inside with a glance over her shoulder. She spotted Martin, head swiveling as he looked for them. She dialed 911. The operator picked up. "What's your emergency?"

"Martin Sheehan is after us." She gave the address and slipped into the hangar. "He's got a gun and he already shot someone." Panic wanted to consume her. She choked it down and held the phone as she looked for a place to hide. Unfortunately their options were limited. A clothing rack full of costumes, the plane, storage boxes. All neat and orderly.

"He's coming," Steve hissed.

"There." She pointed to a large cabinet that was in the corner. Not made to be placed in the corner, there was space on either side next to another door. She didn't know if that led outside or into the house. "If we pull that clothing rack in front of us, we should be good."

They moved quickly, Steve stepped into the small space first, then pulled Riley up against him. She maneuvered the clothing rack in front of them and prayed Martin would be too distracted to do a good search.

"We can go out that door if he gets too close," Steve whispered in her ear.

She glanced through the clothing to see that the door did indeed lead outside.

"Riley? Stop running. I'm not going to hurt you, you know that." Through a part in the clothing, she watched Martin step inside the hangar.

Steve tensed, his hands on her waist flexed, and she could feel a tremor race through him.

Martin held his weapon in his right hand. Riley shivered. He made a three-sixty and then focused in on the clothing rack. Riley tensed.

Martin walked toward them. "Come on, Riley, I know you're in here."

Her lungs constricted. Her heart raced. In the distance she thought she heard sirens. *Oh please, please, hurry.*

Martin came closer, then paused, head turned as though listening. He heard them too and cursed. He swung back to the clothing and raised the weapon. "Come out now, Riley."

She looked up at Steve and mouthed, "Push."

She raised her hands and placed them on

the bar where the clothing hung and then pushed with all her might. With Steve's added strength, the heavy rack flipped over onto Martin. His howl of rage echoed through the hangar as he went to the floor. The gun discharged, but Riley didn't stop to see what he hit as she flung open the door.

Steve's hand on her lower back assured her he was with her. They raced across the backyard toward the wooded area. The yards were large and they were going to be exposed for a good bit. She just prayed he didn't come out of the hangar until she and Steve could find cover again.

Another gunshot cracked through the air and she flinched. So much for finding cover.

"The bridge," Steve gasped. "Go for it."

She knew exactly where he meant. The large airpark neighborhood had a park area about the size of half a football field, but with a lot more trees, hills, and valleys, and a creek with a bridge.

And all kinds of possible hiding places in the woods lining the area.

She ran to the right, then headed straight. Her boots clunked on the asphalt for a brief moment before she hit grass again. The bridge was just ahead. Steve grasped her hand and surged forward. Riley wanted to glance behind but couldn't take a chance on tripping. She stayed with him.

The park stood empty, the cold keeping families away. She followed Steve onto the bridge. Another shot rang out, chipping a piece of the railing in front of her. She let out a low scream and Steve pulled her to a stop.

"Riley! Stay there or I'll shoot again!" Martin's harsh threat shivered through her.

"Go over," Steve said.

"What?"

"I hear the sirens, they're getting closer. Hopefully they'll scare him off. Go over. Try to hit the ground and not the water."

She was right at the edge of the bridge and saw what he meant. The ground sloped down into the creek. If they hit it right, they could dash into the trees. She hauled herself over. Heard Martin's angry roar and the crack of his weapon. She hit the ground with a thud and a grunt, but rolled just like she'd been taught in Katie's self-defense class. She almost landed in the water but caught herself and climbed the slight bank back up to the trees. She whirled to make sure Steve hadn't been shot and saw him launch himself over the rail. He landed beside her and let out a harsh cry. He fell back and grabbed his left leg.

"Steve, what happened? What'd you do?"

"My leg."

Riley looked up to see Martin on the bridge. They had to get into the trees before he spotted them. She tried to help Steve to his feet, but he let out a loud gasp. "I can't put any weight on it."

"Is it broken?" she asked, trying to help her friend and keep one eye on Martin at the same time. Only he'd disappeared. She swiveled to the left, then back to the right. "Come on, can you walk?"

He tried, flinched, and lost what little color he had in his face. "I think so. I don't think it's broken, just sprained."

She grabbed his hand and pulled, glancing over her shoulder. A wave of nausea swept her when she saw Martin coming toward them. He held the gun in front of him, aimed right at her.

"Don't move," he said. The wind whipped his wild hair around his face, his eyes were wide and darting, but the weapon was steady in his hand.

Riley froze. She could run, but there was no way Steve would be able to keep up. She stepped in front of him and he groaned. "Don't do that, Riley." But she stayed where she was, keeping her body in between them.

Martin came to a stop in front of her, the

gun never wavering from her and Steve's general direction. "Now get —"

She lashed out in a kick that caught Martin's forearm. The gun spun from his hand and he roared, leaped forward, and tackled her to the ground. She rolled and got her thighs locked around his neck. "Steve, go!"

Martin grabbed her leg and bent it toward her until the pain gave her no choice but to loosen her grasp. From the corner of her eye, she saw Steve going for the gun.

Martin must have seen him at the same time. He shoved Riley away from him and dove for the weapon. His shoulder crashed into Steve's chest and her friend went down with a grunt. On her knees, Riley scrambled to get the weapon, but Martin beat her by a breath. He whipped it around and smashed it against the side of her head.

Pain flashed and she hit the ground hard. Dark spots dimmed her vision and nausea rolled with the excruciating headache. Darkness threatened but she hung on. She rose to her knees and lifted her head. Her gaze met Martin's. He held the gun against Steve's head.

"Try anything like that again and he dies."

26

Daniel aimed the plane toward home. Anxiety pounded through him. Fear for Riley, shock at Martin's betrayal. "Still can't get Haley?" he asked Katie.

"No."

"Plug that cable into the phone. Since our headsets are linked, you'll be able to hear as well." She did as instructed and then dialed again.

They listened to it ring. And another line beep in. "It's Riley," Daniel said.

Katie switched over. "Riley?"

"No, unfortunately Riley is a bit indisposed right now. This is Martin. I have Riley and her friend, and if you want to see them alive, bring me the coin. And if I see any cops, I will kill Steve or Riley. And I haven't decided which one yet. But I've killed before and I don't mind doing it again."

Daniel paled. "So it's been you all along.

All we've been through together? This is what it comes to?"

"Save it. All I'm interested in is the coin. With three ex-wives, I don't have much left. I'm about to lose the house and —" A sigh. "Never mind. That coin is my ticket out. Give me the security code for the restaurant on Elmwood."

"What? No."

"Do it or I'll beat it out of Riley."

"7625."

Martin hung up.

Daniel slapped the dash. "See if you can get him again, will you?"

She tried, but it went to voice mail each time. "He's cut the phone off."

"Try his cell number." He rattled it off to her and she dialed.

The mechanical voice said, "We're sorry, this number has been disconnected —"

Daniel hung up. "All right, we'll do this another way. Can you find the app on my phone that says 'Security Monitoring' and pull it up."

"Okay. Got it. What next?"

"Scroll down until you see the Elmwood store. Tap it and then start clicking through the different rooms. Once he's there, we should be able to see where they are and what's going on."

She followed his instructions while his heart beat like a hummingbird's wings in his chest. He'd been in dangerous situations before. He'd dodged bombs and been in hand-to-hand combat with enemies as skilled as he. But nothing had scared him like knowing Riley was in danger.

Katie kept tapping.

"What do you see?" he asked.

"I can see all of the rooms except the basement. That screen is just black."

"Then that's where they are."

"I'm going to try and check on Haley again, if that's all right."

"Of course."

"If Martin beeps in, I'll switch."

He nodded, his mind churning. He heard her voice, registered someone answering her, but didn't process the words. He was too busy trying to figure out his next move.

She hung up and pressed her fingers to her lips.

"How is she?"

"You weren't listening."

"No, sorry. It's not that I don't care, I do. I just . . . was thinking about Riley. I'm scared." There, he'd said it out loud.

"Being scared for someone you love is normal," she said. "I'm worried and scared too, but we're going to do our best to make sure she's all right."

"I know. Thanks."

"And Haley's going to be fine. It was a flesh wound. She managed to trip him to give them some extra time. He kicked her in the face and she may have a broken nose, but at least she's alive. She said she closed her eyes and played dead. He was too intent on going after Riley and Steve that he left her alone."

Relief swept him. "Good, that's great news." He drummed his fingers on the wheel and thought, even while his adrenaline raced and worry for Riley and Steve tore at him. "I know Martin." He gave a low, humorless chuckle. "Or at least I thought I did." He drew in a deep breath. "Okay, I've got to think like him."

"How does he think?"

"Right now, he's thinking like a criminal. How to survive. How to get the coin and get out of the country. That coin is worth around four million dollars. He knows he'll never sell it legally while I'm alive, but he also knows he can sell it on the black market for at least half."

"And that's still a pretty good haul."

"Yes. He's not leaving without it."

"Do you think he killed Armstrong?" Katie asked.

"I don't know. What reason would he have?"

"It's crazy, I'll admit. Maybe it was just some stupid, random thing?"

Daniel shook his head. "Maybe, but if Martin killed Armstrong, not only do I wonder what Armstrong was doing there, but what was Martin doing there?"

"Those are questions only Martin can answer, I'm afraid."

"Yeah. We're going to need backup. Can your friend Bree go to the restaurant and scope it without him seeing her?"

"Of course."

"Tell her to call me and stay on the line. I want to see what she's seeing." He rubbed a hand down his cheek while she phoned Bree. He heard her fill the detective in and extract a promise not to do anything that would alert Martin to her presence.

She looked at him. "We really need to get a team on standby in case we need to go in fast."

He shook his head. "Martin's serious. He'll kill one of them if he sees any sign of cops. He's former military. He knows how cops think and he doesn't need two hostages."

She gave a slow nod.

"And if he finds out that Riley's had the

coin the entire time, she's dead too."

Katie didn't respond, and when he looked at her, she had her eyes closed, lips moving slightly. She was praying. For Riley. For them. For him?

The lump in his throat took him by surprise. He reached over and wrapped his fingers around hers, and for the first time since his brother and sister-in-law had been killed, Daniel found himself praying. *Please, God, don't take Riley too.*

Katie squeezed his hand and looked up. "He answers prayers."

"Yes, but will it be the answer I want?"

"I don't know, but that's where faith comes in."

His jaw ached and he realized he was clenching it. He made the effort to relax it. "Yeah, that's what Riley keeps telling me."

"She's a smart girl."

"I know." Daniel cleared his throat and pointed. "We're coming up on my neighborhood. We'll land and drive straight to the restaurant."

"I'm ready when you are."

Riley's head pounded and her right eye hurt. The gun had gotten her solidly on the cheek and grazed her eyelid. The side of her face felt sticky and tight and she assumed it was from dried blood.

A chill that was part weather and part fear sent tremors through her. Her hands were bound behind her and he'd duct-taped her to a column in the basement of her uncle's restaurant. She sat with her back against the column and could feel Steve's hands against hers, felt the heat of his body warming hers. She hadn't been down here since her uncle had found Maurice hanging from the pipe. She swallowed and tried not to throw up from the pain in her head. She just couldn't add that humiliation to her misery and terror.

"Steve?"

"Yeah?"

"Where'd he go?"

"I don't know."

"How's your leg?"

"It hurts, but I think it's just a sprain, not broken."

His monotone worried her. "Do you know what time it is?"

"No." Silence fell between them. "He took my phone," Steve finally added.

A door slammed and Riley tensed. "Hey! Who's there?"

Martin rounded the corner, carrying a bag. "Be quiet, Riley. I don't want to have to tape your mouth shut."

She bit her lip. He looked so . . . normal. He wore a long-sleeved sweatshirt, khaki cargo jeans, and tennis shoes. "Why are you doing this, Martin? Uncle Daniel's your best friend. You've been like another uncle to me."

A pained look crossed his face, then his features hardened. "I know, Riley. And I truly never meant for things to turn out this way." He set the bag on the floor and pulled out several items.

"What are you doing?"

"Waiting for Daniel to get here."

"Okay, never mind the first question. What is that stuff for?"

"You might call it an insurance policy."

"Quit playing with words. What is it?"

"A bomb," Steve said. "It's a bomb. He's going to blow us up."

Riley sucked in a deep breath. "Martin?" she whispered.

He dropped his head and sighed. "I'm sorry, Riley, I really am."

Her heart fluttered in her chest like a trapped bird. Was this really happening? "Then stop!"

He shook his head. "I can't. Daniel's going to give me that coin or this building is going to go boom."

Riley's chest tightened. Should she just

give him the coin? Tell him it was in her pocket? But then he would have no reason to keep them alive. He had no choice but to kill them at this point. "Everyone knows it's you."

"Well, the original plan was to just use the coin for fame and sell off some of the other artifacts. Altogether I've probably uncovered a good three million dollars' worth of artifacts. I didn't need the coin, but now there's no way I can move those things and get the money, because now I have to deal with this situation. Because of you and your uncle and those bodyguards, *nothing* has gone according to the plan."

She wanted to yell, "Good!" but held it in. She didn't figure that would help the situation. When he wrapped a wire around her throat, she shook her head. "What are you doing?"

"This is linked to the bomb. If you try to take it off, you will detonate the bomb. Understand? Your boyfriend's going to have one too. So both of you need to sit real still. I just need to get away. Then someone will come in and rescue you."

He was lying. She knew it. She met his eyes for a brief second and saw that he knew she knew it. Tears welled, then streamed down her cheeks. "Please, Martin, please don't do this."

"Sorry, Riley." He almost sounded like he meant it, but they both knew he didn't.

She wanted to release the scream building in her throat. Instead, she clamped down on the wail and began to pray.

Daniel landed the plane without a hitch and taxied to his drive. Katie raced into the hangar and stopped at the blood on the cement. "She's going to be all right," she murmured.

"Come on, Katie, let's go."

She spun to find Daniel waiting beside her Jeep. She hurried toward him, pulling the keys from her pocket. He climbed into the passenger seat and she hauled herself into the driver's. Within seconds, they were racing down the drive toward the restaurant. His silence worried her. "What are you going to do?" she asked.

"I don't know. I'm winging it."

"That could be deadly. I think we need to stop and come up with a plan. If we go charging in there, someone's going to get hurt."

"As long as it's Martin, I'm okay with that."

She heard the vicious threat in his voice. She got on her Bluetooth and dialed Maddy.

The woman answered on the second ring. "Are you up to working?"

"Of course. I'm just being Snow White and sitting here with Grumpy. What do you need?"

Katie filled her in. "Bree's there now. She's scoping the area."

"I'm on the way. Should I call Haley and Olivia?"

Katie paused. Of course Maddy wouldn't know. "Haley's been shot." At Maddy's gasp, Katie hurried to reassure her. "She'll be all right. It was a through and through and didn't hit anything vital, but she's got a broken nose and lacerated cheek from where the attacker kicked her. She's in the hospital where you are, but you can check on her later. We need you and your surveillance equipment."

"What about Charlie and Lizzie?"

"Yes, call them." The restaurant came into sight and Katie hung up. "Maddy's on the way. She's former FBI, so her presence might come in handy. She's also had hostage negotiation training."

"Is there anything your team can't do?"

"Not really. But let's not use this situation to find out."

"I'm good with that."

27

They parked several feet down on the side of the road next to the cemetery. Daniel's restaurant lay thirty yards ahead.

Katie had Bree on the phone. "What do you see?"

"Nothing much. No cars in the vicinity that match the description you gave me of Martin's vehicle. No license plate that matches, no cell phone use with the number. Nothing. I got up to the window and there's no one in the main area. The only place I couldn't see in was the basement."

"And that's the only camera we can't see working," Katie said. "They're in there and we need to see what's going on."

"Maddy's on her way and bringing her surveillance equipment."

"Is there any way he can monitor what's going on out here?" Bree asked.

Katie looked at Daniel. He shook his head. Then paused. "Only if he's in the office looking at the computer and the computer is password protected."

"And he wouldn't know the password?"

"Only the manager and a few select employees know it."

"Does Riley know it?"

"No."

"Then we may be all right."

Riley tugged against the duct tape. The bomb was strapped around the column right above her head. Martin had gotten it in place, then disappeared up the stairs. "Martin! Martin!"

"What are you calling him for?" Steve sounded rattled.

Riley gave a grunt and another tug on the tape around her wrists. She made sure to keep her head still, even though she didn't think the bomb was active yet. No sense in finding out the hard way. "I want him back in here. I'm more comfortable being able to see what he's doing."

"Well, I'm more comfortable with him out of sight."

"I don't suppose you have anything sharp on you?"

"No, sorry, I wasn't planning on being kidnapped today."

Riley fell silent and listened. Thought.

How much time did they have before the bomb went off? Was it even armed yet? "I'm sorry I got you into this," she said.

He didn't answer for a moment. Was he mad? Of course he was mad. She sighed and the base of her neck started to throb. Her head hurt where Martin had struck her and every once in a while she had to fight a wave of nausea.

"Riley, it's not your fault," he finally said. "I knew about the stuff going on with your uncle and I didn't really care. As in, I wasn't going to let it keep me from hanging out with you. I could see that Beth and Kyle were preoccupied with each other and you needed a friend. I wanted to be that friend and try to make up for the lousy way I treated you."

Riley swallowed against the next round of tears that wanted to flow. She had needed a friend. Beth was supposed to be her best friend, but ever since she and Kyle had started dating, their time together had been significantly less. And Steve had noticed. "Thanks," she whispered. She tugged again. Something loosened and hope sparked. "Can you reach the tape around my wrists and see if you can work on it?"

He shifted. She felt his hand brush hers, then stop. "Hang on. It's too awkward this way." He maneuvered around so that his body was more perpendicular to hers. "He's got me taped to the column but maybe —"

She felt him push his arms back, his fingers dug into her upper back. There was a sucking sound as the tape pulled away from the column and Steve gave a victorious grunt. "Okay, that was almost too easy."

"Don't knock it. Just be grateful."

Footsteps on the stairs froze her. "He's coming back."

"Got it," Martin said. "I'll be back up there in just a minute." A pause. "Yes, yes. I got all of the artifacts. As soon as I have the coin, we'll be set." Another pause like he was listening. "They'll be too busy digging through the rubble to worry about me. Now you do your part while I do mine."

Riley's adrenaline pumped. Who had he been talking to? Martin stepped into the basement. She glared at him. "So how many people are involved in this little scheme of yours?"

He frowned. "Doesn't matter."

"Oh come on, of course it matters. What was that little press conference about? You were glowing, all puffed up with pride. I was proud of you, happy for you that you were finally seeing your dream come true. What's going to happen to your golden-boy image when the press gets ahold of this?"

"*If* they get ahold of it. I told him no cops."

"And you really think he's going to follow your orders?"

Martin rubbed a hand down the side of his face.

"You can stop this now," she said. "Let us go and we'll forget this ever happened."

"I wish I could, but I'm afraid I'm in too deep."

"So the press will know, then everyone will know that you were behind this. What's that going to do to your precious career?"

Martin grimaced and for a moment she wondered if she'd gotten through to him. Then he shook his head. "My name will be mud, of course, and that would be a big disappointment. A huge one actually." His jaw tightened, and she saw him blow out a slow breath. "So. This is what it's come to. I wanted fame and fortune. At this point, I've resigned myself to settling for the fortune and possibly a bit of notoriety."

"Like being labeled a murderer?"

His jaw tightened and his narrowed eyes lasered into her. For a moment she wondered if she'd pushed him too far. "Well," he said, "it's a little late to worry about that one, isn't it?"

Wait a minute. He'd killed someone? Her

fear ran deeper. She hadn't realized that. She'd been talking about her and Steve. "Martin," she whispered, "who did you kill?" His gaze went to the pipe just beyond her and he suddenly looked weary. "Maurice? You killed Maurice? Why?"

"Who do you think found the coin and called me to get an estimate on how much it was worth? He found it before he was fired. When I saw it, I made him tell me where he found it. He showed me and was all excited about making things right with Daniel, that giving him the coin would make up for what he'd done."

"Only you betrayed Daniel and killed a man who wanted to do something right."

Anger flashed in Martin's eyes. "Shut up, Riley, or —"

"Or what? You're going to kill me too?" He didn't respond, so she watched him. Then dared to ask him a question that was at the front of her mind. "Why did you burn down the restaurant on North Lake? You know how important that box is to me. Why?"

He snorted. "I had to fix the situation I'd caused at the other restaurant by hanging Maurice in the basement. I needed the focus taken off of the place."

Riley gaped. "So you burned the other

one?" He opened his mouth to answer, but she beat him to it. "Of course you did. Uncle Daniel would be so busy with insurance and everything else, he wouldn't be paying attention to what was going on at the one on Elmwood."

"Pretty much. It wasn't anything personal."

"Not personal! Are you nuts?"

His anger returned full force. "Shut up or I'll put a piece of duct tape over your mouth."

She snapped her lips shut. That was the last thing she needed but dread shivered through her. He'd killed Maurice Armstrong over a stupid coin.

He patted her head. "That's a good girl."

"I'm not a dog." The words flew from her lips before she could bite them back. She honestly didn't know why she wasn't in a mute puddle of terror, but . . . this was Martin. Would he really kill her? Her aching head said it was a real possibility. His eyes narrowed and he reached for the tape he'd left stuck to the column just above the bomb. "Sorry. Sorry. I won't say another word."

"Good."

A knock on the basement door snapped his head up. "That's probably your uncle."

He held the gun steady. "Now, it's time to wrap this up." He walked toward the door.

Riley tugged again. Felt the tape twist slightly. Was she helping or simply pulling it tighter? Martin hadn't used a whole bunch. He'd been in a hurry. "Steve," she hissed.

"Yeah?"

"Go to work on my tape, will you?" she whispered.

His fingers fumbled, felt around, and she knew he was trying to find the edge of the tape. And finally she felt him press, his fingernail scratching. Then he gave a pull and the tape rasped.

He froze and she waited for Martin to turn, but Martin wasn't paying them any attention at all. Instead, he stood at the door, his hand on the knob. Steve pulled again. More tape moved.

Martin placed himself behind the protection of the door as he held the gun in his left hand and aimed it at the opening. He walked backward, staying behind the door as it opened.

"Keep your hands where I can see them," he said.

Her uncle Daniel appeared and Riley finally was able to take a deep breath. His eyes caught hers and she saw the banked emotion there. He was scared spitless for her. She lifted her chin and narrowed her eyes and she thought she saw the corner of his mouth twitch slightly upward.

He kept his hands away from his body and walked into the basement of his restaurant.

Katie continued to stare at the screen, hoping that somehow the camera would start working and she'd be able to see into the basement. Of course it didn't. She scrolled through the rest of the screens, monitoring each room in case they moved from their current location.

Maddy stepped up to her. "SWAT team is in place."

"Good. Make sure there's no way they'll be seen by Martin."

"Not to worry. These guys are good, you know that."

"Yes, I know, it's just . . ." She shrugged.

"It's never been this personal for you before?"

Katie glanced at her friend. "Something like that."

"He's a good guy?"

Katie tapped the screen that would show her the lobby. "Yeah. The best."

"I thought there was something between you two when you brought him to Quinn's room."

"Yes, there's something. I'm really praying we get the chance to figure out exactly what, because I don't think Martin's plan includes Daniel coming out of all of this alive."

Daniel stared at the man who'd once been his friend. Betrayal cut deep. Katie was right. He'd been way too trusting. "You okay, Riles?"

"Peachy. Except for the bomb sitting above my head, the bomb strapped to Martin, and this wire wrapped around my neck. Other than that . . ."

Her spunkiness relieved him. He could still hear the fear in her voice, but she was going to put up a good fight. Her last sentence registered. A bomb. He looked closer, still keeping Martin in his peripheral vision. He could see the deadly weapon strapped to the column just above the kids' heads. Great. He knew Katie was listening. He just hoped the bomb squad was on the way. And Martin had a bomb on him. Not good. *God, I think it's time we started talking again.* He made sure his fear wasn't registered on his face. He'd get them out of this one way or another. "Steve?"

"Oh sure. 'Peachy' sums it up pretty well, Mr. Matthews."

Good. While he could hear the fear in the

kid's voice, Steve wasn't a wimp. Although considering his circumstances, it would be understandable.

Only now he had to block them from his mind. He had to focus on Martin. "You going to search me?"

Martin licked his lips. "You have a gun on you?"

"No."

"Really? You came in without a weapon. You're a liar." He turned the gun on Riley's head. "You want to get rid of it?"

"I don't have a gun, Martin." He kept his tone even. He pushed back his jacket so Martin could see the empty shoulder holster. Then he turned and lifted his jacket. "Nothing in my waistband." He pulled his slacks up. "No ankle weapons. Come pat me down yourself."

"And give you a chance to use that karate stuff on me? No thanks."

Daniel ground his teeth. He'd been hoping Martin would move closer. "Just, why? At least tell me that."

"Because you're sitting on a gold mine."

Confusion flickered. "That doesn't tell me a whole lot."

Martin let out a laugh that didn't sound completely sane. Nevertheless, the man knew exactly what he was doing. He gestured to the back wall. "Underneath your restaurant, man, are all kinds of artifacts. Where do you think I was getting them?"

Daniel didn't move as the light went on for him. "You were digging them up here and planting them down by the Congaree River site."

"Exactly. Now give me the coin before the cops get here."

"What makes you think the cops are coming?"

"Because I know you. And I know you've got at least that bodyguard woman outside. I'm guessing the cops are on the way."

"As long as you have hostages, they're not going to risk doing anything."

"Exactly. Now the coin."

"First I want answers."

Martin jabbed the gun at him. "And first I want the coin! Hand it over!"

"I don't have it."

The man's face went red and without turning his body aimed the gun at Riley and Steve. "Your call. Who do I shoot first?"

Steve sucked in a breath and Riley squealed. "Uncle Daniel, let me —"

"You're not going to shoot anyone," Daniel said with a calm he was trying to feel. He shot a look at Riley and prayed she'd stay quiet. "I mean I have the coin, but I wasn't dumb enough to bring it with me. It's my only bargaining tool, Martin, surely you understand that. As soon as we're away from here and Riley's out of danger, I'll take you to it. It's close by." Daniel thought Martin might just start shooting. "Why show me the coin in the first place if you were just going to steal it and sell it?" he asked in a desperate attempt to distract the man.

Martin sighed, the gun lowering slightly. He moved to the door to peer out. "What?" The change of topic seemed to confuse him.

"You were planning on selling it all along. Why show it to me?"

Martin scowled. "Because I always seem to be on the losing side of life. I finally had something worthwhile and I wanted to show it off a bit. Stupid, maybe, but —" He shrugged.

"And then you lost it when you tried to kill us at the North Lake restaurant by crushing Quinn's car with the backhoe," Daniel said softly.

"Let's go!"

"I'm not leaving without giving Riley a hug."

"No hugging. Let's go."

Daniel stood his ground. "I know you plan to kill me when you have the coin, Martin." Riley gasped and Daniel ignored her. "And that bomb isn't there because it's pretty. I'm giving her a hug. If you want to blow us all up and forgo getting the coin, well, that's your decision." He walked toward Riley and Martin backed up, the gun never wavering, but his frustration evident. Greed won out as Daniel felt sure it would, but his relief was almost tangible.

"Keep your hands where I can see them," Martin snarled.

"Fine."

Daniel held his hands at his sides and walked over to Riley. He eyed the bomb even as he knelt in front of his niece. He leaned over and kissed her on the head, then placed his hands on her shoulders. "Make a scene," he whispered.

She started crying. "Don't leave me, Uncle Daniel. Don't let him kill us. Don't leave!" The tears turned to sobs and Daniel didn't think it was all an act. His heart shuddered at her distress.

"Hey, Riles," he said loud enough for Martin to hear. "It's going to be okay." His hands slid down her arms. "Which pocket?" he whispered.

"Left." She let out another sob. Without moving her head and neck, she tilted her hips to the right and his hand slipped into her pocket. "Please, Martin, please don't do this!"

Daniel palmed the coin and gave her one last fierce hug. "Be strong," he whispered. "I'm not going far. Katie? You hear me?"

"Loud and clear." Her welcome voice came through the earpiece.

"It's up to you now."

"I'm ready as soon as you have Martin out of there," she said.

He hesitated and kept his arms around his niece, careful not to jostle anything explosive. "It's the only way?"

"Yes, the bomb squad's been contacted. Officers will be following you to take Martin out at the first opportunity."

"What are you talking about?" Martin screamed. "You hugged her, now come on!"

Daniel looked into Riley's eyes. "You hear me?"

Riley sniffed and swiped the tears on her shoulder. She met his gaze and nodded.

"Enough!" Martin marched over and aimed the gun at Daniel. "I said move." With his free hand, Martin reached into the front pocket of his cargo jeans and pulled out a device. His thumb pressed a button and the bomb above Riley and Steve's heads beeped. "It better not be any more than thirty minutes away, because that's all the

407

time they have left." He unbuttoned his shirt and Daniel sucked in a deep breath. Not only did he have a bomb to blow up the restaurant, he had one strapped to his chest. "And this one is for you."

[28]

"He armed the bomb, Bree," Katie whispered.

The basement door squeaked open. Daniel appeared, Martin behind him. Martin had one arm around Daniel's neck and a gun to his head. Daniel's eyes connected with hers. He was going to let Martin get him in a car. So far Martin hadn't spotted the earpiece in his left ear.

Daniel held his hands where everyone could see them. Martin had his shirt undone and Katie could see the bomb taped to his chest. "Great."

"I see it," Bree said. "Does he have a dead-man switch?"

"Yes. Yes, he does. See his arm around Daniel's neck? Look at his hand." Bree groaned. "Daniel?" Katie called. She knew that Martin expected her to be there. She stepped into their line of sight. She'd already heard the conversation between

Daniel and Riley, had heard Martin's plans for Daniel, and knew there was a bomb in the restaurant and one attached to Martin's chest.

There would be no way for a sniper to get him without getting Daniel too. If a sniper took out Martin, he'd release the switch and whatever it was rigged to would go boom.

Daniel held his hands away from his sides and let Martin direct his steps. "Back off, Katie. Stay with Riley."

"Shut up." Martin shoved him toward his SUV.

Daniel shook his head. He didn't want her to try anything. She couldn't see them, but she knew the snipers were there. The command center for this incident was set up somewhere nearby, but if she was just a passerby, she'd never know that either.

She looked around. Where was the bomb squad? They'd been called as soon as she'd realized there was an explosive device involved. But she knew it could take them a while to arrive. She paced, gnawing on her lower lip. But this was Riley's life at stake and that of her friend. The longer it took for the squad to arrive, the greater the chance of detonation. She couldn't just stand here and do nothing. The bomb was ticking, according to Martin. She'd heard his last comment to Daniel. Thirty minutes. She glanced at her watch. Twenty-six and counting.

"I'm going to have to go in, Bree."

"What?"

"We don't have time to wait on the bomb squad."

"You don't have a suit. No protection, nothing." Bree's voice was low, concerned.

Katie watched Daniel climb into Martin's SUV from the passenger side. Martin nudged him on over into the driver's seat, and then Martin slipped into the passenger seat and shut the door.

"I know." Katie blew out a breath. "I know. It's not my first choice."

"This isn't an action-adventure movie, Katie. You go in there, you could die."

"I know that too. But if I don't go in and the bomb squad doesn't get here in time, then Riley and Steve die. I can't let that happen. I'm trained in this. I know what I'm doing."

Bree got on her phone. "I need the ETA for the bomb squad, Ry." She nodded. Swallowed hard and met Katie's eyes. "Twenty-five minutes. Yeah. Got it. Thanks." She hung up. "There were two different bomb threats this morning. They've called for help, but . . . you heard. They're twenty-five minutes out."

"Then get me a tool kit, I'm going in."

Daniel kept an eye on the dash clock while his brain ticked away on coming up with the best action to take against Martin. He knew they were being followed. Martin knew they were being followed and he didn't seem to care. He held the gun with his left hand and sent a text with his right. Martin had deactivated the dead-man switch and set it aside, which meant he wasn't ready to detonate it. Yet. An answering ping had Daniel desperate to know who he was conversing with. Daniel nodded to the detonation device on the dash. "How much range does that thing get?"

Martin looked up from his phone. "We're out of range with this one. I just want the coin and a head start and then you can leave."

Right.

Out of range with this one. What did that mean? Daniel drove fast but with precision. He didn't want to have a wreck and wind up setting Martin off. The fact that the man had strapped a bomb to his chest had Daniel scrambling for a plan B. His original plan had been to just get Martin away from Riley and Steve. "You sabotaged my airplane," he said.

"It was a spur-of-the-moment decision. A moment of opportunity that I took a chance on."

"What if I'd decided to let Riley take the plane up? She doesn't have the skills yet to land it like I did."

"That would have been unfortunate, but you would have been distracted and I would be gone."

Daniel slammed a fist against the wheel and Martin jerked. "Don't you care about anybody but yourself?" Daniel hissed.

"I used to. Before I got tired of being used and discarded. I decided it hurts too much to care about others. My last ex, she was pregnant, you know?"

The news rocked Daniel for a brief moment. "No. I didn't."

"I didn't either until it was too late."

"For what?"

"To stop her from killing our baby. She was already planning to leave me for another man and a baby would have been a decided inconvenience. So . . . she just got rid of it. Like it was a piece of trash to be thrown out."

Daniel sucked in a breath. "I'm sorry. That's awful." He truly did feel sorry for

413

the pain of that situation, but Martin had taken things way too far. There was no room for negotiation in this. Riley's life was on the line. Martin's phone beeped again. He sent another text. Daniel could have landed a punch on the man's jaw several times over at this point, but the bomb Martin wore held him still. He had to get out of this alive or Riley would never forgive him.

"Where are we going?" Martin asked.

"My house."

"You left the coin at your house?"

"I did."

A slow smile slid across Martin's lips. "I wondered if that's where you would put it."

"You didn't expect me to bring it."

"Not really. I had hopes, but I also know you pretty well. Where is it? Your safe?"

Daniel's jaw tightened. Was he really that easy to read? Then again, Martin didn't realize he actually had the coin on him. He let Martin read his expression and interpret it as a yes. "Convenient. Getting me back on your turf, huh? Smart." He sent another one-handed text, then pressed the muzzle of the barrel against Daniel's head. His finger tightened around the trigger. "So what do I need you for now?"

Daniel lifted a brow. "The combination?"

"Hmm . . . and probably as a hostage. I

414

know we'll be followed."

"Yes. We will. But someone's finger is on a bomb that can blow up my niece, Martin. I'm not going to try anything." And he wasn't. Yet.

"Ah yes, well, actually, the bomb is set only on the timer now."

"Then why . . ." He paused. "You just wanted me to think someone was still in control of the bomb in the basement. Then where's your accomplice?"

Martin's lips curled up. "You're a pretty smart guy, I'll let you figure it out."

Static sounded in his ear. And now he was out of range of Katie and her team.

Katie stepped inside the basement door. She'd lost Daniel's signal but knew agents were on his tail. Now it was up to her to get Riley and Steve out. The second detonator was out of range, so now she was just racing against the clock. The thought didn't cheer her. Much.

Her heart pounded a heavy beat inside her chest and she did her best to ignore it. She needed steady hands and a clear head. Daniel was counting on her. And so were the two strapped to the column with a bomb above their heads. She waited for the voice in her head to start screaming at her.

Paul's voice. *"Help meeeeeee."*

But it didn't. Instead, her brother's face flashed in her mind and she heard his deep baritone echoing the phrase he'd said so many times when he'd trained her. "You can do this, Katie."

Tears gathered and she forced them back. She needed to focus. And she was going to need help. Serious help. *God, I need you here in this basement with your hands on mine, guiding me to do the right thing, make the right choices. Please help me.* Her gaze met Riley's. "You okay?"

"Yes. For the next few minutes anyway."

Katie moved toward the bomb, registering the details, noting the placement, the detonator, the fact that she was going to have to defuse it without her tools. No X-rays, no handy little robot that didn't bleed if it got blown up. She was being incredibly stupid. But what other choice did she have? No one else in the area had her skills, and if she waited much longer, they'd all be dead. "Okay, Riley. Let me just take a look, all right?"

"You shouldn't be here, Katie."

"Let me worry about that."

She glanced at her watch. Yeah, she needed to move a little faster. She studied the device. Cylindrical in shape. Just like the one that had been rigged to Daniel's SUV. That helped. It looked like a pipe bomb, but probably held C4 like the other one had. She'd seen the X-rays. If this one was the same, she knew exactly what to do, so she should be good.

Should be. *Please God, don't let this thing blow. And take care of Daniel wherever he is.*

She drew in a deep breath and reached for the screwdriver in the tool kit Bree had provided from the trunk of her car. Everyone had backed off when they'd learned about the bomb. Daniel was being tracked and she simply couldn't worry about him. He could take care of himself. He *could.* Now it was up to her to take care of his niece. He'd entrusted Riley into her care, was relying on her expertise to defuse the bomb. "Bree? You there?"

"I'm here." Bree's voice sounded close in the small device she had tucked in her ear. Her voice now took the place of Daniel's.

"I've got fifteen minutes and thirty-seven seconds," Katie said. "You got that?"

"Got it."

"Start counting down. Tell me when I'm at five minutes."

"Don't let it get that close, please."

"Well, that's the plan, but —"

"No buts."

With steady hands, Katie began working on the first screw. Then the second. There was no containment vehicle to take this one to a safe place. She was simply going to have to take it apart. One piece at a time.

[29]

Daniel pulled to a stop in front of his house. Martin pressed the gun against Daniel's temple. "Don't try anything, you understand?"

"I understand, Martin."

"Then crawl across and get out on my side." Martin opened the door and backed out of the passenger seat, keeping the weapon trained on Daniel. A half-dozen different self-defense moves flashed through Daniel's mind, but until he was sure Riley was all right, he wouldn't try anything. Not yet. The person helping Martin might still be able to get back in range and set the bomb off early.

Daniel climbed out of the SUV, and under Martin's watchful gaze along with the barrel of the gun still pointed at his head, he strode toward the front door. From the corner of his eye, he saw a dark-suited figure slide around the corner of his house. The

SWAT team was here. But they couldn't shoot Martin and risk blowing Daniel up along with him. He glanced at his watch. Katie had ten minutes left.

"Did you lie?" he asked as he turned off the alarm.

"About?"

"The bomb and how much time is on it."

"No."

Daniel nodded. So it really was up to Katie. Leaving Riley had been one of the hardest things he'd ever had to do, but if it meant saving her life . . .

He looked at Martin. "You don't smell like acetone."

"What are you babbling about? Shut up and get the coin."

"There was acetone in Jake's car. I smelled it again at the restaurant when someone pushed a column over on us, then ran. But I don't detect the odor on you. Who else is working with you?"

Martin's eyes narrowed. "For your information, using a citrus-smelling soap gets rid of the odor quickly. I use it all the time. Now if I have to ask you again, I'll just blow the door off the safe." The steel in the man's voice made Daniel take another hard look at his former friend. He was desperate. Completely and totally willing to do anything it took to get the coin and escape.

Daniel figured he had cops all around his property at this point. He waited for the phone to ring with the hostage negotiator on the other end. He also knew that Martin had no intention of negotiating.

He walked toward his office, his mind spinning. He really didn't want to blow himself up, but he knew as soon as he handed Martin the coin, the man would be done with him.

As he stepped over the threshold into his office, the phone rang. He looked at Martin. "It's for you."

Martin simply walked over to the phone and pulled the plug from the back. "The coin. Open the safe and then step back. If you lift your hand to reach into the safe, I'll shoot you. Am I clear?"

"Crystal."

Daniel walked over to the safe. Movement outside the window caught his eye and he hesitated. He could see the hangar garage door was up. But who . . .

A small wire slid under his window and settled in the corner. So, they were listening. He glanced at Martin, who paced in front of the desk, his weapon held steady, the bomb still strapped to his chest. Daniel dropped his hand from the safe. *Why* didn't

Martin seem terribly concerned about the fact that there were cops now swarming all over his property? "I want to know about Riley and Steve."

"What?"

"There are six minutes left. If they're alive at the end of those six minutes, I'll open the safe."

Martin froze midpace. As far as he knew, Daniel had gotten him as close to the coin as he was going to get. With a low growl, he pointed the weapon at Daniel. "If I don't have that coin in my hand immediately, I'll forgo the six minutes and simply start setting the bombs off."

Daniel turned away from the safe. "Bombs?"

Martin held his phone up. "Yeah, bombs." He moved toward the window. Glanced out.

Daniel reached for the safe.

Katie removed the top of the canister and with steady fingers found the C4. She worked quickly, efficiently. Having seen the first bomb and how it had been rigged helped immensely.

"Katie?" Bree's urgent voice came through her earpiece.

"Kinda busy here."

"The agents weren't able to get into the

house, but one of them got a listening device inside. We just got word. There are more bombs in the building."

She froze, but didn't let her expression change. "All right. Well, right now, this is the only one I care about. I've almost got this. Just one more minute."

"That's about all you have. Actually you're down to four. You need to get out. Now."

Katie continued to work, staying focused, yet deeply concerned about the report of more bombs in the restaurant. How much time did she have? Thirty seconds later, she had the bomb defused. She removed wire cutters from her kit and cut the wire around Riley's neck, then Steve's. Riley pushed away the rest of the duct tape Steve had managed to undo and quickly released helped Katie go to work on his. If they hadn't had the bomb to be worried about, they would have been able to get loose eventually.

"Go," Katie said. "Go now. They're coming, Bree."

"We're ready. Just get out."

"Someone's got to search for the other bombs," Katie said, even as she hooked an arm around Steve's waist and Riley did the same. They headed for the exit.

"Bomb squad just pulled in. They've got

the dogs."

Katie breathed a prayer of relief and bolted for the door as the first explosion ripped through the air.

[30]

"Hey! I told you no hands in the safe!" Martin swung the gun and Daniel tried to duck, but the end of the weapon caught him on the forehead. Pain flashed and he reared back against the desk.

"That wasn't necessary!" Daniel winced. He reached up and felt the warm wetness on his fingers.

"It was necessary." Martin breathed fast, a vein in his forehead throbbed. His hand now held the device that would detonate the bomb strapped to his chest.

"The coin's right there. Front and center." Daniel palmed the letter opener he'd left on his desk. If he could get him at the base of the skull, the man would drop and die quickly.

But the bomb . . .

He released the potential weapon. He simply couldn't chance it. A fact Martin knew.

Martin still held his weapon steady when he turned. He'd placed the device back in his pocket and he held the coin in his left hand. "Finally," he breathed. His phone dinged and he blinked, shoved the coin in his pocket, and pulled out his phone. He glanced at the screen and satisfaction crossed his face. "Time to go."

"Go where?" Daniel swiped at the drying blood on his forehead. His head throbbed once again. He was getting really tired of headaches. "You don't need me anymore."

"Funny. Of course I still need you. Now we're going to the hangar. We're going to fly out of here."

"Once you discovered Riley had the coin, this was your plan all along, wasn't it?"

"Well, I didn't know you had the coin in your safe, but yes, we were going to wind up back here and on your plane at some point. This just makes things a little easier. So let's go."

And no matter how many officers or SWAT members were outside, no one was going to shoot Martin and take a chance on blowing him and Daniel up. On the one hand, that comforted him. On the other, it made him just plain fighting mad.

The first blast had taken most of the roof

off the restaurant. Katie and the teens made it to the bomb squad van and the door slammed behind them just seconds before the next blast ripped through the air. The van shuddered and she went to her knees. Riley threw herself into Katie's arms and held on. "Thank you." Tears leaked from the teen's eyes. Steve sat with his head against the side of the van, eyes shut. He looked pale and shaken. She couldn't blame him.

The van moved, taking her and the others away from the scene. She slumped into the seat next to Bree. Sirens rang, fire trucks moved in. And all Katie wanted to know was —

"Where's Daniel?"

Bree looked at her. "He's still with Martin. Cops are all over his house."

Riley flinched. "The house?"

"Yes."

"Then that's where we need to go," Katie said.

Daniel held himself stiff as Martin once again pressed the gun to his head and ushered him through the house, into the mudroom, and then into the hangar. He knew the SWAT members were there. Behind trees, on top of the hangar, everywhere. But they wouldn't be able to see what was going on inside the house or the hangar at this point. He heard the thumping of a helicopter whirling above.

Daniel got a good look at the plane. The doors were open and the engine was running. "What —" Whoever had started the plane had done so before he and Martin had arrived. But who?

"Shut up."

Martin still had a bomb strapped to his chest, which meant law enforcement hands were tied. His former friend shoved him slightly ahead of him toward the plane.

Once again, Daniel considered taking the man down, but he didn't. "If you think I'm going to fly you out of here, you're crazy."

The barrel pressed against his ear. "We'll see."

Through the window, Daniel caught the eye of an officer peering in. He gave a slight shake of his head. The woman nodded, but didn't lower her weapon, which she kept trained on Martin through the glass.

Martin spied her. "Back off!" Martin made sure the bomb was visible, but he didn't need to. Each one of the officers knew it was there. "Back off!"

There was no way the woman could hear

him, but she got the gist. She backed away slightly.

Martin let go of the back of his shirt. "Get in the back."

Daniel glanced over his shoulder. Saw the officers ready to shoot. But they couldn't. Frustration clawed at him, but already he was thinking how he was going to handle this. Martin hovered right behind him. Couldn't put too much distance between them or one of the officers might shoot him.

"Wait a minute. What? The back?"

"You heard me."

"You think you're going to fly this thing?"

"Nope. She is."

Daniel looked into the pilot's seat and found himself staring his waitress, Sarah Durham, in the eye. And caught a whiff of the acetone he now associated with the person trying to kill him. "You?"

"Hi, Daniel."

His lip curled. "What? No citrus-smelling soap available today?"

Sarah frowned her confusion and Martin snorted. "Let's go."

Daniel stared at her. "How'd you get in here without being spotted? There are feds all over this place."

She smirked. "I simply got here before they did."

Martin shoved him. "Get in."

"Come on, Bree, I need an update. What's going on? Where's Daniel?" Once Katie, Riley, and Steve had been transported away from the threat of any more explosions at the restaurant, another officer had picked up Bree and taken her to Daniel's house. Katie still sat in the back of the van with Riley and Steve. His parents were on the way.

Katie itched to get over to Daniel's house herself but couldn't leave Riley just yet. However, she'd promised to make sure Daniel was all right and she was going to do that.

"I'm on the phone with one of the officers," Bree said. "Martin's forced Daniel into the plane and it looks like they're going to try taking off."

"There's a helicopter on the scene, right?"

"Of course. And newspeople are on it now too. Cops are everywhere, a perimeter's been set up. But Martin still has the bomb strapped to him. Right now, all we can do is monitor the situation."

"What if he gets in the air?"

"Well, we can't shoot them down. We'll have to get them where they land."

Katie bit her lip. "What if they're planning to cross the border?"

"Why are you asking questions you already know the answers to? We'll alert the proper authorities and they'll pick them up when they land."

"I know. I know. I'm sorry. I'm thinking out loud more than anything."

"I understand. I'm hoping Daniel is able to come up with a plan to stop it before it gets that far."

"I'm coming as soon as I can get there. Keep texting me updates, I've got a few calls to make." She hung up.

"Is Uncle Daniel all right?" Riley asked, her voice soft. Scared.

Katie met Riley's eyes. "For now."

"Do what you have to do to get him home safe. Please."

"That's my number one priority."

A knock on the back of the van pulled her attention from her phone. The back door opened and a woman and man stood there with anxious eyes.

"Mom," Steve said. "Dad."

"Are you all right?" the woman said on a sob.

"I'm fine." Steve hopped from the back and his mother engulfed him in a stranglehold. Riley jumped down and she hugged her too. Then she pushed them back and looked them both over. "Are you really okay?"

"Yes."

"But Uncle Daniel's not." She turned to Katie. "Find him, okay?"

"I'm just waiting on my ride." A car pulled in beside the van. "And she just got here. Mrs. Patterson, will you keep Riley with you?"

"Of course."

Katie hugged Riley and the teen squeezed her back. "You'll have to go with the officers and tell them what happened. You'll be in one room, Steve will be in the other. Just tell what happened and everything will be fine, okay?"

"Okay."

"I'll call you, I promise."

Riley nodded. "I'll be watching the news."

"And we'll be making it," Katie muttered. "And it's going to have a happy ending." She hurried over to Maddy's car and climbed in. "Let's go."

[31]

Daniel sat in the backseat. And while his hands weren't literally tied, he felt helpless. Sarah expertly handled the plane, and within minutes they were speeding down the neighborhood runway. Riley had obviously been an excellent teacher.

Martin and Sarah wore the headsets and were talking. He could understand some of what they were saying, but the noise in the cabin drowned out a lot of it. He pulled the backseat headset over his ears and caught the words "Mexico" and "black market" and figured they were going to sell the coin and the other artifacts they'd stolen from under his restaurant once they reached their destination. And he knew they didn't plan to take him along for the ride. At least not much longer.

He also knew he was going to have to get himself out of this one way or another. A plan slowly formed, and he worked it over in his mind while they went back and forth about their plans for when they were rich.

While they were preoccupied, as soon as the plane was airborne, he reached back behind the seat and felt for the material that would tell him he'd found what he needed. Once he had the item in his grip, he pulled it over the seat and into his lap. Then slid it down so that it sat between his feet.

He kept his eyes on the two people in the front. Every so often Martin would look behind him. Daniel simply glowered at the man while mentally running through scenarios of escape. Only to hesitate because of the bomb. A bomb Martin still had strapped to his chest. Was he that unconcerned?

"Is that even a real bomb?"

Martin looked back and grinned. "Of course it is. As long as I'm wearing it, no one's going to shoot at me. And as long as you're in the plane, they're not going to cause it to crash."

True enough. For now. Then again, there might be a time when the authorities decided it was better to sacrifice one innocent life to save hundreds of others.

And what did Martin plan to do with Daniel once they'd landed?

The obvious. Kill him.

"Sarah, after everything I've done for you?

Really?"

Sarah didn't turn. "I'm sorry, Daniel, I really am. The money was just too good to turn down."

"You were the one in the Jeep watching my house."

This time she did glance back at him. "What?"

"The acetone that I assume you used on the artifacts. It was in the Jeep you climbed into to spy. My neighbor said it was so strong he had to have it detailed."

"Oh. Yeah, I had brought a small piece to work on while I waited." She smirked. "I didn't want to be bored with nothing to do. I guess I'm so used to the smell now, I don't notice it."

"I never noticed it in the restaurant."

"I always wash up real good before I go there. I was afraid the customers would complain."

"Of course." That's why she always smelled like . . . citrus. But why watch my house? What was the point?"

"To know how to get to the plane when we needed it." She smirked. "I watched your house a lot."

Sickness filled him. How had he not noticed? "And you're the one who pushed the column over at the restaurant. We smelled it then too."

"I'd sent her to look for the coin. Of course you had to show up," Martin said. "Now shut up and let her fly."

Daniel glanced out the window. The police helicopter followed at a respectable distance. Daniel waited. He was going to have to act and pray the bomb didn't go off while he was still in the plane. Finally, Martin shifted and Daniel lurched forward and grabbed Martin around the neck. The man hollered and struggled against the stranglehold.

Sarah yelped and the plane jerked to the left. She righted it. "Stop it!"

Martin slammed the gun into Sarah's lap. "Shoot him," he croaked.

She raised the gun and aimed it at Daniel.

Daniel let go and ducked behind the seat. "You don't shoot a gun in a plane!" Who has to tell someone that? But she wasn't listening. It was either get shot or risk getting blown up.

Sarah had passed the weapon back to Martin, who turned it on Daniel. "You're dead now. I was going to wait until we landed, but I can't take any —"

Daniel lunged at Martin again and grabbed his wrist. Martin yelled, jerked his arm to the right, and pulled the trigger. The first bullet went through the window next to Daniel's head. Wind rushed in, the noise deafening. Sarah screamed and the plane once again bucked, throwing him off balance.

But Martin still held tight to the weapon and Daniel refused to loosen his grip on Martin's wrist. If he did, he was a dead man. Martin fired again. This time the bullet went straight into the back of the plane. Daniel scrambled to jerk the gun from Martin, but couldn't get enough leverage to do it.

"Stop it!" Sarah screamed again. "You're going to make me crash this plane!"

Daniel ignored her. He just needed a few more seconds. He jerked again on Martin's arm and the third bullet grazed his cheek but shattered the rest of the window behind him. Daniel heaved Martin back into his seat and the gun finally fell from his hand. Sarah's screams echoed through the cabin as the plane started to go nose up and she fought for control. Daniel knew he had only seconds to react. He reached for the item he'd placed on the floor, then fell backward through the broken window into the open sky.

Katie and Maddy sat in the command post van and watched the newsfeed on the computer monitor. When the shots were fired, she'd tensed, her stomach doing a three-sixty. Daniel wasn't the one with the gun. Why would Martin start shooting in the plane?

She gaped when she saw a body fall from the airplane. "That's Daniel," she whispered. "No!"

Offscreen, one newswoman let out a yelp. "Oh no. Shots were fired and now someone's fallen from the plane."

Katie stared, stunned, unable to process what she'd just witnessed. "Please. No."

The screen split, one camera on the struggling plane and one on Daniel's falling body. He was moving, grappling with something. Katie gasped. "Wait a minute. He's got a chute!"

Maddy blinked. "What?"

"A parachute. Now he just has to get it on and pull the cord in time." She closed her eyes and tried not to think how fast a free-falling body actually fell. She started praying. *Please, Jesus, let him get that parachute on and open.*

Maddy gripped her arm and she opened her eyes. And was finally able to breathe. It was open. He shot a thumbs-up toward the news camera. On the other side of the screen, his plane continued to fly, followed by the police chopper. But it was in trouble.

"It looks like the gas tank may have been hit," the news announcer stated as the camera zoomed in on the small plane. A long vapor-like trail flowed from the left wing. "Fuel is leaking at an alarming rate. There's no way they'll be able to stay in the air much longer."

As though the plane had heard his words, it dipped and began to lose altitude. "Activate the parachute, Martin," Katie said.

Maddy shot her a look. "What?"

"There's a parachute on the plane. All he has to do is hit the button."

But he didn't and the plane continued to go down, gliding softly on the air. "Is there any place she could land it?"

Maddy shook her head and held up her phone. "Not according to this map. It's all trees."

"She's not experienced enough to fly that plane," Katie whispered. "This isn't going to end well for them."

The minutes ticked by and the plane disappeared into the trees below.

A few tense seconds passed. Katie almost started to breathe again when a fiery explosion lit up the screen. She and Maddy sat there in silence while the news camera kept the flames in sight. And while she regretted the probable loss of life, her focus was on the one still alive.

She watched Daniel float through the air until he landed in the middle of a minor league baseball field. The news announcer went wild. "What an unbelievable thing we've witnessed today . . ."

Katie tuned her out.

"Now you can breathe," Maddy said.

"Yes, now I can breathe." *Thank you, God.* "Head toward the crash site."

"Why?"

"Because if Daniel can get there, that's where he'll go. And if that's where he is, that's where I want to be."

Daniel rolled with the land and did his best not to get tangled in the lines of the parachute. By the time he was free, he could hear the sirens blaring toward him. He'd seen the explosion on his way down and grief tore at him even as relief flooded him.

He still didn't know about Riley, Steve, and Katie. And of course he had no cell phone. He shoved out of the parachute and started walking toward the crash site. He had to see if Sarah or Martin survived.

In his heart, he knew they hadn't, but if there was a chance . . .

His head still pounded from where Martin had pistol-whipped him, but he was able to ignore it. He'd hurt worse. He picked up the pace, running, footsteps pounding in time with his head. He thought the plane had gone down about a mile from where he'd landed on the ball field.

It took him about fifteen minutes to reach the downed aircraft. He felt the heat before he saw the flames. The plane had crashed into a wooded area behind a shopping center, taking out several trees and power lines. He couldn't see the full extent of the damage, but just prayed no innocent by-stander had paid with his life.

"Martin! Sarah!" Smoke billowed and he coughed as the fire trucks raced onto the scene. The news helicopter still hovered above as well as the police chopper.

He tried to get closer, to see into the wreckage and just couldn't. The heat was already scorching. Daniel gave up and backed away. He couldn't get close. And there was no reason to. In addition to the fuel leak, the bomb Martin had so carelessly worn on his chest had done its damage. There was no way Martin or Sarah had survived. He sank to his knees and thanked God for the fact that he had. Now he had to find out about Riley.

"Daniel!" He blinked. Was he hallucinating? "Daniel!"

"Katie?" He turned to find her racing toward him. She didn't stop, just barreled into his chest, her sobs shuddering through him. He gripped her close. She smelled like vanilla and sweat and fear. She pulled back and gripped his cheeks, her eyes searching his. "You're alive. I saw you fall from the plane." She ran her hands down his cheeks over his chest, his arms. "But you're alive."

"The parachute did most of the work."

"I know, I saw you get into it and I saw it deploy, but I couldn't believe you were actually alive until I saw you for myself." She pulled his head down to hers and kissed him, her desperate fear clearly communicated. He felt her kiss, but heard her heart. And he decided he was very, very glad to be alive.

"Riley?" he whispered.

"She's all right."

"I knew the minute I saw you that she was fine. You wouldn't be here if she wasn't." He buried his face in her neck and just held her. She clung to him for long moments and he lost track of time until an officer tapped him on the shoulder.

"We're going to need a statement."

Daniel was not about to let Katie out of his arms. "I know, but it's really low on my priority list right now. Come back later."

Bree walked up and flashed her badge. "I've got this."

The officer nodded. "Sure."

Daniel decided Bree deserved his attention. He met her gaze over Katie's head. "Thank you."

She smiled and saluted him. "Thank you. Anytime you want to get back into police work, you've got my recommendation."

She walked off and Daniel smiled against Katie's hair.

"You're thinking about it, aren't you?" she mumbled against his chest.

"Just thinking. Also thinking I'm very glad to be here with you."

"Ditto."

[32]

Daniel grinned at Katie, who smiled back. Her eyes lingered on his and he knew he'd found the one for him. It hadn't been how he'd pictured meeting his future wife, but he'd roll with it. Only she hadn't agreed to be his future wife just yet. His palms started to sweat and he drew in a deep breath as he banked the plane toward the lighted landing strip just ahead. "We made it," he said into his headphones.

"Of course," she said. "I had no doubts."

His neighbor had let him borrow the plane. Ever since Daniel's romantic plans with Katie had been derailed by Martin, he'd had plans to re-create the idea. And today was the day.

Within minutes he'd landed the plane and rolled to a smooth stop. It had been five weeks since Martin and Sarah had died in

444

the crash. Five weeks of getting his life back on track. And five weeks of falling even deeper in love with the woman next to him.

Katie yawned and rubbed her eyes.

"Are you going to be able to stay awake for this?"

"A walk on the beach at sunrise on Thanksgiving Day? I wouldn't miss it."

He opened his door and she did the same. Before he exited the plane, he grabbed the picnic basket, blanket, and propane heater. Just in case.

Together, they walked the well-lit path that led to the beach. "Nice place your friend has," she said.

"We served together in Afghanistan. He came home and made a fortune in the computer industry. He built this place for his family and told me to use it anytime I wanted. He's only here six months out of the year anyway. The rest of the time he and his family are in the Dominican Republic working in ministry." He clicked on the flashlight he'd brought.

"Sounds like a good man."

"The best."

Once down on the sand, they kicked their shoes off. Katie shivered and Daniel wrapped a blanket around her. She smiled up at him. "Thanks."

"You want the heater?"

She shook her head and slid her arms around his waist. "Nope. I can think of better ways to stay warm."

He laughed and sank to the sand, pulling her with him. "I like the way you think." He kissed her, long and slow, putting his heart into it, hoping she could feel the love he felt for her.

When he leaned back, she blinked. "And I like the way you kiss."

"I'm ready for a repeat performance. In a minute."

She raised a brow and he pointed.

"Look."

Still trying to catch her breath from the kiss, Katie turned her head. And gasped. She forgot about the cold and the fact that her feet were freezing and just focused on the majestic scene unfolding before her. With Daniel at her back, his arms wrapped around her, she snuggled in to watch God show off.

First a deep orange with streaks of fire shooting into the barely there clouds, the sun gradually made its way through the dark sky, painting it with a mixture of orange, yellow, and gold. Finally the ball of orange settled in the eastern sky, revealing dawn's first rays over the ocean of blue. "How can anyone who sees something like this doubt there's a God?" she whispered.

"I don't doubt him anymore."

She didn't turn, just kept her eyes on the Creator's canvas. "You don't?"

"No. I'll admit I've struggled. I've lost a lot."

"I know you have. I'm sorry about Martin and Sarah."

"I am too." Grief tightened his voice. "I'm sorry I didn't realize what was really going on with him." He sighed.

"Bree said they found all kinds of stuff in his house. A notepad that detailed every step of his twisted plans."

He nodded. "I know. He also had a detailed list of all of the artifacts he and Sarah looted. The police and my lawyer are dealing with all of that. But truthfully, I don't want to talk about them today."

"Okay. What do you want to talk about?" She squeezed his fingers, her heart overflowing with love for the man who held her, for the God who gave them a beautiful new sunrise each morning, for . . . life. Just breathing the salty air, hearing the waves crash against the shore, feeling the sting of the cold on her cheeks made her feel alive. And grateful to be that way.

"I want to tell you that once I got past the anger and the bitterness of everything I lost, I was able to see that, while I've lost, I've also been very blessed."

She nodded. "I know what you mean."

He drew in a deep breath and she felt his chest lift against her back. "Katie, I'm not perfect, not by a long stretch. I'll probably always have nightmares. And I have a temper too."

"Um-hmm . . ."

"Hey, you're not falling asleep on me, are you?"

"Not yet."

He tickled a rib through the blanket and she laughed. "Stop."

"I won't take much longer."

She smiled up at him and tilted her head to kiss his chin, then look back at the sunrise. "Take all the time you need."

He cleared his throat and her heart thudded. She wasn't nearly as close to falling asleep as she'd pretended. In fact, she was very close to coming out of her skin. If he was getting to what she thought he was.

"Katie, I love you."

She sat up and turned to face him. "Finally."

"What?"

"I wondered if you were ever going to say it."

"You couldn't say it first?"

"I could have, but . . ."

He gave a low growl and tackled her onto her back. He hovered over her. "You knew I was going to say it."

"I thought so, but a girl never wants to assume."

A low rumble started in his chest, then escaped his lips, resulting in a belly laugh. She grinned at his mirth, her heart lighter than it had been in a very long time. When he stopped laughing and looked into her eyes, she raised her hands to cup his cheeks. "I love you too, Daniel." And she brought his head down to hers for another sweet kiss. A kiss she wanted to last forever, but ended all too soon.

"So what are we going to do about it?" he asked with a kiss to the tip of her nose.

"Well, I think that's up to you."

"Me? Why?" She lifted a brow. "Oh, then will this do?" He helped her into a sitting position, then reached into the front pocket of his jeans and pulled out a small square box.

Katie let out another gasp and met his eyes. "If that's a necklace, I'm seriously going to hurt you."

His brows rose and he snorted on his laughter. Then another guffaw escaped. Soon he was on his back, his chuckles ringing loudly over the roar of the waves of the ocean. Katie shook her head and wondered if she'd ever learn to keep her mouth shut at the right time.

Probably not.

He finally got ahold of himself and wiped the tears from his eyes. "Only you, Katie. Only you."

Sheepish, she grinned. "Sorry."

"I'm not. It's just one of the many things I love about you." He popped the top and turned the box to show her the contents.

All laughter fled and she looked into his eyes. "Are you sure?"

"Never more sure of anything in my life."

"It's not a necklace," she said.

"No, it's not." He slipped the diamond ring from its resting place and lifted her left hand. "Will you marry me?"

"Tomorrow."

"Works for me." He slid the ring on her hand, then pulled her close for another kiss.

Riley met Steve at the door and let him in. She'd seen a lot of him over the past five weeks but was surprised he'd come by on Thanksgiving. "Hi."

"Hi."

They stood there for a moment, then she smiled. "You want a snack?" She'd already discovered that he could eat at any time of the day. And preparing food gave her something to do. Although she had to admit that their conversations and time together had gotten easier the more they were around each other.

"What do you have?"

"Leftover pizza?"

"That works."

She led him into the kitchen. "Every time I see you, I'm surprised all over again that your parents will still let you hang out with me."

"Really?" His lips curled slightly in a wry smile. "I think they're of the mind-set that lightning doesn't strike twice in the same place."

She choked on a surprised laugh. "Well, that's . . . uh . . ."

He grinned. "I'm just kidding. Mostly."

"Cheese or pepperoni?"

"Both."

She pulled the leftovers from the fridge and then got two plates from the cabinet. "You don't have anything better to do than hang around here with me? What about spending Thanksgiving with your family?"

"We're not doing anything until later tonight. And yeah, I had another invitation, but I chose where I wanted to be."

"Hmm. Who invited you?"

"The guys."

"The ones who think I'm boring."

He laughed. "Oh no, they don't think that anymore, trust me."

Now that the danger had passed and everyone was home safe, she could smile at that kind of comment. "I'm okay with boring, if you want to know the truth."

"Yeah. You and me both." He looked around. "You here alone?"

"Yes. Uncle Daniel and Katie went flying." She put the pizza on the plates. "Cold or hot?"

"Cold."

She passed him a plate and he let it sit there. "I'm glad no one else is here. I wanted to talk to you for a few minutes."

She paused and tilted her head. "Sure. What about?"

He stood and came around the island to place his hands on her shoulders. "Riley, I've really enjoyed spending time with you these past few weeks." He reached up with one hand and rubbed his head. "You're still the same in so many ways, the best friend I used to hang out with when we were younger. But you're different now too. Life has changed you."

"Yes. It's changed you too."

"I know. And not necessarily for the better." He looked away, then back. "When Martin had us and that bomb was strapped above our heads, you were amazing."

She looked into his eyes and nearly swallowed her tongue. Somehow she forced it to work. "What do you mean?"

"You stood up to Martin. I was scared to death and couldn't think of anything to do to get you away from him . . ." He looked away and shook his head, then met her eyes again. "But you just gave it back to him and let him have it. You were furious."

"I was terrified," she whispered.

"It didn't show."

She nodded. "But I was mad too."

"Yeah, I could tell."

She blinked back the tears that wanted to fall. Martin and Sarah were dead. Two people she'd cared about. Had believed cared about her. That grieved her but they'd made their choices and there was nothing she could do about it now. Time would ease the hurt. The betrayal. "I'm glad you were with me, though."

"What?"

"Well, not glad that you were in danger,

of course, but I was glad I wasn't alone." She shook her head. "I don't think I would have been able to deal with him alone. Your presence gave me strength."

He gave a slow nod. "Yeah, I know what you mean. I felt the same way about having you there."

"Good."

"Riley?"

"Yes?"

"Will you go out with me?"

Her heart fluttered. "Like on a date?"

"Uh huh."

"When?"

He glanced at the plates on the island. "After we eat the pizza?"

She snickered and he grinned. "That would be great, but I have to be somewhere for Thanksgiving lunch."

"Oh."

"You want to come?"

He gave an eager nod. "Absolutely."

A knock on the door pulled her attention from the guy in her kitchen. Curious, she walked into the foyer and looked out the window. A man in an orange work vest stood on her porch, his back to the door.

Steve walked up behind her as Riley opened the door. "Can I help you?" she asked.

The man spun. "Oh, sorry. I was just looking around. Nice place you have here."

"Thanks."

He held a small cardboard box in his hands. "I'm working on rebuilding the restaurant site on North Lake. Your uncle's been by just about every day asking us to keep our eyes open for a box." He held it out to her. "I think this might be what he's looking for. Will you give it to him?"

Riley's breath caught and she took the package. "Of course. Thank you." She frowned. "You're working on Thanksgiving?"

"Your uncle paid us a whopping bonus for volunteering. I desperately need the money" — he shrugged — "so it was a real blessing."

"Oh, that's good."

"You want to check it and see if that's it? If not, we'll keep looking."

"Yes." She popped the top and looked inside. Tears gathered in her eyes and she reached in to pull out her mother's marble box. "This is it," she whispered. "I can't thank you enough."

The man grinned. "No thanks necessary. Be sure to let your uncle know?"

"As soon as I can."

The man left and she shut the door, still

looking at the box.

"What is it?" Steve asked.

"The box that belonged to my mother. The one I told you about." She walked back into the kitchen and set the box on the counter. Then slowly she opened the marbled lid. And there it was.

Her mother's Bible. She gently pulled it from its resting place. "I can't tell you how much I've prayed that God would let someone find this. I prayed and prayed about it."

"Yes, I know. I've been praying for it too."

"Really?"

He gave a self-conscious shrug. "I know how much it means to you."

Riley looked up at Steve and smiled through her tears. "God really does care about what matters to us. Sometimes things happen that we'll never understand."

"Like your parents' deaths."

"Yeah. But sometimes he answers our prayers in ways to just say, 'I'm here, I haven't forgotten you.'"

"And this is one of those times."

"Definitely." She held up the Bible. "And sometimes when something precious is lost, he makes sure we get it back so that we'll cherish it even more than we did before."

Steve swallowed hard, then pulled her close for a hug. "He sure does."

Katie lifted a brow when Daniel pulled up to the newly repaired and renovated restaurant on Elmwood. The explosions had done their damage but hadn't completely destroyed the building. As a result, round-the-clock crews had accomplished something of a miracle in less than five weeks. "It looks great."

"I didn't think it was possible to rebuild it this fast. There are a few things left to do, but it's functional and that's what I wanted for today. Want the tour?"

"Of course." She climbed out and the wind blew her hair across her face. She shoved it aside. "But what are all these cars here for?"

"I thought we'd have Thanksgiving dinner with a few friends. Sort of a celebration of being back in business and a way of saying thanks for everyone who stood by me."

"What a wonderful idea." A pang centered

itself in the vicinity of her heart. This was arguably the happiest day of her life and yet the thought of not seeing her family on Thanksgiving left a sadness she couldn't shake. *You made the decision. It's for the best. Deal with it.* She looked at her fiancé — *fiancé* — and couldn't help the smile that lifted her lips. She entwined her fingers with his. "Come on."

He led the way into the restaurant. Just inside, he stopped. "Hey, everyone!"

A hush fell over the room and all eyes turned to her and Daniel. Katie saw Riley and Steve standing off to the side and waved. Daniel gripped her hand and she looked up. "Daniel, what are —"

He lifted her left hand. "She said yes!"

Thunderous applause filled the room and Katie felt the blood rush to her cheeks. "Really?"

"Really."

She laughed. She couldn't help it. His joy was infectious. And then people were hugging her, one person after the other. Bree, Maddy, Quinn in a wheelchair. He gripped her fingers. "You got a good one."

She bent down to hug him. "I know." She glanced at Maddy. "You do too. Don't mess it up."

He grunted and rolled his eyes, then

winked. Haley followed behind him. She hugged Katie.

"How's the shoulder?" Katie asked.

"Almost good as new."

"Liar."

Haley grinned. "Getting there though."

"Good."

Then Olivia, Wade, Amy . . .

Her breath caught. "Daphne?"

"Congratulations, sis. I guess seeing me twice this close together is a bit of a shock, huh?" Daphne grinned and threw her arms around Katie. And Katie hugged her back.

"You didn't call them," she whispered in Katie's ear.

"No, I didn't, I'm going to. Today. I promise."

"I knew you wouldn't."

"Sorry."

"It's okay. I worked around you."

"What?" When Daphne pulled away, Katie wanted to protest but then saw the two people standing behind her sister. She froze and felt the smile slide from her lips. "Hi, Mom. Hi, Dad."

"Hi, baby," her father said.

The endearment almost reduced her to tears. She hadn't heard that in a long time. She swallowed. "What are you doing here?"

"Well, since you weren't coming to us for

Thanksgiving, we decided to come to you." Her mother smiled and tears stood in her eyes. "Daphne had a long talk with us."

"An overdue one," her father said.

Her mother sniffed. "And we want a do-over."

Katie's gaze bounced between them. "A do-over?"

"We've all grieved Paul's death and we know you feel like we blame you." Her dad stopped talking and looked at her mother.

The woman cleared her throat. "The truth is, we were mad at Paul. For being so willing for you to follow in his footsteps."

"And then for getting killed," Daphne said.

"The pain was so great we pushed you away without realizing what we were doing," her father whispered. "We kept thinking that we were going to get that call . . ."

"That same call," her mother said, "that same life-shattering call to tell us you were gone too."

"Oh, Mom," Katie said. She felt the tears burn the back of her eyes. She glanced up at Daniel and saw that he'd pulled most of the people to himself so she could have this time with her family. "It's okay."

"No, it's not," her father said. "But we're going to make it right. We're going to make a new start, if you're willing."

Katie nodded and held on to her tears. She grinned. "I'm willing."

Her father engulfed her in a bear hug. The kind of hug she'd so desperately needed for the past three years. "Then this is going to be a great Thanksgiving."

"Absolutely," Daniel said, walking up and sliding an arm around her shoulders when her father released her. "And it starts now. Let's eat, folks. It's a buffet. We didn't want anyone to have to spend the day serving, so here's the plan." Everyone waited. "Serve yourself!"

Laughter rolled and people lined up at the steaming buffet.

Katie followed Daniel into the dining area and saw that his sister-in-law's table had survived the explosions. It sat front and center. "It's a good day, Daniel."

"One of the best."

"And God is good."

"I agree."

A woman in a wheelchair rolled up to him, pushed by a teenage girl. Daniel held out a hand and the woman reached up to grip it. "I can't thank you enough for all you've done."

Daniel smiled. "It was the least I could do, Mrs. Armstrong. Maurice was trying to make things right and it got him killed."

"I wanted to say thank you too," the teen said.

"You're more than welcome, Alyssa. You're a smart girl with a good head on your shoulders. If you ever need anything, you have a friend here."

She nodded. "I know."

Katie's gaze bounced between the three of them.

Alyssa's eyes met hers. "You're marrying a wonderful man. He's paying for my college. All four years."

Katie's heart swelled with pride for the man next to her. "You deserve it."

"I want to do something to help others," Alyssa said. "I want to be an ADA or a DA. Someone who can put the bad guys away. Get them off the street so they can't hurt others. And now because of Mr. Matthews, I'm going to see my dream come true." She reached out to hug him, and Katie could see the moisture in his eyes as he gave Alyssa a gentle squeeze.

Her own throat felt tight.

And then Alyssa and her grandmother were heading for the buffet. She turned to Daniel and hugged him. "You're a good man, Daniel Matthews."

He flushed, then shrugged.

Then smiled and kissed her. "I'm a blessed man."

"And a hungry one?"

"Starving."

"Let's eat."

ACKNOWLEDGMENTS

You know, there are so many people who invest themselves in me and my writing, and I can never thank you all enough. I'm so touched, honored, and humbled that you would deem it worth your time to read my manuscript and give me feedback. Two of the most amazing people are Retired FBI Special Agents Wayne Smith and Dru Wells. I could never get the police procedural/FBI facts right if it weren't for you! Thank you for the time you spend reading and fixing! ☺

I need to give a shout out to Bill Sammons of 88.7 The Bridge in Delaware. I meant to put this in the back of *Always Watching,* but in my dead-writer-brain state at the time, I forgot. I know, shocking, isn't it?? Anyway, Bill Sammons, thank you and Julie for your wonderful friendship to Jack and me, your servant hearts and amazing generosity in sharing your home, many hours of laughter, and your radio knowledge. *Always Watching* earned a 4.5-star review and a Top Pick by *RT Magazine* because of your willingness to share your expertise. I appreciate it very much! Note to readers: Any errors in the radio scenes are mine! ☺ Give Mary and Lola a hug from me.

Thank you to Ken Galloway, a friend of mine who is a fabulous pilot for my favorite airline. I appreciate you taking the time correct my aviation lingo and for the wonderful idea on how to cause flight problems without killing off my characters. It was exactly what I needed! And I really need to give a shoutout to Ken's MD wife, Molly, who is always willing and able to answer all of my medical questions. I love that she's not even surprised anymore when I say, "I need to poison someone, but I don't want that person to die." She just jumps in with all kinds of excellent suggestions! Thank you, Molly, for being my friend and putting up with me and my writerly weirdness.

Thank you to my Facebook peeps who are always willing to offer suggestions and recommendations when I ask for them. I appreciate all of you who participated in my little game of "Name Daniel's Restaurant." It was fun seeing your ideas!

Thank you to my editor, Andrea Doering,

and my agent, Tamela Hancock Murray of the Steve Laube Agency. As always, I love working with you both!

Thank you to my brainstorming buddies. Edie Melson, DiAnn Mills, Mary Denman, Emme Gannon, Vonda Skelton, Lynn Blackburn, and Alycia Morales. I love our weekly get togethers!

Thank you to my family! Jack, Lauryn, and Will, I love you so much. I couldn't do what I do without you!

Thank you, Jesus, for choosing me for this amazing journey. I love you so much and only want to make you proud.

ABOUT THE AUTHOR

Lynette Eason is the bestselling author of the Women of Justice series and the Deadly Reunions series, as well as *No One to Trust, Nowhere to Turn,* and *No Place to Hide* in the Hidden Identity series. She is a member of American Christian Fiction Writers and Romance Writers of America. She has a master's degree in education from Converse College and she lives in South Carolina. Learn more at www.lynetteeason.com.